Cover Design and Interior Format

# SHARON SALA

# BETRAYED

*There are many tests we face throughout a lifetime.*
*Some have to do with choices we've made, while others come*
*unexpectedly and are out of our control.*

*It is those knee-jerk, split-second decisions that prove our met-*
*tle, strengthen our courage, and show us we are strong enough*
*to withstand even the greatest of grief.*

*I dedicate this book to the quiet heroes who walk through the*
*fire of what they've been dealt, and still suffering, find the*
*courage to live with the pain.*

# CHAPTER ONE

A SINGLE GUNSHOT SHATTERED THE ENNUI of a hot Louisiana night, and when it did, sixteen-year-old Logan Conway reacted the way any sane person would who lived on the south side of Bluejacket. She hit the floor belly down, all but certain there would be other shots, and there were.

She began hearing sirens about the same time she heard some-one run past her house—likely one of the shooters trying to get away, and hid her face against her arms, willing herself not to cry. Tears had no place down here. Being weak got people killed, and she wouldn't be so freakin' scared if Damon was home.

"Dammit, brother, where are you?"

The sirens were coming closer and so were more footsteps.

Suddenly they were on her porch, and someone was pounding on the front door.

"Logan! It's me, T-Boy. Let me in!"

She jumped up, grabbed the baseball bat from beside the door, and swung it against the wood frame like she was swinging for the fence. The thud was loud. The door shook on its hinges.

"Thug, you get off my porch, or I'll send my brother after your ass."

"Sorry, sorry," T-Boy said, and bolted.

Moments later the neighborhood was awash in cops, sirens, and red and blue flashing lights.

A cockroach, knocked loose from its hiding place from the impact of the bat, made a run for the baseboards, but she was quicker. She stomped it with her shoe, then stood the bat back in the corner.

"All the creeps are making a run for it," she muttered, then sidled up to a window facing the street and peeked through the shades.

When she saw a body in the street and a spreading black pool beneath him, she froze.

*Oh my God, that is blood.*

The cops would be knocking on doors looking for witnesses, but she knew the code of the southside.

See nothing. Know nothing.

———◆———

DAMON CONWAY WAS LATE COMING home. He should have called Logan a long time ago, but got busy and forgot. Still, he was coming home with a hundred extra dollars for hauling off tree limbs for a woman on the north side of Bluejacket.

He was late because he'd stopped off afterward to drink a beer at Barney's. He was thinking about supper and a shower as he turned onto his street, then he saw the cop cars and the flashing lights, and panic rolled through him.

*Oh Jesus, Logan. Please be okay.*

Seeing part of the street had been blocked off, he took a quick left and circled the block, coming in from the other direction. When he pulled into the drive, he got out yelling her name.

"Logan! Logan!"

The door swung inward moments before he crossed the threshold. She was standing behind it, holding his old baseball bat.

"Are you okay? What the hell happened out there?" he asked, shutting and locking the door behind him.

She shrugged. "Shots in the street. Someone's dead. Two people ran past the house. T-Boy beat on the door wanting me to let him in."

Damon groaned. "I'm sorry, kid. I should have been here. I took an extra job after work hauling off some tree limbs for one of the north side's fine citizens."

"It is what it is, Damon. Your supper is on the stove. Give me a couple of minutes, and I'll heat it up for you."

He hugged her, feeling the tension in her body as she resisted the attention. She was pissed. He sighed. He shouldn't have stopped off for that beer.

A few minutes later, he sat down to eat while Logan poured herself a glass of sweet iced tea and sat with him. Damon glanced up. Her face was expressionless. She was tough, this kid.

"Were you scared, Sissy?"

The childhood name slid past the wall behind which Logan lived. Her chin came up, her eyes glittering with unshed tears.

"Of course I was scared. Bullets can come through walls and they don't care who's on the other side. I wasn't planning to die today, so I did what I could to prevent it. I face-planted on the floor."

She had tears in her eyes, but not a shred of emotion in her voice. It gutted him.

"I'm sorry...really sorry. I made a hundred extra bucks hauling those limbs, but I didn't have to stop at Barney's for a beer and I did." He laid his fork on the plate and reached for her hand. "I don't take very good care of you. Mostly you take care of yourself and me. But I love you, and I'm proud of you. You're pretty, but you're also smart, and it's brains that will take you far in life. Not looks. I may not always be around. Accidents happen. Remember that, okay?"

Her fingers tightened around his hand.

"Don't talk like that. You talk like you're gonna die or something."

He shrugged.

"Everyone dies, Logan. The unknown is the time and place."

He shook off the seriousness and winked at her as he finished his food.

"I'll wash up the dishes. You can have the bathroom first, if you want."

She stood and hugged him, maybe a little too tight, but he was her anchor, and he was home.

Damon had regrets in his life, and not being a better parental figure was one of them. He cleaned up the kitchen and was going down the hall to his bedroom when his cell phone rang. There was no Caller ID coming up, which made him hesitate to answer.

Logan was running water for her bath when she heard his

phone ringing just outside the bathroom door. She paused and glanced at the clock. It was almost midnight. Who would be calling him this late? Always worried about Damon's choices in life, she put her ear to the door.

It rang for the fourth time before he answered, and then she could only hear his side of the conversation, but she didn't like the sound of it.

"Hello? Yes, this is Damon Conway. Who? Oh, yeah, what's up, man? What kind of a job? What do you mean, not over the phone? I don't hire out for shit that can't be talked about in polite company. Yes, but—I don't... Ten grand? Meet you where? Now? Shit man, I just got home and my kid sister isn't—Yeah, okay. I'll meet you there, but I reserve the right to tell you 'no' without a hassle."

Logan panicked. She didn't know what he was about to agree to, but it sounded both illegal and dangerous. When she heard him go into his bedroom still talking, she began draining the tub, then left the water running so he'd think she was in the shower and slipped across the hall into her bedroom. She stuffed her wallet and house key in her back pocket and under the glow of a big, yellow moon, she went out her bedroom window.

Sundown hadn't cooled the temperature a lick. Heat was an immediate slap in the face as sweat broke out above her lip and beneath the long hair hanging down the back of her neck. The buzz of locusts seemed to sound their own alarm at her sudden presence, raising her panic and anxiety. With only seconds to secure a hiding place, she started toward Damon's truck at a lope.

The cops were at the other end of the block, but it was only a matter of time before they came in this direction asking questions, looking for witnesses. With no time to waste, she leaped into the truck bed and got down on her hands and knees, crawled beneath the old waterproof tarp her brother kept over the bed to protect his tools. She was tucking the tarp down around her when she heard the front door slam, and then his footsteps as he hurried toward the truck. She hunkered down in the corner and buried her head against her knees, trying not to think of what else might be under this tarp with her. He started the engine, backed out of the drive, and took off up the street in the opposite direction of the crime scene.

She gripped the loose sides of the tarp to keep it from blowing up and hung on. Not once did she second guess her decision to do this until she realized he was driving out of town. After that, her concern was not getting caught.

She lost track of time, but could tell by the rough road, and number of potholes he hit after he had turned off the highway, that they were now traveling on blacktop.

A short while later, he turned once again onto what had to be a dirt road. She heard the scratch of limbs along the top of the cab and on the sides of the truck bed. When she began smelling what could only be the swamp, she got scared. Who wanted a meeting in the bayou, and how the hell did Damon know where to go?

When he stopped, he put the pickup in park and left it running. Worried about where they were now, she took a chance and looked out from beneath the tarp, only to see cypress trees heavily laden with Spanish moss, the shimmer of moonlight on the black bayou water, and the headlights of another vehicle coming up behind them. She lowered the tarp and flattened herself against the truck cab.

*Oh my God, oh my God! Damon, what are you doing? Go home! Now!*

She heard Damon get out and actually debated with herself about revealing her presence until she realized it was too late. The other driver was already out of his vehicle and talking as he approached.

The distant rumble of a bull gator made her skin crawl. The call of an owl in a tree above her head echoed what she was thinking. *Who* the hell was out there with Damon? The chorus of frogs out in the murky soup of the bayou was as loud as the locusts had been back in Bluejacket, making it difficult to hear everything being said until they came closer to the truck, and she heard Damon's voice.

———◆———

"SO DUDE, WHAT'S THE BIG job you want me to do, and why all the secrecy?" Damon asked.

"I heard you were a guy who'd do anything for extra dough."

"Ten grand is a hell of a lot more than extra dough," Damon said.

"So, what I need you to do involves a degree of danger, thus the rise in payoff."

"I got a kid sister to consider, so spit it out. What do you want me to do, and I'll make the decision on the degree of danger myself?"

"I want you to kill my wife and make it look like an accident. Five thousand right now, five thousand more when it's done."

Damon didn't hesitate.

"No, man. No hard feelings, but I don't kill people. I'm out'a here."

"Wait, wait," the other man said.

Logan held her breath. She could only imagine what Damon was thinking. She knew when she heard the request that he would say no, but how was he going to get out of this? Then she heard fear in Damon's voice.

"Hey dude. What the hell?" Damon cried.

"So, you know what I wanted, and now you know why we're all the way out here, because you'd be the first one to turn me in when she showed up dead at someone else's hand."

"No, no, no, don't shoot, man. I wouldn't tell. I swear."

The first shot was so loud every muscle in Logan's body jerked. The second one broke her heart, because she knew her brother had to be dead.

"My bad," the man said.

She heard him rustling around in the bushes, and then heard something hit the water. Maybe he'd thrown the gun into the swamp. She was shaking so hard she could barely breathe, and when he walked past the truck bed so close, Logan could have reached out and touched him. It was all she could do not to scream.

She heard a door slam.

He was getting back into his vehicle!

Then she heard a motor revving once, gears shifting, then he revved the engine and gears shifted again!

He was turning around!

That's when she crawled out from beneath the tarp and peeked over the tailgate of the truck. She saw just enough of the vehicle to know it was a white, late model Chevrolet Silverado, and then he was gone.

Panic rolled through her as she vaulted out of the truck bed and ran toward Damon's body, moaning as she dropped to her knees beside him. The absence of a pulse shattered the world as she'd known it.

"Oh no. God, no!"

Choking back tears, she was frantic to find out who'd done this and began looking for his phone. She would see the number of who had called him last, but after a frantic search, she realized it was nowhere on or around him.

She jumped back up and ran to the truck, tearing through the front seat, looking to see if it had fallen out of his pocket, or if he'd left it in the console, but it wasn't there either. Then she remembered the splash.

Damn! The killer hadn't thrown away his gun. He'd thrown away Damon's phone. She ran back to his body, dropped to her knees and began patting his cheek, and then his shoulder, as if he might wake up and talk to her.

"Help me, Damon. Oh my God, why? Why? I don't know what to do? Someone... Damon... tell me what to do."

But there was that hole in his chest and the other one in his forehead to consider. When she laid the flat of her hand on his chest, it was the absence of a heartbeat that finally broke her.

She rocked back on her heels and let out a scream that sent the owl into flight and silenced the frogs, leaving the tragic tableau of brother and sister in the headlights of their old truck. Then she staggered to her feet and threw up until there was nothing left within her but despair. The reality of her situation was sobering. Her brother had been murdered.

But now what did she do?

If she told the cops, the killer would view her as a witness, and she'd be next, even though she didn't know who'd done it. If she just went back to Bluejacket and said nothing, she'd wind up in Foster Care.

"Damn it, Damon. Look what you've done," she wailed. "You leave me no choice. I have to hide you, but how...where?"

Then she thought of the tools in the back of the truck and pulled the tarp aside to see what was there. The glow from the moon overhead was enough for her to see what had been under the tarp, and the first thing she spotted was a shovel. She could dig a grave! Because of the gators, she had to dig a grave. It was just a matter of time before they smelled blood, and she wouldn't give him up to the swamp.

In a panic, she leaped into the truck bed, threw the tarp and the shovel over the side of the truck, then jumped out and killed the engine. When she turned off the lights to save gas and battery power, it left her with nothing but moonlight by which to see, and the sight was daunting. The knees on the Cypress trees growing out of the water were shiny, like they'd been coated with oil. On the other side of the shore, the eyes of animals that called the swamp home glowed yellow within the undergrowth—an eerie reminder that she was not alone. With no time to waste, she dragged the tarp over Damon's body, then picked up the shovel and ran toward the thicket of trees a few yards away from the water. Moonlight was stingy here, and so she had to trust her instincts as she began jamming it into the ground until she found a spot soft enough to dig.

Emotion shut down at the first shovelful of earth she dug up, and then it became rote, taking one shovelful out after another without an awareness of time.

Before she realized it, she was down one foot into the grave, then two feet, all the while keeping an anxious lookout for snakes and gators. At three feet, she stopped to take a breath and looked up just as a shooting star shot across the sky. The notion that it was her brother's soul on the way to heaven was fanciful, but poignant enough to shatter her concentration.

Tears rolled, but they did not slow her down as she resumed digging. Hours passed without notice until the hole she was in was so deep she had a difficult time crawling out. There wasn't a dry thread on her body and sweat was pouring out of her hair. She'd lost focus on everything except getting the body into the hole.

She dragged the tarp off Damon's body, knelt beside him once more, but this time, she began going through his pockets, removing his wallet to take out the money, which she put inside the truck. Then she poked around beneath the seats until she found a plastic bag from a grocery store and hurried back. She dropped the wallet with all of his identification into the bag, wrapped it tight, and stuffed it into his pocket.

You couldn't just bury a body in Louisiana because of the water level. After a short time, they always came back up. She also knew it wouldn't take long for the body to decompose. With a strength she didn't know she had, she rolled the body onto the tarp, and then began pulling it toward the grave a few inches at a time.

Long, agonizing minutes passed as she pulled him closer and closer. She was so exhausted her legs were shaking, but she wouldn't look at his face again. She'd see it in nightmares for the rest of her life.

When she was so close to the grave that one wrong step would send her plummeting into the deep hole, she began rolling him up like the cigars he liked to smoke at Christmas, until he was only inches from the edge of the grave. A flash of panic washed through her as she realized what she was about to do. How could she do this? How could she leave him here all alone and in an unmarked grave?

Renewed horror for her situation overwhelmed her as she dropped to her knees and threw herself over his body, sobbing uncontrollably until it hurt to draw breath. It was the sudden splash in the water off to her right that jarred her back to the task at hand.

She rocked back on her knees and began pushing the tarp-wrapped body into the grave, wincing as it hit bottom with a solid thud.

There was a moment of complete exhaustion when she was flat on her belly, her face in the dirt, so tired and so damn scared she wanted to crawl into that hole with him. Instead, she made herself get up and began looking for something to weigh him down so the body wouldn't float up with the first big storm.

There was plenty of deadfall, but very few rocks. So she started with heavy limbs, pulling two large ones to the grave and rolling them over the edge before going back for more. She tossed in a shorter one that landed crossways, unintentionally making it look as if there was now a wooden cross over his body.

She was sad to the bone, but crying time was over. His body still wasn't safe, so she began tossing in limb after limb until the tarp was no longer visible, then she rolled the two largest rocks she could manage on top of the limbs. The grave was almost full, and she still had to cover it with the dirt she'd taken out.

The moon shown witness to her exhaustion as she tossed the first shovelful of dirt down into the hole, followed by another and another until there was no dirt left. Then she began tamping it down with the back of the shovel until her arms were aching and her hands numb. Once she was through, she pulled more deadfall on top of the grave to hide its presence, knowing it would flatten with time. But she'd done it. Damon's body would be safe here.

She turned back toward the truck, shining in the moonlight like a rescue beacon when it hit her. She had no idea where she was. She'd lost her brother, but she couldn't lose his body—not forever. With her last bit of strength, she staggered around behind the tree nearest the grave, and without meaning to, blindly stepped off into water. She came up gasping, her heartbeat thundering in her ears for fear she would become the victim of the nearest snake or gator, and dragged herself out.

"Oh my God, oh my God," she moaned, shaking from the shock, as she felt around for the shovel she'd dropped. Once it was recovered, she began using the edge of the shovel as a knife, chunking off bark until there was a deep, crude version of an X down near the roots.

X marked the spot.

She came out of the bushes, pausing to pull a leech off her arm. It didn't look like a grave, which was vital to keeping him hidden.

Broken in both heart and spirit, she staggered, then caught herself before she fell, and looked around, fixing this place in her mind, accepting that she'd done what had to be done.

"I love you, brother, but this isn't goodbye. I'll be back. I'll find out who did this to you, and make them pay."

She tossed the shovel into the back of the pickup, then slid in behind the steering wheel. She reached up to adjust the rearview mirror, then gasped, shocked by the sight of tear tracks through the dirt on her face. She'd just put her brother in a grave, but she looked like she'd crawled out of one.

"Go home. It's time to hide," she told herself, so she carefully backed up to turn the pickup around, then took note of the mileage before following the tracks back to an old blacktop road. There, she made a mental note of the mileage again, then sat for a moment, trying to remember if Damon had turned left or right when he left the blacktop.

Left, it was left.

She glanced at the sky and then at the time.

Nearly dawn.

"Help me, Jesus," she muttered, knowing she had to reverse every direction she remembered to get back to Bluejacket, and turned right.

Within moments, dawn was happening in front of her, which meant she was heading east. Once she reached the highway, she breathed a sigh of relief. Now she knew where she was.

She glanced at the mileage again before she turned right and drove south, straight into Bluejacket. She marked the mileage one last time at the City Limits sign, then drove to her house the same way they'd left, coming into their neighborhood from the back way and praying the cops had long since gone home.

The street was vacant of people. A few lights were on in houses—people already getting ready for work. The thought that Damon would never wake up again was gut-wrenching, but her focus was on just getting inside. The moment she pulled up into the drive, she began to shake. The adrenaline that had carried her through this ordeal was waning. She was about to crash.

"Steady, girl, steady," she whispered, then grabbed the money from the console, got out, and locked the truck before heading up the steps.

The cool waft of air surrounding her as she opened the door was so shocking she flinched. She'd forgotten there was such a thing as cool. She stumbled over the threshold, turning both locks behind her.

When she heard the water running in the bathroom down the hall, she panicked thinking someone was inside. Then she remembered she'd turned it on before she left and staggered down the hall to turn it off.

The water heater had long since emptied itself of hot water and was running nothing but cold. She was filthy, and wanted to strip where she stood and get in beneath the spray regardless of the temperature, but she still had priorities, and self-preservation was at the top of the list.

Damon never used banks, so she went back into the kitchen to where he kept his stash. Before she did another thing, she needed to know what she was working with. She opened the freezer, pushed aside the bags of frozen vegetables, and reached for what looked like a box of frozen shrimp. She shook out the contents, added it to the hundred dollars in her hand, and started counting.

Twice she had to start over because she was blind with tears, but by the time she had it counted, she was seven hundred and ninety-two dollars to the good which was enough to get her out of Bluejacket and into a new life.

She took the money back to her bedroom, stuffed it inside her purse, and then carried it with her into the bathroom and hung it on the hook on the back of the door.

Self-preservation kicked in once more as she began to strip. The shock of seeing so many leeches on her was lessened by her exhaustion. Once she was naked, she poured bathroom cleaner into the toilet bowl and began peeling off leeches as she went, ignoring the free-flow of blood from the little wounds they left behind. She quit counting after ten, tossing each of them into the toilet and digging the ones on her back off with the long handle of the shower brush. When she was through, she flushed them and closed the toilet lid.

She turned the shower back on, grabbed a washcloth, and stepped into the tub, pulling the shower curtain closed behind her. The blast of cold was shocking, but watching the mud and blood washing off her body justified the shock. Ducking her head beneath the spray, she squirted shampoo into her hand and started scrubbing. Once it felt clean, she soaped up her washcloth and did the same thing to her body until her skin was stinging and the wounds left by the leeches had quit bleeding.

Turning off the water was as shocking as turning it on had been. Now there was nothing to hear but the thump of her heartbeat in her ears. She crawled out of the tub and collapsed onto the toilet seat, intending to just take a breath, but it turned into a sob. After that, she couldn't stop.

She cried until she was emotionally drained and the pain in her chest was too sharp to acknowledge. She couldn't afford to cry again. If she did, she knew she would die.

She got a handful of cotton balls and a bottle of alcohol to begin doctoring all of the wounds left from the leeches, then stepped back into the tub and poured the rest of the alcohol down her back on the little wounds she couldn't reach.

After that, she was on auto-pilot.

She combed the tangles out of her long, dark hair, ignoring the water dripping down her back, and went to get dressed. Clean clothing had never felt so good. Afterward, she paused in the middle of her bedroom, looking around at the dirty clothes and the bits and pieces of things that belonged to her and not the house, trying to gauge what she could take. The reality of leaving Bluejacket was upon her, but first things first.

She gathered up all of her laundry, as well as Damon's, and put them in the washing machine, emptied what was left of detergent in with the load, and turned it on. There was no way to know how long it would be before she got to a place where she could do laundry again.

While the washer was filling, she ran out to the little storage shed in their back yard. Damon had a habit of keeping boxes, and she knew there were plenty out here. She carried what she wanted into the house, and while the clothes were washing, she began packing up their dishes in one box, the pans and skillets in another. After wrapping up the eating and cooking utensils in dish towels, she put them on top of the dishes and sealed the boxes. By that time, the washing machine had stopped, so she tossed the wet clothes into the dryer and then carried more empty boxes down the hall.

Somehow she had moved into survivor mode, calmly sorting and packing what needed to go, including all of Damon's clothing. She couldn't leave them behind without alerting people to the fact that he wasn't leaving with her.

When the dryer finally went off, there was nothing left to pack but the clean clothes. She folded everything and packed them into the last box of clothing, then carried it to the pickup and put it into the back seat. She'd put dishes and pans into the truck bed, knowing if it rained on them as she drove, the only thing that would ruin would be the boxes.

She popped a couple of her brother's no-doze pills, left the front door key on the kitchen table, then backed out of their yard and drove away. She lingered long enough to stop at Friendly's grocery for deli food and coffee, then drove away from Bluejacket and never looked back.

# CHAPTER TWO

*Dallas, Texas - Ten years later.*

THE HOT JULY WIND BLASTED across the dirt-filled lot of the latest build going up in the Talman Estates, while a banner of colored flags tied to a For Sale sign popped and flapped like the business end of a bullwhip at the lot next door. A cement truck was on site, pouring another load of fresh concrete into driveway forms, while the mud crews moved quickly, smoothing it into place.

A black, Texas-size Lincoln, driven by a man named Roy Beatty, came wheeling into the housing addition. Roy was all full of rage and indignation as he headed for the site where they were working, and when he parked, he got out shouting.

"Where the hell is Logan Talman?"

One of the workers pointed toward a group of people standing on the far side of the new build.

Beatty stomped across what would one day be a beautiful lawn, cursing at the dust boiling up on his alligator boots and fancy suit, wishing he'd worn something cooler. He came to a stop a few yards away, jammed the Stetson down on his head to keep it from blowing away, and shouted.

"Which one of you sons-a-bitches is Logan Talman?"

The men stepped back, giving way to the tall, dark-haired woman in work clothes and a hard hat who slowly looked up from the clipboard she was holding.

"Gentlemen, if you'll give me a minute, I'll see what has this dude's drawers in a twist so he can be on his way." And then she strode toward Beatty with obvious intent.

Roy Beatty frowned. Even in blowing dirt and work clothes, she was drop-dead gorgeous. However, he hadn't come here to be side-tracked by some long-legged bitch.

"I need to speak to Logan Talman."

"I'm Logan Talman."

He blinked, then remembered why he'd come.

"I'm Roy Beatty. I own—"

Logan interrupted.

"I know who you are. You own Dallas Brickwork."

Beatty's pig-eyes glittered angrily.

"Yes, I do, and you placed an order with my company for twenty-five pallets of adobe red pavers. Then I get to work this morning and find out you cancelled the order. I want to know why?"

Logan walked into his personal space, punctuating her words every few sentences with a finger jab to his chest, which only made him madder.

"Because you have screwed up my work schedule for the last damn time. You missed your delivery date...again. This is the third order I've given you this year that's been late. I needed those pallets four days ago. I called. Somebody at your office told me there was yet another mix-up, and they were delivered to another contractor. I know how you work. You sell my pavers to some-one who wants an order bad enough to buy it above asking price and make me wait. As you can see, I got tired of waiting and went another direction. I'm pouring concrete instead of pavers, and when I need pavers again, I'll be calling your competitor, Jackson's Rock and Brick Yard for product."

By now, Beatty was furious. He'd never wanted to hit some-one as badly as he did this woman, but his mama had drilled the 'boys don't hit girls' manners into him too well to let fly. All he could do was toss out a pathetic excuse for a threat. His face reddened, and then the wind gusted, blowing dirt into his eyes, which made them begin to water. Now he looked like he was crying. It couldn't get much worse as he began to bluster.

"You can't...you don't...you're making a big mistake!"

Logan's retort was sharp and to the point. "The mistake was

yours. You will not be getting any further orders from Talman Construction. Now get your crooked ass off my property, and don't come back."

Beatty was still trying to figure out how someone so pretty could be so damn mean, when she turned her back on him and walked away.

Hacked that she'd not only gotten the last word, but had dismissed him that casually, was embarrassing to a man like Beatty, especially since work all around them had completely stopped, and every man within earshot had been listening. There was nothing to do but leave, hoping word didn't spread about his business practices. He stomped back through the dust to his Lincoln, leaving rubber on the street as he gunned the engine and drove away.

Logan returned to the conversation with her sub-contractors without missing a beat.

"So, Hank, when did you say the quartz countertops are going in?"

And with that, the briefing continued until all of her questions had been satisfied.

The site managers went back to their respective builds while she spent the rest of the day moving from one job site to the other, keeping track of each crew and the amount of work being done, just as her husband, Andrew, had done.

She didn't leave the new housing addition until the final concrete truck had dumped its load, and Wade Garrett, her general manager, arrived to relieve her and finish out the evening with the last crew.

She mulled over the details of the day through five o'clock traffic on the Dallas Expressway, and by the time she got home, the headache she'd ignored all day was ratcheting up into the beginnings of a sleepless night.

She grabbed the mail on her way inside, tossing it on the kitchen table as the cool air began drying the sweat on her skin.

And, as she did every day when she got home, she poured herself a shot of whiskey, toasted the portrait of Andrew hanging over the fireplace in the den, and downed it like medicine, then stood for a few moments staring at his face.

It was Andrew at his best. Blue shirt the same color as his eyes, open at the neck. His rough-hewn features softened by the hint of a smile and the big gray Stetson casting shade. He'd been a big man—a good five inches over six feet—and the only man Logan had ever trusted on sight. At nineteen, she'd lied to him about her age, and married the thirty-year-old contractor six months after they met.

"Five years wasn't enough. I miss you," she said, and then headed for the shower.

A short while later, wearing shorts and one of Andrew's old t-shirts, she went barefoot back through the house to the kitchen, poured herself a big glass of sweet tea, and sat down at the table, ice clinking in the glass. She began to go through the mail, separating bills from the junk until she came to a large brown envelope. The return address gave her a start.

Blue Sky Investigations—the private detective agency she'd hired a couple of months back. Unwilling to 'go there', she set it aside, booted up her laptop, and proceeded to pay the outstanding bills and answer the day's email.

She didn't think about food until work was done, and now that she'd finished, she was suddenly starving. She took a T-bone from the fridge, seasoned it, wrapped it in aluminum foil, then carried it outside and fired up the grill. It would take a while for it to get hot enough, so she turned an eye toward her pool and the shimmering water reflecting from the sky-blue tile. A dragonfly was dancing above the wind-driven ripples, as if taunting her to come in, and so she did without thought for the clothes she was wearing.

She swam to keep from thinking about that brown envelope and the news it might bring, and when the grill was hot enough, she got out and put the steak on a red-hot grate, taking satisfaction in the sound of the sizzle.

It was just right.

Shrieks of laughter from her nearest neighbor's children rode the air over her eight foot privacy fence, while smoke from the cooking steak drifted across her line of vision. The sound of their joy cut through her like a knife. Had she ever been that happy and carefree? She must have been, but couldn't remember it, if she had.

She'd told no one about her past. Not even Andrew, although it was his passing that had given her permission to finally grieve for Damon as well, which in turn, resurrected the rage of his murder and her desire for justice.

The breeze stirred the scent of grilling meat, reminding her it was likely time to turn it, and so she did. Four minutes on each side, and she was done. She used to cook Andrew's steaks three minutes on each side, and he would have eaten it with less. But she couldn't see blood running on a plate and eat the food it lay on, and she couldn't tell him why.

She turned off the grill, carried the utensils and platter that she'd cooked with to the kitchen, and came back with a clean plate for her steak.

The cold air made her wet clothes clammy against her skin, but she spent most of every day in the wind and sun, so she wasn't going to complain. She made herself a salad while the steak was resting, then grabbed the hot sauce and carried it all to the table. She ate for the body fuel it was, rather than savoring it as food.

It wasn't until she'd finished her meal and cleaned up the kitchen that she picked up the brown envelope again. This time she took it with her into the den along with another glass of iced tea, and settled into Andrew's recliner. It was a poor substitute for one of his hugs, but on most days, it sufficed.

She kicked back, took a quick sip of tea, then tore into the envelope and pulled out several sheets of paper.

*Dear Ms. Talman,*

*Regarding your request for information as to how many men drove white, late model Chevrolet Silverado pickup trucks in and around Blue-jacket, Louisiana in July of 2008, we identified sixteen in that parish as well as two surrounding ones.*

*With regard to how many of those men lost their wives within six months of that date, there are three who lived in Bluejacket:*

*Camren Stephens' wife, Julia, died in a wreck.*

*Roger Franklin's wife, Trena, died during surgery.*

*Peyton Adams' wife, Mona, drowned in the family pool—under the influence.*

*An added addendum to this list is of two other men who were divorced by their wives during that time:*

*Tony Warren divorced his wife, Ellen, who subsequently moved away.*

*Danny Bales divorced his wife, Connie, and she, too, moved away.*
*I am including current addresses and contact information for all the men listed.*
*Awaiting further instructions.*

*Sincerely,*
*Hank Rollins*
*Blue Sky Investigations*

Logan read the names listed through several times, trying to place them in her memory, but couldn't. They were too old for her and would have been people Damon knew. Finally, she laid the paperwork aside and turned on the television to catch the late night news.

She sent an email to Blue Sky Investigations as she watched TV, letting Rollins know she'd received the packet and would contact him again if she needed further assistance. But seeing the names had given her the motivation she'd needed, and by the time she went to bed, her decision to go back to Bluejacket had been made.

———◆———

SHE SLEPT WITHOUT DREAMING UNTIL a siren going by the house woke her. She got up to make sure the emergency was not in her neighborhood, got a drink, and went back to sleep. The next time she woke, the alarm was going off, and it was time to do life all over again.

The thought of going back to Bluejacket had always been in the back of her mind. Knowing Damon's killer got away with murder was the pain in her gut that never went away. Before, she'd never known where to start looking, but now that she did, she had no reason to delay. There was no way to know what she'd find when she got there, but she would figure it out as she went.

All she had to do was make sure her business was in good hands before she left, and later, when she arrived on-site at the new housing addition, her general manager was there and with a coffee waiting for her.

"Black with two sugars," he said.

"Thanks, Wade," Logan said, and took a quick sip before setting it aside. "I have something to tell you."

Wade frowned.

"Should I sit down?"

"Not unless you're tired," she said.

He chuckled.

"So talk to me," he said.

"I have to go to Louisiana. I'm leaving tomorrow, which means you will be in charge of everything until I get back."

"How long will you be gone?" he asked.

"Not sure. I have some loose strings from my past that need to be tied."

There was a long moment of silence as Wade looked at her, and she looked everywhere else but at him. Finally, he asked. "Are you in trouble?"

Logan looked up. "No."

Wade eyed the steady look she gave him until he was satisfied, and then nodded.

"Okay then. So what's on for today?"

"Letting the site managers know I'm leaving, and that you'll be in charge. I won't be here tomorrow, so if there's anything you need to ask me, now's the time."

"I have one question," Wade said.

"Ask."

"What aren't you telling me?"

"The same thing I didn't tell Andrew," she said, then checked her agenda. "The roofing material for Talman eight and nine was backordered. I had an email about it when I got home last night." She handed him the paperwork she'd printed off. "Give them a call, see how long they think it will be, and if it becomes an issue, look into finding the same product somewhere else."

Wade watched the way her lips moved as the words came out of her mouth, knowing there were important things she wasn't saying. He'd always known she kept most of her past to herself, but it had never been his place to push. Now, she had admitted there was a secret, and what she didn't say worried him. Still, she was the boss, so he simply agreed.

"Will do," Wade said.

"As soon as I've notified everyone, I'm going home to pack," Logan said.

"Are you flying?" Wade asked.

She shook her head and looked away. "No. I'm taking the Hummer."

He didn't like that she wouldn't meet his gaze. His instincts were right. Something was going on.

"So, Boss, make me a promise. If you get into trouble, call."

Logan nodded. "Promise made."

———◆———

LOGAN LEFT DALLAS ON I-20 with the new morning sun in her eyes. She crossed into Louisiana hours later and took I-49 South while the heat waves coming off the concrete shimmered eerily in the distance like a doorway into another dimension. If she drove fast enough, could she jump into that realm, and if she did, who and what would she find? Was Damon there, still waiting for justice?

*Hang on, brother. I'm coming.*

———◆———

TEN YEARS HAD GONE A long way in changing the looks of the countryside, but the closer Logan got to bayou country, the more anxious she became. The twinge of eye strain from the trip was turning into a headache, and the nerves she'd ridden with had become a knot in her belly. She was topping a hill about thirty miles from Bluejacket when she hit the brakes, coming to a sliding stop only feet from running over a massive alligator taking its own sweet time crossing the highway. It triggered the memory of hurrying to bury Damon's body before a gator dragged it into the swamp, and that set the tone for the rest of the trip to a feeling of unease.

As soon as the gator crossed, she drove on, but the headache had become a thundering pain, and the knot in her gut was growing. All of a sudden, she hit the brakes again, bailing out of the Hummer just in time to throw up while struggling to catch her breath between one gut-wrenching spasm after another.

Weak tears blurred her vision as she finally crawled back behind the wheel, grabbed her water bottle, and took a few careful sips to make sure they stayed down. With a shaky hand, she turned the air conditioner on high and drove the rest of the way into Bluejacket with it blowing in her face.

It was a couple of hours before sundown when she reached the City Limits. The sight reminded her of the overwhelming grief she'd been in the last time she'd passed by this sign, and she could almost hear her brother's voice.

*Okay, Sister, be careful. You are stirring up ghosts.*

She passed the Bayou Motel on the north end of town, which was new to her, then the Bait Shack with the little diner called the Shrimp Shack sitting next to it. Locals stopped what they were doing to look up as she drove by. She was aware that the grumble of the big engine and the rumbling from the Hummer's muffler sounded like a hot rod, which was why Andrew had liked it.

She wouldn't look, but she sensed eyes on her. They couldn't see her for the smoky glass on all the windows, but she knew they were wondering who was behind the wheel.

She drove all the way through town, past the Police Station, which still looked the same, then past Friendly's Grocery, and all the way to the south end of the street before going back to the motel through a residential neighborhood. She drove slowly for the hell of it, looking for familiar faces and places until she reached the motel.

She parked at the office, grabbed the wallet from her shoulder bag, strode inside, and then stopped abruptly. The woman behind the counter was Teresa Wallis—her old neighbor from across the street. But when the woman glanced up and gave her little more than a cursory glance, she breathed easier. It's not like she expected to remain anonymous, but the longer she could investigate before anyone figured out who she was, the better.

"I have a reservation," Logan said. "Logan Talman."

"Right. I'll need to see your driver's license and a credit card."

Logan pulled the cards out and slid them over the counter.

"Dallas, Texas, huh? Just passing through?"

"I'll be here a while," Logan said, and returned the cards to her wallet.

"Got you in Room 4A, facing the street midway down. There's a small coffee station in your room as well as a mini-fridge and Cable TV."

Logan took the key card.

Teresa was frowning now, staring at Logan.

"You look familiar," Teresa said.

"I get that a lot," Logan said, and left the office.

She drove down to 4A and parked in front of the door, then grabbed her things and went inside.

The room smelled and looked clean enough. It would do. She tossed her bag on the bed, hung up the clothes she'd brought in on hangers, and then turned around and walked out. There was still about an hour of daylight and places she needed to see.

All three men on her list had local addresses.

Camren Stephens and Roger Franklin owned their own businesses here in town, and the last one, Peyton Adams was a local lawyer.

Tony Warren, whose wife, Ellen, divorced him and left town, was retired and in a house not far from the high school.

Danny Bales, also divorced and remarried, lived on the south side.

Five men, and she was certain one of them had killed her brother.

Logan left the motel with her heart pounding. It's been said one can never go home, and yet here she was driving down the street where she and Damon used to live.

The hair crawled on the back of her neck as she drove past the house. It looked like the last ten years might never have happened, and that if she went slow enough, Damon would come the front door and wave her down.

Some man was working on a car in the driveway next door. He paused to watch as she rolled past. A teenager was mowing grass a few houses down, and an old woman across the street was outside watering flowers with a garden hose in one hand and a cigarette in the other. She looked familiar, but Logan couldn't place her.

She drove past the high school, wondering about her friend, Caitlin Kincaid, and if she'd left Bluejacket after graduation like she had said she would?

Finally satisfied she'd seen enough, she entered an address in her GPS and within a couple of minutes, found the residence belonging to Camren Stephens. It was a nice house on the north side with the three cars in the driveway, which attested to a comfortable life.

The second address she entered was for Roger Franklin, the second name on the list. His residence was a grand house on the outskirts of town with ornate landscaping more suited to old-style plantation living.

The third address belonged to the lawyer, Peyton Adams, and as she drove past, was startled to see it was where her friend, Caitlin, used to live. Then she remembered Caitie's mom had remarried when she and Caitie were twelve, and Logan began to remember a well-dressed man always in the background at the house, but she couldn't remember his name. Caitie had referred to her stepdad as Pops, which told her nothing. Or, she might be worrying for nothing. They could as easily all moved away after Logan left Bluejacket and Adams was just the current occupant.

By now the sun had set. It was too late to look at any more houses and her belly was growling. She needed to eat. As she drove back through town, she spotted Barney's Café, a place where she and Damon used to go on occasion, and pulled into the parking lot.

She got out to the scent of hot grease and deep-fried fish as she walked across the graveled parking lot on her way inside. A cop car drove past, moving slowly. She didn't know if someone was curious about the stranger in town, or if this was part of the regular patrol route. Either way, she didn't care.

Within seconds of entering, she recognized the waitress working the first table. Her name was Juniper, but everyone used to call her Junie. Logan noticed her hair was still the same brassy shade of blonde, and she was still too skinny for her clothes. She'd had a big crush on Damon, always flirting outrageously when they came in to eat.

"Grab a seat anywhere," Junie said. "I'll be with you shortly."

Logan had a choice. The table against the back wall, or sit beside a table full of men. She chose the one at the back of the room, and as she wove her way among the seated customers, felt every man in the room watching it happen. She knew she turned heads, but it wasn't anything that gave her pleasure. It was damned difficult to run a male-dominated business when people didn't take her seriously because of how she looked.

Logan chose the chair facing the room, and then reached for the menu already on the table. She was looking through the specials when someone slid into a chair at her table.

"I thought that was you. Lord, lord, but you did grow up fine."

She glanced up, then frowned. So much for anonymity.

"Hello, T-Boy."

"Where did y'all go? You just disappeared."

"Last time I heard your voice you were begging me to let you in the house," she said.

He frowned.

She stared back.

Junie showed up at her table.

"Is he joining you?" she asked.

"No," Logan said. "I'll have a bowl of gumbo and some sweet tea, heavy on the ice."

"You got it," Junie said, and hurried off.

"You've changed," T-Boy said.

Logan eyed the dreadlocks and number of tattoos on T-Boy's pale skin.

"You haven't."

A dark flush spread across his face, and then he shrugged and grinned.

"I guess I can't be pissed about the truth. Where's your brother?"

"Minding his own business," she said.

"You still got that ball bat?" he asked.

"Traded it for a Colt 45."

"Jesus Christ, Conway. I was just trying to be friendly."

"Talman. I'm Logan Talman, and you were never friendly to me. You just wanted in my pants. It didn't happen then, and it's not gonna happen now."

T-Boy held up his hands, then grinned, got up and walked away.

Logan watched where he sat, eyeing the men with him, and then made a mental note to keep her handgun close while she was in town. A couple of minutes later, Junie came back with the iced tea and a basket of hot hush puppies.

"Gumbo comin' up. Hush puppies to tide you over," Junie said, and then gave Logan a second look. "I know you, don't I?"

Logan shrugged.

"I used to live here when I was younger."

It was the sound of Logan's voice that triggered Junie's memory.

"You're Damon Conway's little sister! Wow, you grew up to be a real pretty woman. How is he doing?"

"He's in a good place, Junie. Better than all of us."

Junie sighed.

"You give him my best."

"I will," Logan said.

Junie nodded and hurried off.

Logan popped a hush puppy into her mouth, savoring the greasy crunch and the dash of heat from the jalapenos the cook had added to the batter.

When Junie served her bowl of gumbo, she brought fresh hush puppies to go with it, then left Logan alone to eat.

Logan didn't recognize any other diners, but there was a person in Barney's, who went by the nickname of Big Boy, and he damn sure recognized her. When she'd first come in, she'd looked enough like her brother to stop his heart. He thought for moment he was seeing a ghost, but then he'd changed his mind when he saw the long hair and the swell of her breasts. She was beautiful, but she reminded him of the nightmare he'd lived with for months after offing her brother.

He'd spent days after the shooting expecting someone to knock on his door with an arrest warrant. It wasn't until after the fact that he'd remembered Damon had a younger sister. He'd probably told her where he was going when he'd left the house, *and* who he'd been going to meet. And when her brother hadn't come home, she would have called the cops and given them a name. He should have been the first person the cops came looking for, yet none of that had happened, and he'd never understood why.

All he did know was when he'd gone looking for her, she was gone. Then he'd driven out to the site where he'd left Conway's body, only to find both the body and the truck Conway had driven there were gone. He knew where the body was. The gators had dragged it off. And the truck could have easily been stolen. It had been running with the keys in it when Big Boy had left the site, and wherever the little sister was, it wasn't in Bluejacket.

As time passed, his panic subsided to the occasional nightmare... until today. Now he was sitting on the opposite side of the dining room watching Damon's sister, and her body language was obvious. It said, "don't mess with me". But she'd made a mistake in coming back, because Big Boy was going to mess with her, big time.

# CHAPTER THREE

LOGAN ATE WITHOUT LOOKING UP, unaware she was dining in the same room with the man she'd come to find, and
that he was just biding his time, waiting for her to finish eating.

When Big Boy saw her flagging down her waitress for the
check, he tossed some money on the table and headed to the
parking lot to wait. The inside of his car was still cooling off
when she came out of Barney's and got into a big black Hummer.

Again, he was struck by her resemblance to her brother. In the
darkened parking lot, without being able to see her long hair or
the curve of her body, he would have been certain it was Conway, right down to the way he walked.

He followed at a distance as she left the parking lot, needing to
see where she was staying.

UNAWARE THAT SHE HAD ALREADY become a target,
Logan drove aimlessly through town, feeling better for having food in her belly. She was tired and more than ready for bed,
but still took the long way back, remembering these streets and
the people who'd lived on them. When she finally got back to the
motel, she set the car alarm and went inside.

After a quick shower, she put on Andrew's old t-shirt and a pair
of briefs and wearily slipped between the sheets. The last thing
she did before she turned out the light was put the Colt on the

nightstand by her bed.

---

BIG BOY HAD FOLLOWED HER from a distance as she drove, and was still on her tail all the way to the motel. He watched until the lights went out, thinking how easy it would be to just knock on her door, and when she opened it, put a gun to her head and pull the trigger.

End of her.

End of his worries.

Never one to waste time over-thinking, he drove home to get both his handgun and the silencer, made sure it was loaded, then drove back. He pulled up into the parking lot and was about to park and get out when he saw a shadowy figure moving between the cars in the lot, trying each one to see if any were unlocked.

"Sorry bastard," Big Boy muttered.

This was a delay he had not planned for. He was still in the midst of rethinking his options when all hell broke loose.

One second Big Boy saw the man reaching for the door of the Hummer, and then a car alarm went off in a high-pitched screech that was so startling, the sneak thief froze. Before the thief could gather his senses enough to move, Damon's sister flew out of her room with a gun.

Big Boy grunted.

He wouldn't have taken her by surprise after all, so he quietly put his car in gear and eased out the back way of the parking lot. He rethought his options as he drove home while wondering who would have gotten off the first shot, him or her?

---

UNAWARE OF THE DANGER SHE'D been in, Logan was focused on the thief.

"Get down! Get down or I'll drop you where you stand!" she shouted, and when the thief turned to run, she fired off a shot into the air.

He dropped belly first with his hands above his head screaming, "Don't shoot! Don't shoot!"

Logan kicked the bottom of his shoe.

"Don't fucking move."

The night clerk came running out of the office and saw the woman from 4A holding a gun on some man on the ground.

"Call the police!" she shouted.

He turned and rushed back inside as people began emerging from rooms around her. Having strangers at her back made her nervous, but she was too deep into this to back out.

Now that the shock was passing, the thief's thoughts were spinning, trying to come up with an explanation for what had happened besides the fact that he'd intended to rob her.

"Look lady, I—"

"Shut up," Logan said.

The tone of her voice made his skin crawl. He went silent.

Logan kept staring at him, wondering if she knew him, but in the dark, it was hard to tell. Hearing the sound of approaching sirens was a relief, and then all of a sudden, two police cruisers were in the parking lot.

———◆———

JOSH EVANS HAD BEEN THE chief of police in Bluejacket for nine years. He'd seen a lot of things during his years of service, but nothing quite as memorable as the tall, half-naked woman standing in the parking lot with a gun trained on the man at her feet.

Both Evans and his officer, Kenny McKay, came out of their cruisers armed.

"Drop your weapon!" Josh shouted.

Logan backed up and laid it on the ground, then raised her hands. The alarm in her car was still going off.

Josh picked up her weapon, then pointed to the Hummer.

"Ma'am, please silence this alarm."

"I have to get my keys," she said.

He nodded.

She went inside, and moments later, the alarm ceased. She came back out and pointed to the man still on the ground.

"The alarm went off when he tried to break into my car. He tried to run. I fired a shot in the air and he dropped."

McKay already had cuffs on the thief before he dragged him to his feet. Then the thief saw the woman's face, ducked his head and cursed.

"Ah shit...the bitch with the baseball bat. Where did you come from?"

Logan eyed him in disbelief.

"Paul Robicheau...the boy voted most likely to wind up in jail. How nice to see you living up to your fame."

Josh frowned. This woman was driving a Hummer with a Texas tag, and yet the two obviously knew each other.

"So, talk to me now, lady. What's your name, and what's going on here?"

Logan's anger was quick and hot and directed at the cop speaking to her.

"You ask *me* what's going on? I already told you. You should be asking your poster boy here that question. He's the one who got caught committing a crime. I'm just the one who stopped him."

"I know who she is, Chief. Her name is Logan Conway," Robicheau muttered.

"Ten years changes a lot of things," she said, and looked straight at the chief. "My name is Logan Talman. I used to live here. So, Chief... which one of us are you taking to jail?"

Josh ignored the challenge.

"Kenny, take Robicheau in and book him for attempted robbery. I'll be there shortly," he said.

"Yes, sir," Kenny said, loaded up the prisoner, and left.

Josh shifted his stance.

"Ma'am, I'm Chief Evans and I'll need to see some identification, but if you'd like to put on some more clothes, I'll be—"

"I'll get my wallet," she said, strode back into her room for her wallet and room key, and came out, this time shutting the door behind her to keep the cool air in and the bugs out.

Josh was taken aback by both her forthright manner and her lack of modesty, guessing she might have had way more to worry about in life than bare legs.

"Driver's license, contractor's license, license to carry a handgun," she said, and handed them over.

"You're a contractor? As in building houses?

"Yes," she said, and slapped at a mosquito on her leg.

He eyed her bare legs again, then laid her ID on the hood of his cruiser and used his cell phone to take pictures before handing them back.

"What are you doing here in Bluejacket?" he asked.

"Visiting friends," she said.

She was lying, but he already knew it was the only answer he was going to get.

"Plan to stay long?" he asked.

"Is there a time limit on hospitality now?"

Josh frowned.

"I don't appreciate a smart ass," he said, then watched her give him a look of such disdain it was embarrassing.

"Well, Chief, I didn't expect to be treated with suspicion after being the victim of a crime my first night here, either."

He gave her handgun back.

"Don't fire that in the city limits again."

"Then keep your blue-ribbon citizens away from me and mine," she said, reset the car alarm, and went back to her room, slamming the door behind her.

Josh frowned, then got back in his cruiser and headed to the station.

Paul Robicheau was already in a cell when he arrived. He gave him a cursory glance as he walked in through the back and then headed for his office to write up the report. Normally he would have been home in bed asleep beside his wife, Lorene, but his Deputy Chief was on his honeymoon, and two officers were out sick, which left him pulling double shifts and sleeping in his office.

He sat down at the computer and opened up a new report, then sat there thinking about Logan Talman instead. She was full of secrets, and she'd brought them to Bluejacket along with that Colt 45, which made it his business. Tomorrow he was going to run a thorough background check on her so he'd know what he was working with, but tonight was all about adding to Paul Robicheau's rap sheet.

———◆———

LOGAN COULDN'T GO BACK TO sleep. Her routine was off. She missed her nightly toast with Andrew and missed that dip in the pool. Coming back to Bluejacket had also resurrected buried nightmares, and now that she was here, she was cognizant of what her presence would mean to the killer. When word got around that Damon Conway's sister was back in town, he would likely suspect she had come for him.

She opened her laptop and logged onto the *Bayou Weekly* website. With the list of names from Blue Sky beside her, she clicked on Archives, then began with the January 1issue of 2008 and started reading. She fell asleep around two a.m. with her finger on the mouse pad, reading about the Fourth of July shrimp boil in the Town Square, and woke up to the sound of someone slamming the trunk of a car outside her door. The sun was shining and her laptop had long since gone dark.

Time to put away the past for now and deal with today. She threw back the covers and headed for the shower. As always, the first thing she saw when she looked in a full-length mirror were the two tattoos above her navel.

7-29-2008

1/4 - 2 - 9

The first was the date Damon died. The second one was the directions she'd taken from his grave back to town.

A quarter mile from the grave to the blacktop—two miles of blacktop to the highway, and nine miles back into Bluejacket.

Andrew had asked her what they meant once, and when he'd seen her reaction, quickly told her it didn't matter, that it changed nothing about how much he loved her. And for that, she'd loved him even more.

She showered quickly, dressing for the heat and exploration. Until she relocated where she'd buried his body, she had nothing but her say-so that he'd been murdered. She would need that location before she could go to the law, and after the unfortunate meeting with the police chief last night, she didn't know if she could trust him.

Confident that she had a plan, she made up her own bed and left the Do Not Disturb sign on her doorknob as she went back to Barney's for breakfast.

Junie saw her come in and waved.

Logan smiled as she headed for the table she'd had last night and scored a different waitress, a woman who had lived a few houses down from where she and Damon had lived. Charlotte obviously didn't recognize Logan, because she took the time to introduce herself when she came to take her order.

"Hi, I'm Charlotte. Y'all want coffee this mornin'?"

"Is it chicory?" Logan asked.

Charlotte grinned.

"Yes, ma'am, it sure is."

"Then yes, please," Logan said, and quickly scanned the menu as Charlotte poured coffee into the cup already on the table. Logan stirred in two sugars, which made her think of Wade. He'd spoiled her by bringing her fresh coffee already sweetened to the job every morning.

She thought about calling in, then decided against it. She didn't want him to think she didn't trust him.

"Know what you want to eat?" Charlotte asked.

"Biscuits and gravy with a side of bacon."

"Comin' up," Charlotte said, and left to turn in the order.

Logan was waiting for her coffee to cool when her phone signaled a text. It was Wade. She read the text and sighed.

*Are you okay? Did you reach your destination? I'm not snooping. Just need to know you're alive somewhere.*

Her fingers flew as she sent one back

*I'm here. I'm fine. Thank you.*

And that ended their conversation.

She leaned back in the chair and looked up at the diners around her, catching some of them staring. Some faces seemed familiar, but most did not. She wondered if any of the men in Barney's were on her list, but couldn't ask without explaining why she wanted to know.

Charlotte came back with her food.

Logan settled in to eat, savoring the peppery bite in the sausage gravy and the melt-in-her mouth biscuits. The hickory-smoked bacon was just like she liked it, bordering on a crunch, but not quite there. Andrew would have loved this.

She ate until there was nothing left on her plate but gravy smears and biscuit crumbs, then washed the last bite down with the sweetened chicory coffee.

She picked up her check again, left a hefty tip for Charlotte, and paid on her way out. She drove up Main, then stopped at a gas station across the street from Friendly's Grocery to fill up before she went exploring. Just to be safe, she grabbed a couple of water bottles and a snack bar, and then drove north out of town. Once she passed the city limits sign, she began marking the mileage.

She drove for nine miles before turning west onto the blacktop to her left, marked the mileage again on the speedometer, and accelerated, but the closer she got to two miles, the more confused she became. The whole south side of the blacktop was fenced now, and the turnoffs she remembered were gone.

"What the hell?"

She kept on driving, thinking she could have made a mistake about the distance. Maybe it was more than two miles. Anything was possible. She'd been so tired and nearly blind with grief.

She drove two miles farther until she ran out of blacktop, then turned around and retraced her trip to the highway thinking to herself that maybe it wasn't nine miles - maybe it had been ten. So, she drove back to the highway and went a mile farther north before she turned west onto another blacktop road.

The first thing she noticed was no fences. Ah, this had to be it. She began marking distance to two miles, but there were no little side roads along that blacktop on which to turn. She drove a little farther, past the two-mile mark and finally found a narrow path on the south side leading into the swamp.

"This is more like it," Logan said, as she took the turnoff.

Now she was straddling swamp grass and little bushes that had grown up between the tracks as she went, attributing all of that to the ten years she'd been gone.

But when she finally reached water, the inlet was nothing like she remembered. She kept telling herself ten years was a long time for a swamp to evolve, but the old growth trees that should have been there were missing.

She grabbed her Colt and got out anyway, looking through the trees that were there, searching for that X she'd dug into a tree trunk so long ago. She was just walking through a small grove of trees when a snake dropped right in front of her from an overhead limb.

She screamed, her heart pounding, as it slithered into the underbrush.

"What the hell? What the hell? Nothing looks right," she moaned, as she began backing away.

She circled the trees from another direction, but there were no marks of any kind on these either. Disappointed, she was on her way back to the Hummer when she walked up on a six-foot gator hiding out on the swamp grass.

Her hand was on her gun as the gator opened his sizeable jaws and made a hissing noise that sent her running.

By the time she got back to the Hummer, she was sweating profusely. Locking herself in, she jacked up the air conditioner then paused to take a drink. Once she'd calmed herself down, she turned around and drove out, her heart still pounding.

She was on her way back to Bluejacket and feeling defeated. Fear was mingling with frustration as she drove up on the same blacktop at the nine-mile mark she'd taken the first time. It still felt right, even though nothing was the same.

She was scared. She must have been out of her mind after burying her brother. What if everything she'd believed for all these years was wrong?

"Oh, Damon... I don't understand. I didn't lose you. I couldn't lose you."

Making a knee-jerk decision, she made a quick turn west on the blacktop again. This time she ignored the fencing and drove straight to the two-mile mark, then stopped and got out.

"My gut says this is it. I don't know why this changed, but this is it. Now how the hell can I prove it without tearing down a fence?"

She was seriously thinking about jumping the fence and walking in when she heard a car engine. She started to drive away, and then it was too late. An old man in a run-down truck was coming toward her.

*Ask him, dammit.*

The voice in her head was startling, and she found herself lifting an arm to flag him down.

He slowed down as he neared her, then braked.

"Havin' car trouble, ma'am?" he asked.

She eyed the dip of Skoal bulging in his lower lip, the years weathered into his sun-burned face, and then noticed the fishing poles hanging over his tailgate.

"No sir, just revisiting the past a little. I lived in Bluejacket when I was a kid, and I'm trying to find a place where my brother used to take me fishing. I thought it was down this road, but I don't remember any fences. Is this new fencing, or am I likely on the wrong road?"

He leaned out to spit, then wiped his mouth before he spoke.

"I can't say that you're on the right or wrong road, lady. But I can tell you this fence here hasn't been up more than seven or eight years. Before that it was all open land."

Logan breathed a sigh of relief.

"Thank you! I thought I was losing my mind."

He grinned.

"Happy to help. I'm going to do a spot of fishin' myself."

"Well, good luck to you," Logan said, and waved as he drove away.

Even though she was nervous about abandoning the Hummer here and walking a quarter of a mile back into the swamp on foot, she had no other choice. She buckled on her holster and gun and paused to look around.

The sun was a ball of fire in the sky that had already turned the air to steam. The assortment of insects, both flying and crawling, would have been an entomologist's dream, but she wanted no part of them. So she pulled out a can of bug spray from the console and sprayed herself all over, then put on a ball cap to shade her eyes and set the alarm.

Once she was over the fence, she found a clear-cut in the trees where a road had once been and started walking. She was a good hundred yards in before she found the road.

"Please God, let this be it," she said, and lengthened her stride.

She moved carefully through the overgrowth, dodging the occasional snake with an eye for gators, grateful for the high-top cowboy boots she was wearing and wishing she'd thought to wear long sleeves. She was out of sight from the road when she heard another car engine somewhere on the road she'd just left. She stopped, torn between where she was and the vehicle she'd left behind. But when the car drove past without slowing down, she relaxed. It was, however, a reminder to hustle.

She lengthened her stride and was drenched in sweat by the time she reached water. Ten years had done a number on under-brush as well as the knobby-knees of the cypress trees wading in the edges. The Spanish moss hanging from the limbs looked like old men's beards—long, gray, and untrimmed, but the place felt familiar.

Her heart was pounding so fast now that it was hard to breathe. She'd never seen it in the daylight, but the horror of what she'd witnessed still lingered. While there were breaks in the canopy letting the sunshine come through, the place where Damon had died was in shadow. Now, she just had to find where she'd buried him.

She headed for a clump of trees off to the left, pushing through brush and stomping down more swamp grass as she went.

Sweat was running from her hairline when she circled the trees and looked down. She was expecting to see that X gouged into the bark, but when it wasn't there, she started to shake.

"This can't be," she moaned. "It was there."

She squatted down and began digging at the lichen and moss on the tree and found the X beneath. Relief was instantaneous as she traced the faint scar in the bark with her fingers. Then she came out from behind the trees and looked down, her eyes blur-ring with sudden tears. She couldn't see a grave, but she knew it was there.

"I told you I'd be back. I'm sorry it took so long."

She stood in silence, listening to the occasional bird call, and the splash of water as a turtle slid off the bank into the bayou. She was rejoicing in the fact that she'd found it when it dawned on her that she shouldn't be seen in this vicinity. She'd found the location of her brother's grave, but she needed the shooter.

She started walking back to the blacktop, but the farther she went, the more she lengthened her stride. Anxiety grew as she kept moving at a faster and faster pace, until she was running when she ran out of the trees into the sunshine. She climbed over the fence in haste and leaped the shallow ditch between her and the Hummer, shaking in every muscle.

Once the alarm was off, she tossed her hat onto the dash, put the gun and holster into the passenger seat, then began brushing leaves and bugs off her jeans. Suddenly, she thought of the leeches from before and yanked up her pant legs. To her relief, there were none.

When she'd removed enough of the swamp to get inside, she started the engine and amped up the air conditioner, welcoming the cold air blowing across her face and neck.

Nothing felt better than this, except sex.

She drank the last of her first bottle of water and opened the second, taking one more drink before heading back to town.

# CHAPTER FOUR

———◆———

IT WAS ALMOST NOON WHEN Logan drove past the city limit sign. Her belly was growling, and she didn't want the snacks she'd bought, but she was in no condition to eat in public. Then she saw the Shrimp Shack and pulled up to the drive-thru window, ordering a shrimp po-boy and a Pepsi to go.

The clerk eyed her disheveled appearance and then the big fancy Hummer before turning away to fill her order. A few minutes later, he was back with her order sacked up and the big cup of Pepsi already wet from condensation.

"You sure look familiar," he said.

She shrugged.

"I lived here when I was a kid."

He nodded, took the twenty she gave him.

"Keep the change," she said.

Money talks. Just like that, his suspicious nature vanished.

"Thanks, lady."

"Thank you," she said, then stowed her food and drove away.

It was a short trip back to the motel, but by the time she'd set the car alarm and gotten into her room, she was as exhausted as if she'd worked a whole day on the job in Dallas.

She washed her hands and face, then sat down at the little table, turned on the television for company, and ate while her food was still fresh. It was surprisingly tasty, and she made a mental note to go back again before she left town.

Once she'd finished eating, she headed for the bathroom, stripped, then checked herself closely for hitchhikers from the swamp before she got into the shower.

She soaped herself twice and then shampooed her hair. It felt so good to be clean that she stood beneath the water long after the soap had been rinsed from her hair and skin.

She was drying off when she heard her phone begin to ring and raced out of the bathroom to grab it.

It was Wade.

"Hello? Is everything okay?" she asked.

"That was going to be my question to you," he said.

She sighed.

"I'm fine."

"I'm not," he snapped. "I have nightmares about you that are probably far worse than the truth. Put me out of my misery. What are you doing?"

After all these years of living with this secret, the urge to tell him was huge.

"It's a long, ugly story," she said.

"I haven't been afraid of anything in years, but I am now officially afraid for you. Every instinct I have tells me you are in danger."

"I could be," she said, and heard him groan.

"Come home."

She clutched the bath towel up against her chin and sank down onto the bed. "I can't, Wade. Not yet."

"Are you doing anything illegal?"

She frowned.

"Hell no!"

"Then why the secret?"

She sat in silence for so long, she wondered if he'd disconnected.

"Are you still there?" she asked.

"Yes."

Andrew was the only man who hadn't run out on her...until he'd died. Now it seemed Wade had some of his best friend's traits. She pinched the bridge of her nose to keep from crying.

"I am looking for my brother's killer."

"Jesus H. Christ! I am sorry I asked. The reality is worse than my nightmares," he muttered.

Logan caught the dribbles of water running out of her hairline with the towel while trying not to freak out that she'd said that much. Maybe it was because the phone was an impersonal link and she didn't have to look at him when she said it.

"Why you? Why not the police?" he asked.

"It's complicated," Logan said.

"Then tell me where you are so I'll know where to come claim your damn body."

She heard fear and anger, and a kind of panic in his voice she hadn't expected.

"Wade...don't."

"No! *You* don't!" he shouted. "I know how to run a trace. Do you want me digging into every place you've used a credit card since you left Dallas? If I have to, I will do it."

And just like that, the secret spilled.

"No one knows my brother is dead but me and the man who shot him. Ten years ago, he got a phone call late at night to go meet some guy to talk about a job. It was really late and I was afraid for him to go alone, so I hid in the bed of his truck." Unknowingly, Logan's voice slipped into a whisper, and she was starting to shake. "When we got to the meeting place, I heard them talking. The man wanted Damon to kill his wife. He offered him ten thousand dollars and Damon refused. The man killed him to keep him from telling anybody about the offer, and I heard it all. I didn't see his face, but I saw what he was driving when he left."

"Why didn't you tell the police?" Wade asked.

She groaned.

"I just told you! Because I didn't see his face! I would have been his next target! They would have put me in foster care!"

Foster care? Wade was moving into personal territory he didn't understand, and he didn't want her to clam up.

"How old were you?" he asked.

"Sixteen."

"Damn. Oh. Wait. How did people not know your brother was dead?"

Logan threw the towel onto the floor as she stood and then began to pace, unable to sit calmly and speak the horror of what she said next. "Because I buried him in the bayou, marked the spot and drove home, packed up everything we owned, and was gone just after sunup."

Wade shuddered, trying to imagine the guts that must have taken, and the fear that had driven it.

"And now you're looking for the place where you buried him?"

"I found it this morning."

"Then go to the police!"

"And tell them what? I still can't identify the killer."

"So then what the fuck are you doing there?"

"A few months ago, I hired a private investigation agency. I have the names of all the men in the area who were driving late model Silverado pickups who also lost a wife in 2008."

There was a long silence, then Wade's voice.

"How many?"

"Three," Logan said.

"You are a sitting duck," Wade said.

Logan sighed. "I know."

"Please don't die," he said.

Her eyes welled.

"My parents were killed in a wreck when I was ten. I was the only survivor. Damon came back into my life and took me with him, saving me from a life in foster care. He was my brother and what stood for a father-figure, and the only hero I had left. I promised him I would come back to find who did this to him, and so I have."

"Did Andrew know all this?" Wade asked.

"No one knew. You're the first person I've told, and I expect you to respect my decisions."

"Shit," he muttered.

"I'm sorry," she said.

Wade wasn't satisfied. "I need to know where you are."

Logan tensed. He was beginning to push her and she didn't like it. "Bluejacket, Louisiana, and your job is to take care of my business there, not my business here. Understand?"

"Shit."

She picked up the towel and swiped it across her face to catch the tears.

"'Shit' is not an answer," she said.

"Yes, I understand. Yes, I will take care of the damn houses you aren't going to live to see built. Are you happy?"

She swallowed past the lump in her throat.

"I haven't been happy even one day since Andrew's death," she admitted. "But losing Andrew reminded me that I'd made a promise to my brother that I had yet to honor. I came to find my brother's body. He came for me when I needed him most. I can do no less for him."

Wade knew if he didn't back off, she would shut him out. "Know this! I will call you every day, and no matter where you are, you better answer or I'm coming after you. Do you understand me?"

"Yes."

He hung up on her.

She dropped the phone back down on the bed and went to comb the tangles out of her hair, but her hands were shaking so bad she dropped the comb twice. Telling that story to someone had been almost as scary as witnessing it.

She put on one of Andrew's old t-shirts for comfort and a pair of her own shorts, then curled up on top of the bed with her laptop, found the place in the *Bayou Weekly* archives where she'd fallen asleep, and resumed her research. In a town this small, there had to be something that would drive a man to murder. She made a couple more notes and then put in a call to Blue Sky Investigations.

The phone rang to the point she thought it was going to go to voice mail, but then she heard a familiar growl.

"Big Sky, Hank speaking."

"Hank, this is Logan Talman."

"Yes, ma'am. What can I do for you?"

"A couple of things, and if you can, put a rush on this request."

"Depends on what you need," he said.

"Regarding the three deceased women on that list you sent me, I need to know if there were any life insurance policies on them...and while you're at it, see if the two divorced women had life insurances policies on them as well."

"Ah...good one," Hank said. "What else?"

"More regarding the two women who divorced their husbands and left Bluejacket. I need to know if they really left and are alive somewhere."

"Right. It won't take long to get these answers for you."

"I'm out of town, so just email me the information as soon as you get it."

"Will do," he said, and disconnected.

She laid the phone aside and went back to reading, making notes as she went.

———◆———

JOSH EVANS ALREADY KNEW WHAT Paul Robicheau was about. He was in jail because he was a thief. But he didn't know what Logan Talman was about, and he didn't like surprises.

The two officers who'd been out sick had shown up for work this morning, which gave him much needed time in the office. He was finding out plenty from the background check he was running on her—but nothing that sounded any warnings until he began to follow up on her brother.

She'd been the sole survivor in a wreck that had killed her parents. At that point, her brother had become her legal guardian. Her brother didn't have a rap sheet and neither did she.

He found school records for her that ended here in Bluejacket's high school her junior year. Her brother had worked for a plumber in town, but never filed an income tax statement after 2008. And as more information came in, he realized there was no record whatsoever of her brother working again.

The next information he got on Logan was that she'd earned a GED in Dallas, Texas while she had worked waitress jobs. Nothing was flagged on her driving record or her work record, and she'd never been arrested.

He saw a copy of her marriage license to an Andrew Talman, and then a death certificate for the man five years later. The best he could tell, Logan had stepped into her husband's shoes after he died in an on-the-job accident, and at the age of twenty-four, had begun running their contracting business on her own and had kept it in the black.

So now he knew a lot about her, but not why she was here.

The business about her brother going off the grid in Bluejacket bothered him. He thumbed back through the paperwork and found that the address where they used to live was one of Martha

Beaudine's rental properties.

He glanced at the clock. It was nearing noon, and Martha usually went to the Senior Citizens Center to eat dinner. It might not be a bad idea to talk to her about the Conways and see what she had to say.

He grabbed the keys to his cruiser and walked out through the back past Robicheau's cell.

Robicheau saw him and yelled out.

"Hey, Chief! When am I being arraigned? I'm supposed to get my day in court!"

"Judge won't be here until tomorrow," Josh said, and slammed the door behind him as he left.

Robicheau threw himself backward onto his bunk, cursing.

"I'm supposed to get a phone call," he muttered, ignoring the fact that he had no one to call.

———————◆———————

JOSH DROVE STRAIGHT TO THE Senior Citizens Center and parked in the shade, although it did little in the way of blocking heat. The sweat stains on his shirt continued to spread beneath his armpits as he got out and went inside.

There were at least two dozen of Bluejacket's older citizens scattered about. A couple of old men were playing dominoes and talking about the newest widow in the room. But the same woman they were talking about was sitting off by herself, staring out a window. The lost expression on her face tugged at the chief's heart. He didn't want to imagine how lost he'd be without his wife.

The scent of fried shrimp was immediate, but the rest of the odors coming from the kitchen were unrecognizable, which didn't bode all that well for the elderly diners—or maybe it did, depending on how important these meals were to all of them.

He stood in the doorway for a bit, trying to pick Martha out from the others. A few of them were already at the dining tables waiting for food, but most of them were at the other end of the room playing Bingo.

Someone yelled Bingo, and when he glanced that way, saw

Martha Beaudine. She looked a bit rough, but then she always had, so he didn't assume she was as feeble as she appeared. He was looking around for the coordinator when the man walked up behind him.

"Hello, Chief. Did you come to eat with us?" he asked.

Josh shook his head.

"Hi, David. I'll pass on lunch, but I need to talk to Martha for a couple of minutes...in private."

"Why don't you go on into my office, and I'll get her for you?"

"Thank you," Josh said. "Much appreciated."

He slipped into the half-open door and waited for just a couple of minutes before Martha tottered in.

"Here I am," Martha said, frowning. "I got a hot bingo card, so speak your piece."

He grinned.

"Yes, ma'am. I appreciate this. I'm trying to run down some information on a brother and sister who once lived in one of your rental properties."

"What's the name?" she asked.

"Damon and Logan Conway, and they would have moved away about ten years ago."

Her rheumy blue eyes suddenly blazed.

"I remember them. Ran out without telling me. Left food in the refrigerator and the keys on the table without so much as a note."

"Did they skip owing you money?" the chief asked.

"No. Nothing like that. They were good tenants. Kept stuff clean and paid the rent on time."

"Do you know why they would have left?"

"Not a clue, but I asked a couple of neighbors, and both of them told me they saw the girl, Logan, driving away, but no brother in the truck."

Evans nodded.

"Did anyone ever come around asking for them?"

She frowned.

"There was someone, but I can't remember who. It's been too long, you know?"

"Yes, ma'am. If you do happen to remember, would you please give me a call?" Josh asked.

Martha shrugged. "Sure, if it matters that much, but don't count on it. My memory isn't what it used to be."

Josh hid a grin as she tapped her head to punctuate her statement. "Yes, ma'am, I understand, but do try. Thank you for your time. Better get back to that hot bingo card before the mojo is gone."

"Fosho, dat," Martha said, slurring her words in a slow Cajun drawl, and left the office.

She was already back in her chair and complaining about losing her place in the game as he was leaving.

———◆———

B IG BOY WAS NERVOUS, AND when something bothered him, he always went to his garden for peace and calm. The roses he grew were his pets—his babies. He talked to them as he walked, dead- heading those in need, and fussing at them as if they could hear. Their scent was sweet, intoxicating. They gave him the only high he'd ever need. As he worked, he kept thinking of Conway's sister.

People were starting to talk about her now. The majority had figured out who she was, referring to her as Damon Conway's sister all grown up. The fact that she'd come back alone immediately brought up questions about her brother. This all had to go away and fast.

He finished up in the rose garden and went inside, pausing in the work room to trade his gardening shoes for his loafers. Ruthie, their cook, was baking pastries as he came through the kitchen.

"Something sure smells good, Ruthie."

"Thank you, sir."

He smiled, thinking about how good they would taste at dinner tonight, and was halfway up the stairs when he heard footsteps coming from behind him.

"Where have you been? When are we going to New Orleans? You promised me a shopping trip. I hate this little hick town so much. There's nothing here I want. Absolutely nothing."

Big Boy stopped, frowning at his wife's chatter.

"I'm in this hick town, so are you saying you don't want to be my wife anymore?"

She blinked, then threw her arms around his neck.

"No, no, no, baby. I didn't mean it that way. I love you more than anything. Forgive me?"

The fact that she now had her hand on his dick made it easy to say 'yes'.

———◆———

LOGAN FINISHED READING THROUGH THE archived copies of the weekly paper for the entire year of 2008. Other than reading notices of the three women's deaths on her list, and subsequent obituaries announcing services, there was nothing to indicate a scandal, a loss of business, or anything else that made her alert on the deaths.

Having come to the decision that there were no answers here, she decided to wait and see if Blue Sky came up with any new leads she could use. So she logged out of the archives, checked her email on the off-chance Hank might have responded, but he had not, so she logged off the laptop and set it aside. Tired of inactivity, and with the beginnings of an ache between her shoulders, she stretched out on the bed and soon fell asleep.

———◆———

CAITLIN HAD JUST HEARD THE news that Logan Conway, Logan Talman now, was back in Bluejacket and staying at the Bayou Motel. Caitlin was alternating between the excitement of going to see her, or still being put out with her by ignoring she was here.

They'd been best friends in high school, and when Logan and Damon left town without even a goodbye, she'd been devastated. She'd kept telling herself that Logan would at least write to tell her what had happened, but after a year had passed without a word, she'd let it go.

The ensuing years had battered teenage Caitlin's dreams. The death of her mother, an unplanned pregnancy, one hasty marriage, and two babies later, she was a far cry from the bubbly blonde she used to be.

Part of her reluctance to go see Logan was that she had let herself go, but the Logan she remembered would not have cared about that, and in the end, curiosity won out over vanity. Regardless of wishing she looked better, she made the decision to reconnect. A few minutes later, she was dropping her kids off with a girlfriend before heading to the Bayou Motel for a high school reunion of her own.

She stopped off at the motel office to get the room number, then had to remind the clerk that she and Logan had been best friends in school and she was just coming to say hello, before the clerk would divulge her location.

Still rolling her eyes, Caitlin walked the short distance down to 4A, eyeing a black Hummer parked right in front of the door. If that was Logan's vehicle, she was seriously impressed and couldn't wait to hear all about what was going on in her friend's life.

She smoothed down the front of the loose yellow blouse she'd chosen, which helped disguise her muffin-top. She was as ready to face this reunion as she would ever be, so she took a deep breath and knocked.

———◆———

THE ABRUPT KNOCKING AT LOGAN'S door startled her awake. She rolled over and reached for the Colt before she went to the window. When she saw who it was, she put the gun back by the bed and unlocked the door.

The smile on Logan's face eased Caitlin's nerves.

"Hi stranger!" Caitlin said.

Logan swung the door inward.

"Caitie! Oh my God...I am so glad to see you! Come in, come in! How did you know I was here?"

"Oh you know Bluejacket. Nothing stays secret for long. I hope you don't mind, but I talked the clerk up at the office into telling me your room number by reminding him we'd been friends in school."

"Of course I don't mind! Come in!" Logan said.

Caitlin stepped over the threshold into a big hug, then eyed Logan's long, lean legs and body with envy as Logan closed and locked the door behind her. She didn't think anything of the added security measure until she saw the big handgun on the table by the bed.

"What's with the gun?" she asked.

Logan blew it off with a shrug.

"A woman traveling alone these days has to take care of herself." She dropped back onto the bed, pulling Caitlin with her. "Sit. Tell me what's going on with you."

Caitlin scooted up on the bed to face her like they used to do when they were kids.

"You first," Caitlin said. "You're the one who disappeared over night. I worried about you for months."

Logan reached for Caitlin's hand and gave it a quick squeeze.

"I'm so sorry. It's part of why I'm back, but nothing I can talk about yet."

"Are you in trouble?" Caitlin asked.

"Not like you mean. It's all good, honey."

"So you married," Caitlin said.

"I was. My husband died two years ago. Accident on the job. I miss him every day of my life."

Caitlin's eyes welled with tears.

"Oh my God. I'm so sorry."

"It happens," Logan said. "What about you?"

Caitlin's shoulders slumped.

"I was pregnant when I graduated high school. Johnny and I got married right after."

"Johnny Baptiste?" Logan asked.

Caitlin nodded.

"Yes. He's good to me and the kids. They're both boys, which made Johnny happy, but they are hell on wheels and keep me jumping. Of course, the oldest just had his ninth birthday. My little one is seven. Do you have kids?"

"No," Logan said.

"What about Damon? Where's he these days? Is he in Texas, too?"

"No, he stayed in Louisiana. I moved with the marriage,"

Logan said. "Hey...it's almost lunch. Have you eaten?"

"No, but—"

"Let me change, and we can go to Barney's. My treat."

Caitlin grinned.

"Yes, I'd love it."

Logan rolled off the side of the bed, stripping off Andrew's old t-shirt as she went. She grabbed a clean shirt from the little closet and slipped it on, then was putting on a pair of jeans when Caitlin spotted the tattoo above her navel.

"What's that on your belly?"

"Oh, just a tat," Logan said, and began buttoning up her shirt.

"What does it say?" Caitlin asked.

"Nothing that matters," Logan said, and began buttoning up the shirt.

Caitlin didn't argue, but it was becoming obvious that her old friend had secrets, and ten years was plenty of time to make them.

A few minutes later, they were on their way out.

"Want to ride with me or follow?" Logan asked.

"I'll follow you, that way I can go straight home from Barney's. I have a friend watching the boys, and don't want to leave her hanging too long."

"See you there, then," Logan said.

She turned off the car alarm and stowed her gun and holster beneath the seat before following Caitlin's car.

# CHAPTER FIVE

———◆———

FROM THE LOOKS OF THE parking lot, Barney's was already busy with noon diners. Caitlin parked her smaller car up near the entrance, but the Hummer took up space and required more maneuvering room, so Logan opted to park near the back of the lot.

Heat slapped her in the face as she got out, but it wasn't anything new. It was hot in Dallas, too. An old gray cat was lying in the shade of the bushes along the side of the parking lot and looked up as Logan walked by.

"Hi, kitty," Logan said.

The old cat's mew was as weak as it looked. It was a day fit for cold drinks and languid breezes—languid being a word fit only for places like Louisiana. Logan had known little happiness here, but it had been home until that night. Now it was just a landmark for murder.

She looked up to realize Caitlin was waiting for her and lengthened her stride.

"You always did dawdle," Caitlin said, giggling as they met at the front door.

They were still grinning at each other as then went inside.

"Oh, feel that blessed air conditioning," Caitlin said. "I wonder if other people appreciate it quite like we do, you know? And, I don't get out much alone, so this is a real treat."

"Same here. I'm on the job all day with a bunch of men, so getting to spend time with a girlfriend is a treat for me, too."

"You work with men? What do you do?" Caitlin asked.

"I'll tell you all about it as soon as we get seated," Logan said, and once again, headed for the same empty table at the back of the room.

She chose a seat against the wall, leaving Caitlin to take her pick of the other three.

Junie and Charlotte were both working the room again, and this time, it was Junie who came to their table with glasses of iced water.

"Well now, seeing you two together again sure looks familiar," Junie said.

Caitlin giggled.

"It feels like it, too, Junie. What's the special today?"

"Meatloaf and two sides," Junie said.

"I'll have that with mashed potatoes, gravy, and corn."

"You got it, honey. How about you, Miss Logan?" Junie asked.

"Gumbo still on the stove?" she asked.

Junie grinned.

"Gumbo is *always* on the stove. Bowl of that and hush puppies again?"

"Yes. I haven't had good gumbo since I left Louisiana. Don't want to waste a chance to eat my fill of it before I go home," Logan said.

Junie went to turn in the order, leaving the two women alone.

Caitlin leaned forward, her elbows on the table as she lowered her voice.

"So, what's that all-male job you work at?"

"My husband was a contractor. He built houses, lots of houses. I worked on the site with him after we married because I wanted to, and when he was killed on the job, I stepped into his shoes and kept it going. I have good men on my crews, and a general manager named Wade Garrett who is my right-hand man."

"Wow," Caitlin said. "You did what I wanted to do. You got out of Bluejacket."

"I guess it would seem that way," Logan said. "But you have what I always wanted. You have a family. As hard as I try, I keep losing mine."

Caitlin knew about the death of Logan's parents, and now her husband? She hurt for her friend as she reached across the table.

"I'm sorry, sweetie. I do love my boys." Then she leaned closer and giggled. "And most days, I love Johnny."

Logan laughed. It felt good to be caught up in Caitie's nonsense again.

Junie came back with their food, and they quickly dug in.

As they began to eat, their conversation was little more than asking for the salt, laughing at an old story from high school, asking about people they had in common. But as always, Logan was hyper-aware of the people eyeing her, always wondering if one of them was the killer.

A couple of men were staring at them from across the room and had been since they'd come in, and it was making Logan nervous. She leaned forward and lowered her voice.

"Hey Caitie, do I know either of those two men at the table under the front window? Don't look at them now. Just do it casually in a couple of minutes."

Caitlin nodded, then took another bite of meatloaf, chewed and swallowed, then turned in her chair, as if looking for their waitress, and saw the men.

"The one with the longest hair owns the fish and bait store on the north edge of town. He and Damon used to go fishing together. The man in the white shirt and slacks is our illustrious mayor, Barton DeChante."

"What does he do?" Logan asked.

"Much of nothing. He makes his money playing the Stock Market. I don't know what he did before that. Why he lives in Bluejacket and not New Orleans is beyond me. He'd fit right into their social circle."

"He doesn't fit into the social circle here?" Logan asked.

Caitlin giggled.

"Oh honey, Bluejacket doesn't have a social circle. Just the right side and wrong side of town."

Logan nodded. The man was probably staring at her because she looked familiar. She didn't remember the men Damon hung out with, but they likely remembered her.

Logan thought about the house where Caitlin grew up. One of the men on her list lived there now, and she'd decided to ask outright about her family.

"How is your Mama these days?" Logan asked

Caitlin's smile shifted sideways.

"She passed away not too long after you left."

Logan's stomach knotted.

"I am so sorry to hear this. What happened?"

"She drowned in our pool."

Logan didn't bother to hide her surprise.

"I can't believe it! That doesn't make sense. All those races we had when we were kids, and she out-swam both of us every time."

"I know...but she was changing. A year after you left, she started drinking...a lot. She was drunk the night she died. They said she hit her head when she fell in the pool, and that's why she drowned. I was on a date with Johnny and my step-dad was out of town on business. I found her when I came home."

"Oh my God, I am so sorry, Caitie."

Caitlin shrugged.

"It had a lot to do with the choices I made later on. Pops, my step-dad is okay, but he never wanted to be a parent. He just wanted my mother. I made the decision easy for him afterward, and even though Johnny and I didn't get married until we graduated, I moved out. We were living in an apartment here in town within four months of Mama's passing."

"Did your step-dad stay in your family home or did he leave town?"

"He's still there in the same house," Caitlin said.

Logan filed that info away for future reference as she pushed her plate away.

"It would seem life slapped us both down a little, didn't it?"

"Yes, but we're both survivors, too, and that's enough sad stuff. Let's eat pic," Caitlin said.

Logan grinned, and waved at their waitress on her way past the table.

"Junie, we're having dessert."

"Chocolate or coconut cream pie...Apple cobbler or bread pudding?" Junie asked.

"Oooh, I'll take the chocolate," Caitlin said.

"Make it two," Logan said.

Junie gave them a thumbs up.

Logan was trying to stay in the moment and get back to light-hearted chit-chat with Caitlin, but her head was spinning. How

was this news about Caitie's mother going to tie in with the new
info Blue Sky Investigations would send? Would she find a big
life insurance payout on Mona's death?

However, Caitlin's constant chatter moved to family when she
pulled out recent pictures of her boys. Logan nodded and smiled
in all the right places, listening to her talk about the two little
redheads and how they were just like their father. Her old friend's
easy-going personality made their time together enjoyable and
the conversation easy—almost too easy, because when Caitlin
finally asked another personal question, Logan was tempted to
tell.

"Logan, honey... why did y'all run? And don't tell me you just
up and decided to move in the middle of the night."

Logan glanced at the look on Caitlin's face. She was sincere to
a fault, and she'd always kept their secrets. But telling her any of
this could put her in danger, too, and that couldn't happen.

Logan shrugged.

"All I can say is that it was because of something Damon got
mixed up in."

"Oh Sugar... I'm so sorry," Caitlin said. "Does that have something to do with why you're here? Why you lock everything
behind you? Why you carry a gun?"

Logan shrugged.

Caitlin frowned. "Is there anything I can do to help?" she asked.

Logan started to tell her no, and then she thought of Wade.

"There is one thing," Logan said.

"Anything," Caitlin said. "Just ask."

"Do you have anything I can write on?" Logan asked.

Caitlin picked up her purse and dug through the contents until
she pulled out a long grocery receipt and a pen.

"Will this work?"

"Yes, thanks," Logan said, turned it over and wrote Wade's
name and phone number, then handed them back.

"If anything happens to me, please call this man. Will you do
that for me?"

"Oh my God, Logan! Yes, of course I'll do it, but you're scaring
me," Caitlin said.

"That's pretty much what Wade said." Logan watched as Caitlin folded the paper up and put it into a zippered pocket inside

her purse.

Caitlin's hands were shaking as she set it back down on the floor. "Can the police help you?"

Logan shrugged. "Maybe, but not yet. Don't worry. I'm tough and I'm careful."

Then Junie came back with the pie, filled up their drinks, and left them to enjoy. They ate with their heads together, talking and laughing, which had diners looking up at them more than once.

Caitlin scraped the chocolate off the plate, licked the fork, and then leaned back with a groan.

"That was the best cheat meal on the diet I have yet to start, and the most fun I've had in years, but if I don't get back and pick up my boys, my friend will kill me."

"And I need to get back to the motel and check my email," Logan said, but she was eyeing the pie crust she'd left on her plate and impulsively wrapped it up in a paper napkin to take with her.

She left a tip on the table, picked up the check, and went up front to pay. Caitlin waited beside her, and then led the way outside. As soon as they were alone, Caitlin paused.

"I am so happy I got to see you. This time when you're through with your business, don't you dare leave without telling me goodbye."

"I promise," Logan said, and hugged her. "Take care, and tell Johnny I said hello."

"Will do," Caitlin said, then waved as she drove away.

Logan watched until she was out of the parking lot before returning to her car. The old gray cat was still in the patch of shade beneath the bushes. Logan paused to unwrap the crust, and then laid it down only inches from the old cat's nose. The cat sniffed, managed another weak "mew" and then unwound itself before getting up to eat it.

Satisfied, Logan turned off the alarm on the Hummer and reluctantly slid across the seat. The temperature inside was like an oven. She wasted no time starting it back up to cool off, and as she was waiting, decided to go by the grocery store and get some snacks to take back to the room. She drove four blocks down Main, and then pulled into the parking lot of Friendly's.

She sat for a couple of minutes thinking about Caitlin's mother.

What had made her start drinking? Had she really fallen into the pool or had she been pushed? She was still thinking about Mona's death when someone knocked on Logan's window. She turned to look and then frowned.

*Chief Evans? What does he want now?*

She rolled down the window.

Josh wasn't sure this was the time to approach this subject, but he wasn't the patient kind.

"Can we talk?"

She shrugged. "Get in."

"I'd rather you stopped by the office," he said.

"Well, I'm going in to get some groceries, and then I'm going back to the motel to check email. I have five builds going on at once in my housing addition and a lot to deal with, so I'd rather you talked to me here."

He blinked.

She didn't.

"Then would you mind getting into my cruiser to talk?" he asked.

"Only if you keep the air conditioning on high," she said.

He grinned. "Yes, ma'am."

She killed the engine and locked her car, then strolled over to the police car where he was waiting. He opened the door for her, and as she got in, pushed the seat back as far as it would go to accommodate her long legs.

Josh got in, then realized they would be having this conversation over the squawk of the police radio, so he decided to make this quick.

"Miss Talman—"

"Mrs."

He flushed. "Right. Sorry about that. Mrs. Talman, I talked to your old landlady."

"Mrs. Beaudine? I didn't think she'd still be living. I need to look her up and say hello," Logan said.

"Yes, well, as I was saying. Several people have told me that you left Bluejacket very suddenly, and when you did, you left alone."

Logan's heart skipped, but her expression never changed.

When she didn't volunteer anything, he frowned.

"Why didn't you answer me?"

Logan pretended surprise. "Because you didn't ask me a question. You just stated some third-party gossip, which should not have a damn thing to do with why I'm visiting. I am still in shock that I have become a 'person of interest' to you, when I have done nothing but come back to a place where I once lived."

He heard tension in her voice, but guessed it was because she was trying not to get angry. He knew he was pushing for answers to questions he didn't have the right to ask.

"Mrs. Beaudine said you left without telling her."

Logan frowned. "Well, back then my brother took care of all that stuff, and I didn't know she hadn't been notified. What I do know is that we left with all bills paid and the house keys on the kitchen table. It's not like we'd signed a lease. We were month-to-month renters, like all of her other properties, and we didn't owe her notification or a reason for leaving."

"Where is your brother?"

She glared. "Is he wanted for a crime?"

"No, but—"

"Am I wanted for a crime?"

He sighed.

"No, but—"

"Then you, sir, need to go find someone else to question. If at any time during my visit I feel the need for police protection, rest assured, I will not hesitate to call. And just so you know... if anything should happen to me while I'm here, then and only then will you have yourself a reason to be all up in my business. Okay?"

"Why would you think something might happen to you?" he asked.

Her eyes narrowed. "Life has a way of cutting the legs out from under me now and then, so I always hedge my bets. If we're through here, I really need to go."

Josh frowned. "I suppose I'm—"

She got out and shut the door without looking back.

He watched until she went into the store, and then he put the car in gear and drove away. She was hiding something...and she'd side-stepped commenting on her brother for a reason. He had a feeling her business would become his business, too, before they were through.

L OGAN GRABBED A SHOPPING CART and headed for the produce aisle. After picking up a small bunch of bananas, a couple of apples, and some grapes, she went to look for cheese snacks and a box of crackers. She added those to her cart and moved next to the soft drink aisle. Two six packs of Pepsi later, she was finished and on the way to check out. She put everything on the conveyor and then moved up to the register where the checker was running her purchases through the scanner.

She was waiting for the total when a man walked into the store, then suddenly stopped. She glanced up and caught him staring. He looked familiar, but then so did a lot of people here, so she ignored him, swiped her credit card, and then signed her name.

"Do you need any help with carry out?" the checker asked.

"No, ma'am. I've got this," Logan said. She put everything into her basket and pushed it toward the exit.

The man hadn't moved. When she got closer, she realized he was shaking.

"Excuse me, ma'am. I didn't mean to be staring, but you look like someone I used to know. By any chance are you related to Damon Conway?"

"I'm his sister, Logan. Do I know you?"

"Probably only by name. I'm George Wakely. Wakely's Plumbing? He worked for me, you know, and I used to see you around town, but you were just a kid then."

"Yes, Mr. Wakely. Nice to see you," Logan said, and went through the exit door, pushing her cart.

When she realized he had followed her back out, his dogged persistence added to the tension.

She stopped, then turned around to face him, which elicited a quick red-faced apology.

"I don't mean to stare," he repeated, "and I'm sorry to keep bothering you, but what happened? One day y'all were here, and then you weren't. He was a good employee. I worried."

"It was all really sudden," Logan said, then turned off the car alarm and put the sacks in the passenger seat.

"So, did he come back with you?" he asked.

"No. After I grew up, I married and live in Texas now."

Wakely nodded.

"Well, when you see him, tell him I asked about him."

"Yes, I'll do that," she said. "Nice to meet you."

Then she got in and drove away, well aware her behavior had bordered on rude, but it couldn't be helped. She just wanted to get back to her room, see if she had any more information from Big Sky, then solve this mess and go home.

She pulled up to the motel and parked, then began carrying her purchases inside before going back to get the gun from under the seat, reset the alarm, and locked the door.

She was kicking off her boots when she realized there were fresh towels in the bathroom, which meant the maid had been here. Damn it! She'd forgotten to put out the Do Not Disturb sign. She immediately began looking to see if everything was still here, and it was.

She put a few bottles of Pepsi into the mini-fridge, as well as the cheese and fruit, then changed back into her shorts and t-shirt, grabbed her laptop, and crawled back onto the bed.

She was about to check email when her cell phone rang. She glanced at Caller ID and sighed. It was Wade.

"Hello. I'm fine, how are you?" she said.

He chuckled, and the sound rolled through her like silk against her skin.

"Okay, then. Good to know. We had an issue with flooring on McGuire's crew. The delivery truck wrecked on I-35 North-bound, scattering pecan brown laminate all over the place this morning. They're sending a new flooring shipment tomorrow, so it won't throw them behind enough to stress about."

Just hearing Wade talk about everyday business was calming.

"As long as the cost is on them and not us, then it's all good," she said.

"Agreed," he said, then cleared his throat. "Doing anything new?"

"I had lunch with the woman who was my best friend in high school. It was good. Her name is Caitlin Baptiste. She married her high school sweetheart, Johnny, and has two red-headed boys like him."

"Okay...but you didn't go there for a school reunion. What else is going on?"

She leaned back against the headboard, staring up at a small water stain on the ceiling and squinted her eyes, trying to decide if that was a bug or a dirty spot on the wall below it.

"Logan! Damn it!"

"Don't yell at me. I'm trying to decide how much I'm going to tell you, and if you piss me off, I will hang up."

"Then talk to me, and you know better than to threaten me."

She frowned. "I'm waiting on more information from the private investigator. I want to know if any of the surviving spouses collected on big insurance policies, and if the two women who divorced and moved away are alive in the world somewhere."

There was a slight pause. "Good thinking," he said.

"Thank you."

"If you need me..."

"Yes, I know," Logan said.

"I'll call tomorrow."

"Was that a promise or a warning?" she asked.

He chuckled again.

She closed her eyes, suddenly wishing she was safe at home and not down here taking chances with her life. But there was her brother and that promise she'd made.

"Take care of yourself," he said.

"I will."

The line went dead in her ear.

She laid the phone aside and pulled up her email. There was a new message from Hank Rollins. She opened it, and as she began to read, realized this information would likely eliminate two of the five on her list.

There was a half million-dollar life insurance policy on Julia Stephens, who'd had died in a wreck.

There had been no life insurance policy on Trena Franklin, who'd died on an operating table.

There had been a two hundred and fifty-thousand-dollar policy on Ramona (Mona) Adams, which had had a double indemnity clause if the death was accidental. The half-million had been paid out after a lengthy investigation to rule out suicide.

Regarding the divorcées, Connie DeChante Bales, was living

in California, but Ellen Warren, the other divorcée, had dropped off the radar and was believed to have gone to Alaska to live off the grid. Logan noticed Bales' maiden name was DeChante and wondered if she was related to the mayor, then let it go.

Hank Rollins ended the report by including a bill and the same instructions. "If you need further information, just let me know." And then he'd signed it.

She thought about handing all of this over to Chief Evans right now, but she didn't know him well enough to trust him.

But to safeguard what she *had* learned, she needed to share it with someone, and who better than Wade?

She paid the current bill to Blue Sky through PayPal, and then began typing up a cover letter to Wade, writing a detailed listing of everything she knew and how she'd come by the info, then attached the latest email from the P.I. as well. She re-read it twice and then hit "Send" before she changed her mind.

When she looked up and realized it was almost four o'clock, she groaned. One last task before she went to bed. She wanted to see where the two divorced men lived. If their living conditions were such that they would never have been able to offer ten thousand dollars to get rid of a wife, then she was going to eliminate them.

She dressed once more and then left. Once inside the Hummer, she entered the first address into her GPS system, then followed it, weaving her way through the streets, then out to the south edge of town to an ordinary-looking house. It wasn't large, but it wasn't a hovel, either. There were three late model vehicles in front of the house, and an older man washing a car in the shade of two live oaks. She wondered if that was Danny Bales. He looked the right age, and he did not look like a man who would ever be able to throw money around.

She entered the second address into the GPS and headed for the other side of town, looking for the residence of Tony Warren—the man whose wife had dropped off the grid. She couldn't assume this meant anything sinister, because she'd personally known two different people in the last ten years who'd done that very thing. One had moved up into the mountains in Colorado to live off the land, and the other had chosen Alaska and done the same thing Warren's wife had supposedly done.

As she was driving, she began to notice the clouds building off in the distance. It would rain soon, certainly before the night was over. She braked at a stop sign near the high school, allowing herself a few moments of reverie, and noticed a heavy-set guy mowing out on the football field. When she accelerated through the intersection and passed the man on the riding mower, she looked closer, wondering if she would know him, too.

Then she saw his face.

"Wow. How far the mighty have fallen."

Rhett PreJean, the star quarterback from high school, who had been generous enough to give every cheerleader on the squad his own brand of tryouts, was mowing the football field.

She shook her head as she drove past, and within a few minutes, came up on the property belonging to Tony Warren.

The house was nice. Not on the same level of elegance as Peyton Adams' home, but a really nice home with a quartet of white Grecian-style columns gracing the two-story verandah.

There were two cars under the portico—one a racy little sports car, and the other one a big white Lincoln. Either he had company, or he'd remarried, neither of which was suspicious.

She drove past, not knowing what to make of either of the residences. She accepted she wasn't much of a detective, but she was a really good judge of character. Too bad there was no way to meet all five of these men on equal ground and see what kind of vibe she came away with. It was for certain that one of them had her presence on their radar.

She was still thinking about how to move forward when the first drops of rain hit the windshield. She looked up, then frowned and accelerated, hoping to get back to her room before the main part of the storm hit. She made it by less than a minute and had just stepped into her room when the clouds unloaded.

# CHAPTER SIX

———◆———

IT WAS AFTER MIDNIGHT BEFORE Big Boy could get out of the house unobserved. He needed another look at the Bayou Motel and didn't want Sugar all up in his business. So, he'd waited until she'd taken her nightly dose of sleeping pills and passed out.

The air smelled fresh from the passing storm. The tree frogs were starting to tune back up, but the cicadas were still silent. The tiny niggle of concern that he'd be found out was digging in like a tick on a fat dog. He had committed many sins in his life, but he'd always gotten away with it. This time felt different. It was the first time he knew what it felt like to be hunted.

He started his car, then eased out of the driveway. Once out on the streets, he headed for the Bayou Motel via neighborhoods, rather than down Main.

A skinny hound slunk back into the shadows as he passed, and a few blocks down, he braked for a raccoon waddling across the street. He'd probably been digging in someone's garbage.

Big Boy had his own sense of what was right and what wasn't, and didn't see the irony in the fact that he chose not to run over a raccoon, but was willing to end a human life.

He came into the motel parking lot from the alley with his lights off, and again, stopped near the back beneath the live oaks. God, but he wanted this over.

The lights were out in 4A. He thought about setting off the alarm on that Hummer to bring her out again, but that would bring everybody else outside as well, and he couldn't have witnesses. He sat with the cold air blasting in his face, waiting for an epiphany.

After a while, he came up with a plan. If he was already here when she came out of the room in the morning and used the silencer on his handgun, he could pop her right on the threshold without anybody hearing a thing. She'd drop, and he'd be long gone before anyone discovered the body.

The more he thought about it, the better he liked it. Satisfied with his plan, he headed home. Then to assure himself that he would get out of the house again unobserved, he slept in his downstairs recliner with his cell charging on the table beside him, the alarm set for six a.m.

---

IT WAS SUNDOWN IN DALLAS before Wade got home from the jobsite. He'd stayed late to be on hand to receive a rush order of flooring to replace the shipment that wound up in the wreck at the I-35 junction.

He was tired, filthy, and hungry when he reached the bathroom and started to strip. While he showered, he debated with himself as to whether he was too tired to eat, or too hungry to wait until morning. By the time he'd dried off and dressed in gym shorts and a t-shirt, he felt better. He went barefoot to his kitchen to make his go-to meal—a three-egg, cheese and jalapeno omelet.

As always, his thoughts went to Logan. She'd been upbeat when they'd spoken earlier, but he couldn't let go of a looming sense of dread.

He finished cooking the omelet, turned it out on a plate, and carried it to the table so he could go through email while he ate. He inhaled the first three bites with relish before opening the email and responding to the ones that needed answers while reading and deleting others. He didn't find Logan's email until he'd finished eating, but when he saw it and the words *For Safe-keeping* in the subject heading, he opened it immediately.

The message consisted of a one-page explanation of what she wanted him to know, and how important it was for someone else to have the info in case something happened to her. A cold chill ran through him as he read the last paragraph.

*I have a tattoo on my belly. It is the date of Damon's death and how to find where I buried his body. But to find the grave, you need to read them in reverse. Start at the city limit sign on the north side to begin the count. Reading in reverse, the first number is how far north you drive on the highway. Turn west. The second number is how far you go on the westbound blacktop road. Then, once you stop, you have to walk south the last quarter of a mile into the swamp. The land didn't used to be fenced, which was why it was a bit difficult for me to locate. However, when you get to the inlet of the bayou, you will see a grouping of old cypress trees to your left. Find the one with the X marked on the back.*

*I buried Damon in front of that tree.*

His skin crawled.

The reason she was telling him this now was because she had accepted the fact that she might not live long enough to see this to the end. He read through the information that followed, stunned by the attention to detail.

He was sick to his stomach as he sent the email to the printer, then went to retrieve the hard copies from his office.

He put it all in a file folder and left it on his desk before going back to the kitchen to clean up.

He was equal amounts heartsick and pissed by the time he got to bed, certain he'd never sleep. But instead, he fell asleep immediately, dreaming of the night he and Andrew had first seen Logan working the lunch shift at a café near their job site.

*Wade pulled into the parking lot of the Bluebird Café and parked.*

*"Looks pretty full. If there aren't any tables open, I'm not waiting. We can go through a drive-thru somewhere on the way back, okay?" Andrew said.*

*"I don't care one way or the other," Wade said, and got out.*

*It was a chilly November day and had been spitting a mix of snow and sleet all morning, but at least the work they had left on their latest build was all interior finishes.*

*"I'm going for some chili," Wade said.*

*Andrew nodded.*

*"Me, too. It'll be quick to serve, and we'll be back on the job, ASAP."*

*They headed for the door with their shoulders hunched against the cold and their heads tilted sideways against the sleet.*

*Warm air met them at the entrance, along with enticing aromas coming from the kitchen. They were looking for a place to sit when they saw the young, long-legged waitress moving confidently among the tables.*

*"Oh man, would you look at her," Wade said.*

*Andrew's eyes had narrowed.*

*"Dibs," he said.*

*"No way! I saw her first," Wade said.*

*Andrew turned and looked at his best friend.*

*"I said, Dibs."*

*Wade couldn't remember ever seeing that look on his friend's face. He took a deep breath and then let it go.*

*"Whatever, man. Do your thing."*

*Even as they sat down in her section, Wade kept watching the cat-like pace of her stride, and the way her body moved as she walked. It took him a few moments to realize how young she was, and at that point, let go of the momentary vision he'd had of waking up beside her for the rest of his life.*

*When she stopped at their table, he watched Andrew make the biggest play for a woman he'd ever seen. Wade also ignored the twinge of heartache he felt when Andrew reeled her in.*

*In the dream, he was standing beside Andrew, watching her coming down the aisle, and reliving the pain of giving her up for good when he awoke.*

———◆———

LOGAN DREAMED OF DAMON ALL night long. Everywhere she went in her dream, he was with her, helping her search for a red door in a very large house. She knew if she could find the right door, the answers she needed would be behind it. In the dream, she turned a corner and finally saw it at the end of a hall. She was running toward it when she woke, then rolled over in bed and groaned.

"Damn it, Damon. Why didn't you just tell me his name? I need this over with."

She glanced at the clock. It was just after seven. She'd eaten fruit and cheese the night before and wasn't in the mood to snack again this morning, so she got up and headed for the shower.

A short while later, she was dressed and putting on her boots, getting ready to go eat breakfast at Barney's. She picked up the Colt and, instead of wearing the holster, dropped it in her purse, slung it over her shoulder, and headed out the door with her keys.

———◆———

WHEN THE ALARM ON BIG Boy's cell phone went off at six a.m., he groaned. It felt like he'd just closed his eyes. Still wearing what he'd worn last night, he grabbed a bottle of Coke from the refrigerator for caffeine and slipped out of the house. When he reached the car, he checked to make sure his gun was still beneath the seat, then got in and took a big swig of the cold Coke. He would have rather had coffee, but this would have to suffice.

In the bright light of day, the good idea he'd had last night seemed like a joke, but he had to do something and this was it. He took another drink of pop as he traveled through neighborhoods still asleep and winced when he saw the road-kill ahead. Looked like the raccoon had made one trip too many across the street.

When he finally got to the alley behind the motel, he eased up into the back of the lot and parked with an open view of her door. Once she came out, he would have a clear shot.

It occurred to him as he was waiting that he hadn't taken any kind of security cameras into consideration and quickly scoped out the site.

Old lady Doolittle, who owned the motel, was obviously too tight to put up cameras, or else she'd purposefully omitted them to maintain the anonymity of her pay-by-the-hour guests. His tinted windows were dark enough that no one could see him sitting inside the car, so he pulled the gun out from beneath the seat and cradled it in his lap before reaching for the Coke.

———◆———

LOGAN WALKED OUT INTO THE sunlight, aiming the remote control toward the Hummer to turn off the alarm, when something hit her in the back so hard it threw her forward against the front fender. There was a sharp flash of pain and then everything went black.

The unending screech that erupted as Logan Talman fell against the Hummer was an unexpected explosion of sound. Big Boy groaned. He'd forgotten about the alarm. Damn it. He should have let her turn it off first.

"Son-of-a-holy bitch!" he muttered, threw his car into reverse, backing out of the lot into the alley, before speeding away toward home.

This wasn't what he'd planned. She'd come out of her motel room so abruptly that he'd shot before he thought, and then when the shot had hit her in the back, the impact of her body falling against the vehicle had not only set off the alarm, but he'd had to leave without waiting to see if she was dead. His heart began hammering so hard it hurt to breathe, and he was still driving home when he figured out that his hammering heart was not part of his panic. He grabbed at his chest with one fist, feeling the heavy, erratic thud of his own heartbeat and moaned.

"Oh hell, oh no! I am not having a heart attack. I am not. I am not. I just need to get home."

Snot was running down his upper lip, even though he wasn't crying, and he was mumbling to himself over and over, trying to convince himself everything was okay.

There had been no shot to be heard, and he'd gotten out of the parking lot before anyone had come out to see what had set off the alarm. He was fine. He was fine. No one had seen him there. And even if someone had seen him in his car driving too fast through the streets of town, he would just be speeding, not a suspect in a shooting.

He reached home with a huge sigh of relief, and was already in the house before the first ambulance arrived on the scene at the motel.

———◆———

T-BOY WAS DRESSED AND ABOUT to leave last night's 'date' in the motel bed to sleep it off when he heard the alarm.

He'd seen Logan Talman's Hummer in front of her door as he and Francie were going into their room around one a.m. The fact that he was only two doors down from the female he'd spent his teenage years trying to screw gave him a hard on, and Francie hadn't complained about it. As for T-Boy, he'd closed his eyes and pretended it was Logan he was fucking, not his forty-dollar whore.

His hand was on the doorknob when the alarm went off. He'd already heard about what happened to Robicheau, and was wondering whose ass was on the line now when he heard a car peeling out of the parking lot. He grabbed for the door, wanting to see who it was, but was stopped by the safety chain. By the time he'd gotten the door open, the car was long gone. That's when he looked toward the Hummer, saw Logan crumpled up on her side and the spreading pool of blood beneath her, while the alarm continued to scream out a warning that had come too late.

He ran to her, kneeling in the spreading blood. The bullet hole in her back was impossible to miss, and when he rolled her toward him to check for an exit wound, he groaned. The front of her shirt was blood-soaked, too.

"No, no, girl. You do not end like this!" he muttered, and grabbed his cell and dialed 911.

"What is your emergency?"

"A woman has been shot in the parking lot at the Bayou Motel. Send police and an ambulance and hurry. She's bleeding out."

Then Francie came stumbling out of their room.

"T-Boy, what's going on?"

"Bring all the towels from the bathroom!" he shouted, as he rolled over into a sitting position against the front fender, pulled Logan's bleeding body up between his legs, letting her head rest against his chest as Francie turned and ran. Seconds later, she was back, her face as white as the towels she was holding.

T-Boy grabbed one towel and pressed it against the entrance wound, and another towel on the exit wound, then pushed against them as hard as he could, sandwiching her body between them.

By now, people were spilling out of their rooms. The motel

owner, Bea Doolittle, came flying from her room behind the office, trying to be heard above with the blasting car alarm.

"What's going on?" she screamed, and then came around the back end of the Hummer and saw for herself. "Oh my God! Is she dead?"

"I don't know," T-Boy said, but he was in a cold sweat. The muscles in his biceps where already burning from the pressure he was exerting, and there were tears on his face. "Where the hell is that ambulance?"

When he finally heard a siren, he looked down at the woman in his arms.

"Hang on, girl. I've got you. You're gonna be okay!" he said, and then pushed even harder against the wounds.

———◆———

WADE HAD JUST DRIVEN UP to the jobsite and was getting out of the truck with coffee in hand, when he was hit with a pain in his shoulder so sharp that he staggered. The coffee slipped out of his hand, splattering all over his work boots.

"What the hell?" he said, and then Logan's face flashed before his eyes.

Trying not to panic, he grabbed his cell phone and called her. The call rang and rang and rang and then went to voicemail. He called again, and then again, and then again, and by the seventh call, he was already on the way back to his truck.

He called off and on all the way home with the same result, then dropped the phone in his pocket upon arrival and went inside to pack. He didn't know what had happened, but when she hadn't answered her phone, he'd known she was in trouble. He was on his way to his bedroom when his cell rang. He stopped in the hall, his whole body shaking with relief as he looked down, expecting to see her name. Instead he saw, "Unknown".

*Aw hell.*

He was shaking as he answered the call.

———◆———

EVERYBODY IN BLUEJACKET HEARD THE sirens. Police, fire, and ambulance all had different sounds, but when they heard all three at once, they began making calls. Within minutes, more than half the town knew the woman in the Hummer had been shot in the parking lot of her motel.

Johnny Baptiste was outside about to leave for work when he heard them. He stopped on the porch steps, looking to the sky to see if he saw smoke, which would indicate someone's house was on fire.

Caitlin came running out the front door.

"What's happening?" she cried.

"I don't know," Johnny said.

"Call Arnie at the police station and ask," she said.

"Oh hell, Caitie. I don't want to bother them when—"

"Call him!" Caitlin screamed.

Johnny blinked. He hadn't seen her this way since the night she'd found her Mama floating in the family pool. He made the call.

"Hey Arnie, it's me, Johnny. What's going on?"

"All I know is Logan Conway got shot in the parking lot of the motel."

Johnny staggered and then grabbed hold of the porch post.

"No way? Is she dead?"

"I don't think so. The call came in that she was shot. That's all I know. I gotta go," Arnie said, and disconnected.

Caitlin was standing in the doorway, as pale as the white blouse she was wearing.

"Is Logan dead?" Caitlin asked.

Johnny frowned.

"How did you know the sirens were for her?" Caitlin moaned and dropped to her knees.

"Oh my God, oh my God," Caitlin cried, and covered her face.

"No, baby, they didn't say she was dead. They just said she was shot. Come back into the house. We'll say a prayer for her, okay?"

He was helping her up when she suddenly tore free and ran inside.

"What's going on?" he asked, as he followed her into their bedroom.

"I promised Logan if anything happened to her I would call her friend," Caitlin said, as she dug through her purse for the paper, then remembered she'd zipped it up in one of the pockets.

"You mean she thought this would happen?" Johnny asked.

Caitlin ran for the phone, the paper clutched in her hand. Her fingers were trembling as she made the call, and then she took a deep breath and closed her eyes, trying to calm herself enough to speak.

When the phone began to ring, she said a quick prayer. Then she heard him answer.

"Hello."

"Is this Wade Garrett?"

Wade's heart sank.

"Yes."

"This is Caitlin Baptiste. I'm Logan's best friend from high school. She told me to call you if anything happened to her, and I'm sorry to tell you this, but she was shot in the parking lot of her motel this morning."

"Oh Jesus," Wade said, and grabbed onto the wall for support. "Is she alive?"

"We don't know. All they would tell us was that she was shot. They didn't comment on her condition. I'm so—"

"Thank you," Wade said, and disconnected, then called a friend who worked at a private airfield in Dallas.

"Pony Express Airways, this is Junior."

"Junior, this is Wade Garret. I have an emergency."

"Hey bro, what do you need?"

"I need to get to Bluejacket, Louisiana ASAP. Logan Talman was ambushed this morning in a motel parking lot. I need to get there now."

"The hell you say!" Junior said. "Of course I'll help. I'll go service up the Bell Jet. She's a fast little bitch. By the time you get out here to the airfield, I'll be ready."

"Thank you, Junior. I'll be there within the hour."

He disconnected on the way to his bedroom, made one more call to the job site as he threw clothes and a shaving kit into a suitcase, listening to it ring and ring. When it was finally answered, he didn't give his man time to say hello.

"McGuire, this is Wade. Listen carefully. I don't have much

time to talk. Logan's been shot. She was ambushed this morning as she came out of her motel. I don't know if she's dead or alive. I'm flying out to Louisiana within the hour. Text or call if you need me, but for now, I am putting you in charge. Spread the word among the work sites, and tell the crew bosses to contact you for troubleshooting."

"Holy crap, Boss. I can't believe this," McGuire said. "Yes, yes, I'll take care of everything, and we'll say prayers for the boss lady."

"Thanks," Wade said.

The last thing he packed was the file he'd printed off last night, then he left the house on the run.

---

THE AMBULANCE ARRIVED A CAR length ahead of the police and the EMTs exited running. The car alarm was still a raucous screech, exacerbating the chaos of the scene as they reached the victim.

Chief Evans and both on-duty officers came racing into the parking lot, all three skidding to a stop. The chief had one brief glimpse of T-Boy holding Logan's unconscious body, both of them bloody as hell, before the EMTs took over.

By the time Josh Evans got out of his cruiser, T-Boy was leaning against the outer wall of the motel with his hands on his knees, almost as bloody as the woman on the ground. He was bent over as far as he could go to keep from passing out, with his dreadlocks dangling in front of his face.

"What happened here?" Josh asked.

T-Boy shook his head, his words coming in jerks and stops.

"In a room two doors down...heard that car alarm go off. Trying to open the door. Heard a car peel out of the lot. Then I got out of the room and found her. She was shot in the back, but I never heard a gunshot. I think she set off the alarm when she fell against the Hummer. Jesus, Chief. What's going on here? Who would do this to her?"

Josh was sick. He'd known something bad was connected to her return when he'd seen her standing over Robicheau with that big revolver, but he hadn't expected anything like this.

He shook his head, then turned to both his officers.

"Someone silence that damn alarm and bring me the keys. Cordon off this parking lot. No one comes in or goes out except the ambulance, then start looking for shell casings and maybe some tire tracks. A witness said he heard a car exit fast enough the driver laid rubber." He turned around, surveying the layout of the parking lot. "She was shot in the back, so the shot had to come from that direction."

"Yes, sir," they said.

Moments later, the alarm was silenced. Evans gathered up her purse and keys as evidence at the scene of the crime, while the officers scattered. One began walking the perimeter of the parking lot and quickly found a spent shell, which he bagged and tagged, while the other began going through the crowd one-by-one, taking statements.

————◆————

LOGAN WAS FLOATING SOMEWHERE BETWEEN earth and sky, trying to find an anchor. There was a hot, burning pain in her shoulder, and the feeling she'd left something undone. She kept hearing a scream, but it wasn't her. Damon was with her again, but too far away to talk to.

*Help me. Help me.*

No one heard. Or else they didn't care, because no one came. Then Andrew was standing beside her.

*Where did you go? Why did you leave me?*

He didn't answer. Maybe he couldn't hear her, either.

There was a dark, rolling cloud coming toward her, and she couldn't move, couldn't run. Damon was gone. Andrew had disappeared. There was only the darkness—coming to take her under.

————◆————

THE AMBULANCE WAS BACKING INTO the unloading zone at the local hospital when a doctor and a handful of nurses came running out to meet them.

An EMT jumped out of the back, and then everything began happening at once. There was already one IV in Logan's arm as they wheeled her into the ER. Although both entrance and exit wounds had been packed, she was still bleeding profusely.

"What are her stats?" Dr. Venable asked.

"BP is 110 over 40 and dropping. Pulse is weak. She has one bullet wound in the back with an exit wound near her collarbone. Her breathing is shallow. Blood type was in her personal effects: O positive. Blood loss on the scene was massive," one EMT said.

They began cutting her clothes from her body to look for other wounds and revealed the tattoos on her belly.

"Does anyone know her name?" the doctor asked.

"Logan Talman. She used to be Logan Conway. She once lived here," someone offered.

"Hell of a welcome home," the doctor muttered.

A nurse cried out.

"Doctor! Her blood pressure is dropping fast!"

He looked up at the readings.

"She's going to crash. Notify surgery that she's coming up. Who's on duty?"

"Dr. Silas is already scrubbing," the nurse said, and grabbed a phone to notify the surgical unit.

"Get her to surgery, STAT," the doctor said.

Moments later, she was wheeled out of ER as quickly as she'd come in.

# CHAPTER SEVEN

---

WADE HAD NEVER BEEN SO scared. Not knowing if she was still in this world was frightening, but for his life to make sense, she had to be.

Andrew had been his best friend since first grade, and losing him on the job had been a nightmare he had yet to escape. The thought of losing Logan was too painful to consider. She was not only his last link to Andrew, but a woman he loved without reservation, and she didn't even know it.

They'd been in the air almost an hour and a half now. He glanced at the chopper pilot and then back down at the geography below. Junior had been right. This jet chopper was a fast little bitch, just not fast enough.

"Hey Junior, time wise, how much longer?" he asked.

"Fifteen, maybe twenty minutes, tops," Junior said, without breaking concentration.

Wade glanced at his watch, then leaned back and closed his eyes. He wasn't much for prayers, but if there was ever a time, this was it. In his mind, he started and stopped a dozen times without being able to make a complete sentence. Finally, all he could say was, *Please, God. Please.*

---

CAITLIN GOT TO THE HOSPITAL five minutes too late to see Logan before they took her to surgery. She felt more than just a responsibility to be there for her friend and heartsick that such an ugly thing had happened in her hometown. She didn't know who'd done this, but at this moment, if justice could be served by pushing the bastard into a gator-filled inlet, she'd volunteer to do the pushing.

She was pacing the waiting room when Chief Evans walked in. Before he could open his mouth, she was in his face.

"Do you know who did this? Do you have them in jail?"

"No, we don't know who did it, but I've been looking for you. Your husband, Johnny, told me you two were friends when she lived here, and I need somewhere to start. I need you to help me with her background. Was there someone here who might hold some kind of grudge?"

Caitlin shoved trembling fingers through her hair.

"I have to sit or keep walking. My legs are shaking too bad to stand still."

"Then we'll sit," Josh said, and pointed to the seating.

Caitlin dropped into one of the chairs and then took a deep breath, trying to calm herself enough to talk.

"Even though I hadn't seen her in ages, she was and still is my best friend. If she had a personal problem with someone, I never knew about it. Everyone liked her and Damon."

"About the brother, what has she said about him?"

Caitlin frowned.

"All she said was that he'd gotten mixed up in something which was why they left town. She married later and lives in Dallas, and I assumed he'd stayed in Louisiana? Why?"

Josh kept watching her face for a sign of lies, but there was nothing, so he told her what he'd found.

"Because he hasn't held a job since the one he had here in Bluejacket. Not anywhere."

Caitlin stared.

"What? How can that be?"

"I don't know, but if she lives through this, it would be helpful if you'd see what you can find out."

Caitlin gasped.

"Don't say that! She has to be okay. That is all."

Josh nodded.

"Yes, ma'am. I'm sorry. By any chance, do you know who her

next of kin would be, other than her brother?"

"Oh! Yes. When I had lunch with her yesterday, she asked me a favor. She said if anything happened to her, I was to call a man named Wade Garrett in Dallas. She gave me his name and number. I called him right after I heard what happened."

Josh's thoughts were scattered. If Logan Talman was so insecure about her welfare here, then why did she not tell him? Then he considered how they'd gotten off onto the wrong foot. So, who was she afraid of and why? His gut told him it had to do with the missing brother.

"Do you mind if I wait here with you?" Josh asked.

"Of course not," Caitlin said, but she couldn't sit still.

She took some money from her purse, got a cold drink from the vending machine at the end of the room, and then began pacing from the window overlooking the parking lot to the hallway, then back to the window again. She was so focused on waiting for the surgeon, she'd almost forgotten the chief was still there until his two-way squawked, and she heard him answer.

"Evans to dispatch."

"Chief, just got an incoming message from a chopper bringing in Ms. Talman's next of kin. Landing at the hospital helipad in ten."

"Ten-Four. I'm on site. Evans out."

Caitlin ran to the window. The helipad was in plain sight. She turned to ask Chief Evans a question, but he was already gone, so she focused on the sky, watching for sight of the incoming chopper, instead.

A few moments later, she saw Chief Evans exit the hospital and then backed up to stand in the shade at the ER entrance as he awaited Wade Garrett's arrival.

———◆———

FROM THE AIR, BLUEJACKET LOOKED like someone had hacked out a clearing in the middle of a swamp and built a town. And while there was no room for the town to grow, somehow it had still managed to thrive. The football field was a lush green, as were the yards in the neighborhoods.

Wade could see parking lots, so it was easy to assume those were businesses. Not a lot of them, but more than he'd expected.

Even though there were no actual railroad tracks running through town, from this view it was easy to see where the division began of the right side, from the wrong side of the tracks. And now that he knew that's where Logan had lived with her brother before he'd been murdered, he couldn't help but wonder which house had sheltered her.

The chopper banked slightly, and as it did, the helipad came into view. The little hospital scared him, wondering if there was anyone there with the needed skill to save her.

"Goin' down," Junior said, and landed within the parameters of the helipad like a dragonfly on swamp grass. "Good luck to you, Wade, and tell that girl of yours I said a prayer."

"She's not my girl. She's my boss," Wade muttered, settled his Stetson on his head, and reached for his bag.

"Whatever," Junior said. "You save all that for people who don't know better. If something happens and you need a ride back, you got my number."

"We'll drive the Hummer home," Wade said, and opened the door.

The rotors were still spinning when Wade stepped out. He ducked and walked with one hand on his hat, the other carrying his bag. The chopper lifted off behind him but he never broke stride as he headed for the uniformed policeman standing near the ER entrance. He had a question that needed an answer, and that man would have it.

———◆———

JOSH HAD NOT EXPECTED A cowboy, and was chiding himself for being surprised. Texas put a stamp on their people just like Louisiana did on theirs. He stepped out from beneath the portico with his hand extended.

"I'm Josh Evans, Bluejacket's Chief of Police."

Wade shook it briefly, wasting no time in getting to the point. "Wade Garrett. How's Logan?"

"Still in surgery. Follow me, and I'll take you up to the waiting room."

The moment they were in an elevator, Wade quizzed him again.

"Anyone in custody?"

"No. No witnesses, and so far, no clue as where to start. I hope you can fill in some blanks for me."

"I can give you a whole list," Wade said.

Josh was startled and it showed.

"What do you know?"

"She witnessed her brother's murder. Or at least overheard it. She never saw a face, but she heard it all go down."

"Good Lord. That explains why I couldn't find him," Evans muttered. "Why didn't she tell someone when it happened?"

"While she couldn't ID the killer, she'd heard everything as it was happening, which would have made her the next victim if the killer had found out."

"Where's her brother's body?" Evans asked

"She buried him in the swamp...right where he was murdered, and then she ran. She feared it was just a matter of time before the killer remembered Damon had a sister and would assume Damon told her where he was going that night along with who he was meeting. The truth was that she didn't know any of that and was hiding in the truck because of something she'd overheard from her brother's phone conversation. She hid beneath the tarp in the bed of the truck so her brother wouldn't go meet the man alone."

"Why was he killed? What am I missing?" Josh asked.

"The man was looking for someone to kill his wife, and when Damon turned him down, it cost him his life," Wade said.

Josh hadn't seen that coming. Now he was not only dealing with the attempted murder of Logan Talman, but the murder of her brother, and someone else's wife.

Then the elevator doors opened and they stepped out.

"This way," Josh said, leading the way to the waiting room.

Caitlin was in the doorway as they entered.

"Mr. Garrett, this is Caitlin Baptiste. She's Logan's friend."

Wade dropped his bag near a chair and hugged her.

"Ma'am, I cannot thank you enough for calling me."

Caitlin was impressed. Good-looking *and* a gentleman?

"Logan asked me to. I would do anything for her, but I don't understand what's going on? Why would someone want Logan dead?"

Wade had told the police chief what he knew, but it wasn't something to just spread around.

"I can't say as I can answer that," he said, and was saved from further explanation as a man in scrubs entered the waiting room.

"Anyone here for Logan Talman?"

Wade pivoted.

"We all are," he said.

"I'm her surgeon, Dr. Silas. She lost a lot of blood, but she's stable. The bullet was a through and through, even though it nicked her collarbone. Given some time for healing, I expect a full recovery."

"Thank you, Jesus," Caitlin said, and sank into the nearest chair and started crying.

Wade's knees went weak. *Thank you, God.* "When can I see her?" he asked.

"She'll be in recovery for at least an hour, and then she'll be moved to the Second Floor. You can check there for her room number."

"Thank you, Dr. Silas. Thank you for saving her life," Wade added.

"You're most welcome," Silas said, and left.

"There's one more guy you can thank for keeping Logan alive," Josh said.

"Who?" Caitlin asked.

"T-Boy Locklan found her bleeding out by her car and had the presence of mind to apply compresses to both wounds until the ambulance came. It will be a long time before I forget seeing him sitting in all that blood with her in his arms."

"Wow," Caitlin said. "He was her nemesis all through school, but he came through for her when it mattered. I have a whole new respect for him."

Wade frowned.

"What do you mean, he was her nemesis?"

"He wanted her, and she wouldn't give him the time of day," Caitlin said, then sighed. "Heck, lots of boys wanted Logan, but she didn't mess with any of them. Between her ball bat and her brother, she kept them at bay."

Shock spread across Wade's face.

"Ball bat?"

Caitlin nodded, then grinned wryly.

"They all knew she was home alone a lot, so they would be knocking on her door begging her to let them in. She'd shout at them to go away, and if they persisted, she'd swing that bat against the doorframe so hard the front windows would rattle. Then she'd tell them the next time she swung, it would be at their heads. They always cleared out because they knew she meant it."

Knowing this was her life before he and Andrew knew her was shocking. He wondered if she'd ever talked about it to Andrew. He wanted to hear more, so he backed up and sat down.

"Where was her brother when all that was happening?"

Caitlin shrugged.

"Always at work. But they knew if they messed with her, she'd tell Damon, and he would make them sorry in a variety of painful ways. If it wasn't for him, she would never have been safe where they lived."

Wade was trying to absorb all this new knowledge, but it was definitely another reason why she'd run after her protector had been killed. He was staring off into space when Caitlin reached across the chair between them and patted Wade's arm.

"Now that I know you're here and she's going to be okay, I better get home. You have my phone number. I would consider it a courtesy if you would please let me know how Logan is doing, and I'll be back tomorrow to see for myself."

"Yes, ma'am," Wade said, and stood as Caitlin got up and left.

As soon as they were alone, Josh sat down beside him. "Talk to me," he said.

Wade went after his bag, then sat back down and pulled out a copy of all the info Logan had sent him.

"This is everything I know," he said. "She knew two things for sure. That the killer drove a late model white Chevrolet Silverado pickup, and that he would likely have lost his wife soon after he killed her brother. So she hired a private investigator some months back and started them searching for men in the year 2008 who fit that description. She's narrowed her list of possible suspects to five men who live in Bluejacket. All of them owned white, late model Silverados at the time of the murder. Three of them lost their wives within the year after her brother's death in supposedly random ways. Two divorced their husbands, but the agency could only find one actually living elsewhere. The other one is supposedly living off the grid in Alaska, but no one knows that for sure."

Evans was stunned by the depth of detail in the report, and to have a list of suspects just handed to him didn't happen every day.

"I'm going to the office with this. For the time being, keep everything between us. I don't want anyone else knowing this." Then he remembered one other detail. They would need a body to prove there had been a murder. "I don't suppose she remembers where she buried her brother's body?"

"You underestimate Logan Talman," Wade said. "The date of death and the directions to where she buried the body are tattooed on her belly, and she's already back-tracked to the location and verified it."

Josh shook his head.

"I sure wish she'd talked to me when she first arrived. We might not be here like this if she had."

Wade shrugged.

"She doesn't trust people, men in particular."

Josh frowned.

"Okay then. We'll be in touch. I'm going to keep a guard on her door, and I'm leaving orders for no visitors other than Mrs. Baptiste and you. And I'll tell you right now, if someone in this town had ten thousand dollars to pay to have someone murdered, they don't live on the south side of town. They're on the north side where the money is, and I don't like knowing that a murderer has hidden behind a cloak of pseudo-respectability in Bluejacket. As soon as Mrs. Talman is able, we're gonna set ourselves a trap and catch a killer."

"Fine," Wade said. "You can rest assured I won't be leaving this place until she goes with me."

———◆———

BIG BOY HAD ALREADY HIDDEN the gun and silencer in a secret compartment in the library within the bookshelves, then had gone upstairs to shower and shave.

Sugar was still sleeping, so technically, no one at home knew he'd left the house. He finished up in the bathroom and then dressed and went downstairs. It was Ruthie's day off, and he was in the kitchen making coffee when Sugar finally came down.

"Good morning, baby," Sugar said. "I overslept. Have you eaten?"

He kissed her forehead and grinned.

"I was waiting for you."

She beamed.

"You are so sweet. You know what I'd like to do?"

"What?" Big Boy asked.

"Go to Barney's for breakfast."

He grinned.

"That sounds like a plan. Want a coffee to go?"

She nodded.

He poured coffee in two of their insulated cups, grabbed the car keys, and they headed out the door.

The police were everywhere as they headed down Main.

"Wonder what's going on?" Sugar asked.

"I have no idea, but I'll bet someone will share that with us while we're in Barney's."

She giggled.

"Gossip central."

"Yes, but with buttermilk biscuits and sausage gravy," Big Boy said, and then took the turn off Main into Barney's and parked.

The place was busier than usual. Big Boy guessed it was because everyone had come down to Barney's for the latest news on the shooting, and he was right.

They'd barely been seated before Junie came flying by, filled the cups already on the table with coffee, and took their order.

Sugar slowed her down long enough to ask about the traffic.

"What's going on around here this morning? There's traffic everywhere."

Junie leaned over and lowered her voice

"There was a shooting at the Bayou Motel this morning," she said.

Sugar gasped.

"Oh, my Lord! Who shot who?"

"Someone shot Logan Conway in the back as she came out of her room—no, not Conway. She's Logan Talman now."

"How awful! What a loss," Big Boy said.

"Oh, she's not dead. Last I heard, she was in surgery. I can't imagine who would do something like that, or better yet, why? She never hurt anybody."

Big Boy was in shock.

*She wasn't dead? Son-of-a-bitch!*

"Well, thank goodness she's all right," Sugar said. Curiosity satisfied, she moved on to her creature comforts. "I'll have a stack of buttermilk pancakes with a side of bacon."

Junie glanced at Big Boy.

"How about yourself? What tickles your fancy this morning?"

"Sausage gravy and biscuits with a side of bacon."

"Comin' up," Junie said, and went to turn in the orders.

Big Boy glanced up at the clock, then down at his wife. As always, she was talking, talking, talking.

He took a sip of coffee, then stirred in a packet of sugar to take the edge off the slightly bitter taste and tried it again.

He frowned.

Maybe it wasn't the coffee. Maybe it was his failure this morning that left such a bitter taste in his mouth.

---

COGNIZANCE CAME SLOWLY.

At first there was just pain, then the bed Logan was on began to spin. Before she could panic, someone grabbed her hand. It was the anchor she needed. Then she heard a voice— deep and husky with emotion.

"Hang on, girl. Ride it out. Meds are coming."

"Who..."

"Shh... It's Wade. I'm here."

There was a moment of silence, and then her voice was so low he almost didn't hear her.

"My Wade?"

He squeezed her fingers.

"Yes, your Wade."

"Safe..." she sighed.

It was humbling to know he meant safety to her. Before he could say anything else, she was out again.

———◆———

JOSH HAD JUST COME BACK from the Bayou Motel and was in his office making notations in the case file that he'd started. He wanted Logan Talman's motel room undisturbed and had put crime scene tape across the door to 4A to make sure no one went inside. Then he went up to the motel office to express his unhappiness regarding the lack of security footage to the owner, Bea Doolittle, who lived in the apartment behind the front desk.

Bea hemmed and hawed around the truth, which was that most of her income was derived by her hourly customers and their preferences for anonymity.

"I'm not breaking any laws," Bea muttered.

"Yes, ma'am, I know that. But what if it had been you? What if someone had come in and robbed you, then didn't want to leave a witness and shot you? How would you feel about no security cameras then? With all the technology available these days, it's very careless of you to assume you'll never need it. Hell, Miss Bea... Bluejacket isn't all that big. We know on a nightly basis who's screwing who on these premises because we all know what everyone drives. There aren't any surprises happening here. Or at least, there weren't until someone tried to kill one of your guests. Now we have ourselves an unknown resident of Bluejacket running around shooting people in the back."

"I didn't hear no gunshot," Bea said.

"Yeah, neither did anyone else, which means he used a silencer, but that changes nothing for Mrs. Talman. She's still fighting for her life."

Bea had glared at him, and now that's where they stood.

# CHAPTER EIGHT

JOSH WAS FINISHING UP HIS report when he remembered he needed to put a guard on Mrs. Talman's hospital room.

He called Jack Fontaine, one of his off-duty officers, and sent him to the hospital. Then he opened the file Wade Garrett had given him again. What bothered him most was how well he knew all five men on the list, and he'd gone to a couple of the dead wives funerals. The fact that one of those women had likely been murdered, and that her killer sat through her service posing as a grieving husband, made him sick.

He pulled the case file on Julia Stephens' wreck. It was before he'd been hired as the chief of police. Supposedly, she'd died in that wreck, but he needed to go over the autopsy and satisfy himself there was nothing he'd overlooked.

She'd run off the highway and hit a tree head-on. The autopsy stated she had died of massive head injuries. From the pictures in the file, there was no mistaking the injuries to her head and face.

He then turned to the results of all the toxicology tests and immediately caught a notation regarding the high levels Diphenhydramine and Doxylamine found in her body, all antihistamines found in sleeping aids. Typically, toxicology reports always took weeks, sometimes even months to get back, but he had no memory of ever seeing them. Not even when he first arrived. The original assumption as to why the wreck occurred was that she'd just run off the road.

Then he glanced up at the date and frowned. This was after the previous police chief had died and before Josh had taken over the position.

He buzzed his clerk, Arnold Dubois, who'd been the clerk here almost twenty years.

"Hey, Arnie, come to my office for a second, please."

"Be right there, Chief," Arnie said, and true to his word, was knocking at the door in less than a minute.

Evans waved him in.

"What's up, Chief?" Arnie asked.

"You file autopsy reports in the case files, right?"

"Yep, yep, I do...after you review them."

"So, who was reviewing the reports in the interim after Chief Arthur's death?"

Arnie stood a minute, thinking back.

"You know, Chief? I don't remember anyone doing it."

Josh nodded. "When reports came in, you just filed them without review?"

Arnie frowned.

"No sir...I wouldn't have done that. I'm trying to think..." His eyes suddenly widened. "Oh hey! Remember that guy the City Council hired to stand in as chief until you started?"

"Yes! I do. Was he responsible for all of Chief Arthur's duties?"

"Yes, sir. Is there a problem?"

Evans sighed.

"Don't worry about," Evans said. "And thanks for the help."

Arnie smiled.

"No problem, Chief."

Evans waited until Arnie was gone, then pinched the bridge of his nose, and stifled a curse. Lord only knows what went by the wayside while the appointee was in charge. But this autopsy does not support her cause of death. Julia Stephens didn't just run off the road. With all those drugs in her body, she had to have fallen asleep. What bothered him was why she would have been driving if she'd taken such an inordinate amount of sleeping pills?

He went back through the accident report and then began sorting through the photos taken at the scene, looking for any of the interior of the car. There were two showing different aspects of the front seat, and the first thing he noticed was an insulated coffee cup with the letter "C" on the side. The lid had come off in the wreck and was lying in the seat on top of the coffee stain.

So, what if she hadn't knowingly taken the sleeping pills? What if someone had slipped them into the coffee? Someone like her husband?

He went back through the file Wade gave him, looking for the info regarding payouts on life insurance. How much had Camren Stephens gotten for his wife's accidental death?

"Well now, double indemnity for accidental death to the tune of half a million dollars," Josh mumbled, and wrote down Camren Stephen's name.

He'd just become the chief's top suspect.

---

BARTON DECHANTE LIKED BEING MAYOR of Bluejacket, even though it was hardly more than a village. It gave him a sense of authority and control without any problems.

He felt a bit presidential sitting in his office, and he liked signing the minor decrees and paperwork that came across his desk, using the gold-plated pen set that came with the job.

His official portrait hung on a wall next to photos of previous mayors, and he always judged himself as better looking than all of them, except possibly for Justin LeCroux, who had been mayor from 1952 to 1964. Barton had to admit the man was movie-star worthy, but their photos were never going to be hanging so close together that people might think to compare them. And Justin was long since dead, so there was that.

On most days, Barton enjoyed coming in to the office for a few hours, and then going about his day, but his phone had been ringing off the hook ever since that woman from Texas had rolled into town in that big fancy Hummer.

It began with her taking down a local who was trying to break into her car. Barton frowned. What woman does that? The behavior was too masculine for his taste. And then to top all that off, he learns from the spate of calls today, that she had been ambushed coming out of her motel room and was now in the hospital, clinging to life.

He made the sign of the cross, muttering as he picked up his cell phone and dropped it into his pocket as he left his office muttering, "Jesus, Mary, and Joseph, this shit needs to stop."

He paused beside his secretary's desk, frowning at the sight of her touching up the color on one of her fingernails. "Priscilla, I'll be across the street talking to Chief Evans if you need me."

"Yes sir," Priscilla said, as she screwed the lid back on her polish and began to blow on the nail to dry it.

Barton frowned, but said nothing. Truth was, he was a little bit scared of old Prissy. She was nearing sixty if she was a day, and yet kept her hair dyed as black as a witch's heart and wore it straight and long, like she must have when she was younger. Between the hair and those pale, watery, green eyes of hers, he was partially convinced she was a witch.

---

JOSH EVANS FINISHED WITH THE old accident file and got up to refill his coffee before sitting back down with a grunt. His right knee was hurting like it did when the weather was going to change. As long as it wasn't some dang tornado, he wouldn't mind a little rain.

The next name on the list of suspects was Roger Franklin. Everyone in Bluejacket knew his wife, Trena. She'd grown up here, and at the time of her death, had been the high school guidance counselor. When she'd died unexpectedly during surgery from an aneurism, her death had shocked the community.

If her death had been suspicious, then that meant a surgeon would have been in on the murder, too, which the chief considered very unlikely. And a quick check of the list revealed that there was no life insurance policy on her.

He moved to on to Peyton Adams, whose wife, Mona, had drowned in their pool. Caitlin, Mona's teenage daughter, had been the one to find the body. According to the report, Peyton had been out of town on business.

The Chief pulled the old file on the incident and began reading through reports. To his surprise, there had been a lengthy investigation before the death was ruled an accident and not a suicide. He checked the name against the life insurance list and saw that the policy had been a two-hundred and fifty-thousand-dollar policy that would have doubled if the death was accidental. So, half a million dollars paid out here.

When he pulled autopsy files, the first thing that stood out was the blood alcohol level in her body. It had been three times the legal limit. And then he read that she'd also suffered a head wound. There had been blood on the deck as well as in the pool, so they'd assumed she'd fallen in drunk, hitting her head when she fell.

What was it that took so long to clear the case? Maybe she didn't normally drink. He needed to talk to the daughter who'd found the body, and Peyton Adams too, then added his name to the list.

Of the two divorced men, he eliminated Danny Bales almost immediately, both because the wife was alive and living elsewhere, and because Bales would never have had ten thousand dollars to give to anyone.

Tony Warren was the other divorcee, and the last name on the list. But his wife had supposedly gone off the grid in Alaska, so there was likely no way to verify if she was still alive. There was no mention of a life insurance policy on her, either, but he was still going to investigate. There were more reasons than money to get rid of a disagreeable spouse.

He had just started a search for reports of domestic violence on both Peyton Adams and Camren Stephens when the mayor, Barton DeChante, strode into his office without knocking.

"Chief! What the hell is going on in Bluejacket? We go along all calm and friendly for years, and then all of a sudden, we have guns being fired in the streets, and a woman being ambushed like this, as if it was some back alley in New Orleans. What are you doing about that?"

Josh sighed. DeChante was a prick, but he was harmless.

"Nice to see you, too, Barton. Have a seat."

DeChante frowned. "I don't have time to sit down. Just answer my question."

Rude, authoritarian people never got far with Josh Evans, and DeChante's mayoral title didn't impress him one bit. Josh stood up on purpose, well aware he was a good foot taller than DeChante, and walked out from behind his desk to where the mayor was standing, then waited for DeChante to look up.

After he did, Josh nodded.

"We are working the case, none of which is available for public knowledge, which includes you. This is my office. Yours is across the street. I am not rude in your world. You don't get to be rude in mine."

Barton flushed. It wasn't often anyone called him down like this, but he acknowledged he'd been a shit to act this way.

"You're right. I'm sorry. It's just damn unnerving, and I have people calling the office wanting answers I don't have."

Josh patted Barton on the shoulder as he gently pushed him toward the door.

"Then you tell those people that the law is in charge of the investigation, and when there's something to be told, it will come from the police, not the mayor. That should get them off your back, okay?"

Barton relaxed, happy to have been relieved of the burden.

"Yes, I will do that, and many thanks. My apologies for prior rudeness. Have a good day."

He was gone as quickly as he'd arrived.

Josh shut the door to his office, and was settling back into the case, when he began hearing radio traffic between his officers and dispatch about a two-car wreck in front of the bank. He put everything into his desk and headed out to the scene.

———◆———

WADE HAD TAKEN UP RESIDENCE in Logan's room. His bag was in the corner, and he'd claimed the recliner. So when she started waking up, he jumped up and reached for her hand.

"Hey lady, I'm here."

She blinked.

"Wade? What happened?"

"Someone shot you in the back. You just had surgery and you're doing great. Are you in any pain?"

"Shot me?"

"Yes," he said.

"Shit."

Wade grinned. That was the Logan he knew.

"Who?" she asked.

"They don't know. No one heard a thing, so it's assumed he used a silencer. I'd say you are officially a threat to the dude who shot your brother. And just so you know, I gave the police chief copies of everything you sent me so he could do his job."

Logan groaned.

"I wasn't ready to—"

"To what? Die?" he asked.

He watched her nostrils flare. Then she sighed.

"Yeah...that."

"You're welcome."

He watched her eyelids close and her breathing level out. Just when he thought she'd gone to sleep, he heard her whisper.

"Thank..."

He plopped down into the recliner again and leaned back.

*God. She is my Achilles heel.*

There was a soft knock at the door. Wade opened it to find an armed, uniformed officer.

"Yes?" Wade said.

"Are you Wade Garrett?"

"Yes," Wade said.

"I'm Officer Jack Fontaine of the Bluejacket P.D., and Chief Evans sent me here to guard Mrs. Talman's door. I have been given to understand medical personnel, Mrs. Caitlin Baptiste, and you, are the only people allowed in the room."

"Yes, that's true," Wade said.

"Let me know if you have any concerns," Fontaine said, and took a seat in the chair provided for him out in the hall.

———◆———

IT HAD TAKEN JOSH AND his officers a good portion of the morning before they'd cleared the scene of the accident. He had one driver in jail who was high on meth, and the other had gone to the ER with what looked like a broken arm. Both cars had been towed. By the time they had opened the street to traffic again, it was nearing noon, so he stopped by Barney's to get some food to take back to the office.

He was sitting at a table near the door while he waited for his order, and while there, three of the men on Logan's list walked into Barney's within minutes of each other.

Before, he wouldn't have given them a second thought, and now he couldn't quit staring, trying to imagine them as cold-blooded killers, but he couldn't see it. No wonder the killer had gotten away with it. The shroud of propriety within society had way too much to do with money and appearance.

Despite his belief that he could eliminate one name from the three with deceased wives, he had full intentions of interrogating all three, plus the man with the missing wife. There could always be something he'd missed, or information one of them might give up that wasn't on the report.

He was trying to think of a way to open the investigation without alerting anyone he was looking for a killer when he thought of the interim police chief. That would be the perfect excuse. Josh could claim there was paperwork left undone on each case, and he was just following up.

He glanced up, wondering how Logan Talman was doing as Junie brought his order to the table.

"Thanks, Junie."

"My pleasure," she said, and then added. "Hey Chief, do you have any kind of update on Logan's condition?"

"As a matter of fact, I do. I was there when the surgeon came to the waiting room. He said she came through surgery just fine, and barring any unexpected problems, he expects a full recovery."

Junie beamed.

"That's wonderful news. Thanks a lot."

"Sure thing. Have a good day."

"You, too," Junie said, and went back to work as the chief paid for his food and took it back to his office.

---

BIG BOY WAS STILL ON edge as he drove down Main Street, but he had a business meeting he couldn't ignore and had convinced himself that business as usual was a good move—until he walked into Barney's.

Seeing the chief sitting at the door was so startling that he almost turned and ran.

In his mind, he saw Chief Evans standing up and reaching for his handcuffs.

Heard Evans reading him his rights in front of everyone in the room.

Being branded as the killer he was.

Instead, the chief just nodded at him and looked away. The relief kept him upright and walking.

He spotted his stockbroker, already seated and waiting for his arrival, then noticed the table was close to where the chief was seated. Fate was still messing with him.

"Hello, Edwin. How's it going?" Big Boy said, as he took a seat.

"All's well," Edwin Farris said. "Let's order first, and then we can talk."

"Works for me," Big Boy said.

He was reading the menu when he heard the chief talking to Junie, and when he heard Junie ask about Logan Talman's welfare, he was afraid to hear the answer.

The words, "full recovery" made him sick to his stomach. His gut was still in knots long after Evan's departure, and it was all he could do to get through lunch and the brief business meeting afterward.

Big Boy's stockbroker left first, claiming a pending appointment, leaving Big Boy momentarily alone to answer a text from Sugar. By the time he left Barney's, he didn't want to go home. The urge to run while he had the chance was huge. But habit drove him down the same streets, and before he knew it, he was walking into his house. His inability to make a decision had decided for him.

Sugar was in the bathroom giving herself a facial, so he changed into old clothes and headed for the garden.

Wisteria was hanging from a trellis in lush, purple clumps. Irises were in full bloom along the borders and bougainvillea abounded, but it was the roses he coveted most.

He started walking along the path, dead-heading as he went,

pausing with a smile as he watched a bumblebee chase away a hummingbird before moving all the way to the center of the roses, to the bench where he sat to admire the beauty and the antiquity of all that was his.

---

CAITLIN WAS MAKING LUNCH FOR her boys, but her thoughts were still on Logan. It was horrifying to know there was a killer in town who was targeting her best friend, and she didn't know why it was happening.

"Mama, we're hungry!" the boys cried in unison.

"Go wash. Your lunch is almost ready," she said, and then grinned as they pushed and shoved their way out of the kitchen.

She put their food on the table, along with glasses of iced, sweet tea. They came running back, pushing and shoving again, and then slid into their seats.

"Someone needs to say the blessing," she said, which stopped them from reaching for their food.

"You do it, Mama."

"No, Wiley, you do it. Robert did it last time."

Her oldest boy sighed and bowed his head.

"Dear God, thank you for Mama's good cooking and Daddy's job, and please help Robert to quit wettin' the bed. Amen."

Robert ducked his head.

Caitlin hid a grin.

The boys dug into their food as Caitlin got up and made herself a glass of tea, too. But she couldn't bring herself to eat. She was thinking about Chief Evans asking her to question Logan further about what had happened to Damon. She didn't know Wade Garrett had already furnished those answers, and she didn't want to pump her best friend about anything. What they shared, they'd shared willingly. She'd talk to Logan, but she wouldn't pry.

---

L OGAN WOKE ALONE AND THOUGHT she'd just dreamed Wade was here, which left her with an empty feeling in the pit of her stomach. Then she heard his voice and turned toward the sound. He was standing in the doorway talking to a policeman.

Her eyes welled. He was really here.

"Hey," she said.

Wade looked over his shoulder.

"Hey, yourself," he said, then parted company with the cop and closed the door. When he got to the bed, he felt of her forehead. It was cool enough. "How do you feel?"

"Did you tell me I was shot?" she asked.

He nodded.

"Do you need anything? Something for the pain?"

"It will make me sleepy. I want to talk. Did I dream it, or did you tell me the police chief has the files from Blue Sky?"

"No dream. I gave them to him. You're done playing detective."

When her eyes narrowed, he knew he'd ticked her off and was waiting for a dressing down when she reached for his hand.

"I didn't trust him," she said.

"I know, and it nearly got you killed. He said when you get better, that the two of you were going to set a trap and catch a bad guy."

Her eyes widened. "He said that?"

"Yes, ma'am."

"How long do I have to stay here?" she asked.

"I don't know, but considering the fact that you nearly died today, we aren't rushing it. Oh...and who's T-Boy?"

Logan frowned. "He's a guy a little older than me. Mostly just a thug. I saw him once since I've been back. He hasn't changed a bit."

"Chief Evans told your friend, Caitlin, and me, that he saved your life."

Logan's lips parted in shock. "You're kidding."

"Nope. The Chief said he's the one who found you and was holding compresses on your wounds when the ambulance and the police arrived."

"Wow," Logan said, and looked away. "I guess I owe him."

"I would agree," Wade said.

Her eyes closed again, and she was drifting back to sleep when she groaned. Breathing was suddenly a thing of pain, and every breath she took exacerbated the muscles in her back that had begun to spasm. She moaned beneath her breath.

"What's wrong?" Wade asked.

"Muscle spasms. Oh my God, they hurt. Where's the thingy to ring for the nurse?"

"Clipped to your bed," he said, and pulled it down into her line of sight.

She pressed the buzzer.

Moments later a voice came over the intercom.

"Hello, Mrs. Talman. How can I help you?"

"I need something for pain."

"I'll check your orders," she said, and disconnected.

Logan closed her eyes as another wave of pain rolled through her.

Wade had two options. Walk away before he revealed his true feelings, or just hold her anyway. He chose the latter, lowered a bedrail and raised the head of her bed, apologizing as he eased down onto the bed beside her.

"I can't watch you hurt," he said, and slid his hands behind her back. He could already feel the muscles knotting beneath his palms as he eased her forward. "Rest your head on my shoulder and try to relax."

Logan was in too much pain to pay attention to how close they were. What she felt were the tips of his fingers pressing on the knotted muscles—pressing hard for several seconds and releasing. Then doing it again, applying pressure over and over with his fingertips. The relief was staggering.

"Ooh, my God," Logan moaned.

Wade's heart skipped.

"Am I hurting you?"

"No, it's stopping the spasms. Thank you. . .thank you."

"I'm happy it's helping," he said.

The nurse walked in, and then smiled.

"Looks like I'm a little late with the TLC."

"It's not what you think," Wade said, as he eased her back down onto the pillow and lowered her bed.

"The spasms are easing up," Logan said. "How did you learn

to do that?"

"I was in a wreck when I was a teenager. Had a lot of back spasms from the whiplash. A physical therapist taught me how to stop them myself after my therapy had ended."

The nurse nodded.

"Yes, yes. Intermittent pressure on the muscle in spasm does help."

She injected the pain meds into the IV and then checked Logan's bandages.

"Do you think you could eat something?" the nurse asked.

Logan started to say no, then changed her mind.

"Ice cream."

"We can make that happen," the nurse said, and left.

Wade sat back down to put space between them again. It had been too easy to hold her, and he didn't have that right.

The nurse came back with a little cup of ice cream and raised the head of her bed, but Logan was having a hard time feeding herself left-handed.

"May I?" Wade asked.

"Knock yourself out," Logan said, and gratefully gave up and let him feed her like a baby.

"Want more?" he asked, when that was gone.

"Not now, and thank you."

"Then rest. Sleep. I'm here and there's a cop at the door. You're safe."

Her eyes closed. Within seconds she succumbed.

Wade watched her until he was sure she was asleep before texting the bosses of the work crews back home.

For the next hour, texts flew back and forth as the crews all wanted to know Logan's status and then sent messages to her. Wade answered those in between problem-solving at the different job sites. By the time the messages had tapered off, he was tired. He put his phone on the little table beside him and closed his eyes.

He'd lived a lifetime between the phone call this morning and now. He felt tired *and* he felt old. For a few hours today, he'd feared he had outlived everyone he loved.

# CHAPTER NINE

———•———

BIG BOY WAS SITTING ON a corner of the bed, staring out the window into the dark, starry sky, wishing he'd made a different choice and had never called Damon Conway. If he hadn't been such a coward, he would have just found a way to kill his wife without involving anyone else. But it was too late for regrets.

He'd thought about pulling a disappearing act all evening, but didn't have the guts to walk away from the money. Most of it was tied up in investments, and it took time to liquidate.

He glanced over his shoulder at the woman in his bed. Without makeup and in the dark, she could have been any woman. He'd been so caught up in the lust of a pretty face and sexy body that he'd cold-heartedly done away with his woman of substance. He hadn't had one serious conversation with his second wife in the entire time he'd known her. The only thing she understood was using her body to get what she wanted. The only thing she was good at was sex.

Disheartened by his choices, he got up and went to the window. His bedroom overlooked the rose gardens at the back of the house. Even in the dark, they were beautiful. He used to walk among them at night, their fragrance more concentrated in the evening when the air grew heavy and still.

He hadn't walked at night in a very long time and followed the urge all the way to the closet for shoes. You didn't walk barefoot at night in Louisiana unless you were a gambler willing to risk your life on a snake.

With a quick look at the bed to make sure Sugar was still sleeping, he slipped out of the room and then hurried down the stairs and turned off the alarm.

His tennis shoes made little squeaky sounds on the marble flooring as he moved down the hall into the library, his steps hastening with anticipation as he exited through the French doors onto the back verandah.

The scent of jasmine met him at the bottom steps and then followed him through the winding path until he came upon the roses. The aroma of glorious blooms was an aphrodisiac, lulling him into a false sense of all is well.

The soft, nearly soundless flap of wings behind him was all the warning he was going to get from an owl on the hunt. The rustle in the bushes stopped him momentarily until he identified the sound with the possum that came waddling out.

The tree frogs were singing loudly, announcing his presence with a most splendid show of their music, giving way only to a low buzz from the cicadas—the white noise of the night.

It was the familiar he'd known as a kid, sleeping in the back bedroom of his mama and daddy's shack down on the bayou. With windows open to catch the faintest of breezes, but tightly screened to keep out what didn't belong inside, he'd fallen asleep to this midnight lullaby. Then he'd grown up, gotten rich, and was living a life as a man with two faces.

The winding path through the roses was paved with reclaimed brick from an Antebellum property outside of New Orleans. It pleased his fancy to imagine the countless feet of people long dead who had walked on this brick in ages past—before he'd had them moved here to Bluejacket—back when he'd believed that owning what someone else had lost somehow counted as one-upping the Universe.

The path ended at a stone bench within the center of the roses. The words "Angels Among Us" had been carved into the back, with angel wings forming the arms of the bench. He sat, then tilted his head up to the vast infinity of a dark, starry sky. So beautiful, and a far better view from the window of his room.

There was no priest on the seat beside him, and even though he hadn't been inside a church since the day after he'd buried his wife, he still felt the need to seek absolution.

"Forgive me Lord, for I have sinned. It's been something over ten years since my last confession."

He spoke in whispers, because confessing aloud to anyone but God would put him in prison. And then the longer he spoke, the quieter the night sounds became.

Cicadas quit singing. The tree frogs fell silent.

And when he had finished, he realized the sweet scents of his garden had faded into the background, giving way to a more predominant scent—the putrid scent of death.

He stood abruptly, looking first at the bench, then to the ground below it, imagining at any moment his first wife's skeletal fingers thrusting up through the earth, digging her way out of the place where he'd buried her.

"You're dead. Stay where you are," he muttered, and then started toward the house.

But the farther he walked, the more certain he became that he was being followed. Afraid to look, he lengthened his stride, and by the time he reached the house, he was running.

———◆———

AT HOME, CHIEF EVANS WAS just Josh to the woman who shared his life. He and his high school sweetheart, Lorene, had been married nearly fifteen years. She meant more to him now than she had even when love was young and new, and the research he'd been doing on Logan Talman's case was both horrifying and depressing. He couldn't imagine losing his Reenie, let alone be the one to end her life.

Now that most of his officers were back on duty, he made a point to go home on time, and tonight after their supper, he got up from the table and began helping her clean.

Lorene glanced at him more than once before she finally spoke up.

"Sweetheart, I don't know what's gotten into you, but I like it."

Josh looked up from loading dishes into the dishwasher, and saw past the wear and tear of her day, to the blue-eyed girl who'd stolen his heart.

"Reenie, I don't tell you nearly enough how much I appreciate you, or how much I love you," he said.

Her eyes widened with surprise.

"Well, my goodness honey...thank you. I love you, too."

He dried his hands and took her into his arms, resting his chin on the crown of her head.

Lorene had known him for too many years not know that this was more than a husband's guilty conscience for his recent absence from home.

She laid her cheek against his chest and wrapped her arms around his waist. The steady thump of his heartbeat was her touchstone to the rhythm of her life.

"What's wrong, Josh, and don't say nothing. I know you better than that."

"I can't talk about all of it right now, but soon. Suffice it to say, it's the negative part of my job, okay?"

She hugged him tighter.

"As long as it's not me causing you pain, I can handle anything," Lorene said.

"We're good. We'll always be good," Josh said, and took the dish towel out of her hands. "You. Go. Run yourself a big old bubble bath and soak yourself into a little prune."

She giggled.

"I won't turn down an invitation like that," she said, and left the kitchen with a skip in her step.

Josh sighed, then turned back to the dirty dishes and kept rinsing and loading.

"If only it was this easy to wash away sin."

———◆———

THEY WOKE LOGAN UP WHEN they served the evening meal, hoping she would feel like eating something.

She picked through some of it and drank her iced tea while watching Wade eat the meal he'd ordered, plus what was left of hers. Soon afterward, her nurse came into the room to check vitals.

"Do you need me to leave?" Wade asked.

Before the nurse could answer, Logan interrupted.

"No. I don't want you to leave," she said, and then blushed. "I just meant, you don't have to," and looked away.

Wade's heart hurt for the lost expression on her face.

"Don't worry...I've got your six, Boss."

Logan looked up at him.

"You've always had my six. I just don't think I ever recognized how much you do on my behalf, so, thank you, Wade."

The seriousness caught him by surprise.

"You're welcome, but I don't need thanks for doing something I wanted to do."

"Okay then," the nurse said, and began going through the routine.

She was kind and friendly, and properly horrified that something this awful had happened in Bluejacket. She kept saying things like, "This kind of stuff never happens here," but Logan knew better. She'd seen a body in the street in front of their house the same night Damon had been murdered.

Finally, the nurse finished. "Is there anything else you need? I'll bring fresh ice water in a little while."

"No, I'm fine. I don't need anything," Logan said, then heard Wade mutter something about "being fine and getting shot in the back are not synonymous," but she didn't argue. She knew she'd scared him. For that matter, she'd scared herself, too.

Wade didn't comment, even though he knew she'd heard him, and then gave her a look before checking texts on his phone.

"Is everything okay back home?" Logan asked.

"According to McGuire, who I left in charge, there were no big snags today other than Carter shot himself in the foot with a nail gun."

"Oh my God," Logan muttered, and raised the head of her bed up enough so she could talk. "Is he okay?"

"He's going to be okay, but he's off work for at least a week. That's going to make that crew one guy short."

"Then tell McGuire to either call Xavier Santiago or Joey Chavez. They've filled in for us before."

"Ah...yes, good call," Wade said. "I've got their numbers, I think."

"I have their numbers in my phone, which is in my purse, wherever that is."

"I have them, too," Wade said, and made the calls.

Xavier was busy, but Joey Chavez was glad for the work. Wade told him where to show up tomorrow, and that McGuire was in charge, then he sent McGuire a text to that effect and hoped that was the last problem to solve for the day.

"All is well," he said, as he put his phone aside, then looked up and noticed Logan had fallen asleep.

He lowered the head of her bed so she could sleep better, then straightened the covers. The last thing he did was smooth the hair away from her face. He'd often wished he could spend more time with her, but not like this.

He rubbed the back of his neck, trying to ease tense muscles as he moved to the window on the other side of her bed.

The sky was littered with starlight as far as the eye could see. It looked beautiful, but dark in bayou country was dangerous.

Weary all the way to his bones, Wade finally gave up and stretched out in the recliner, pulled the extra blanket they'd given him up past his waist, and closed his eyes.

He was asleep within minutes, but his sleep was restless. Too focused on making sure she stayed safe, he never really blocked out the sounds. The shower in her bathroom had a drip, and the scent of antiseptic was too strong to ignore. Outside in the hallway, one police officer traded duty with the other, and he heard them talking about the case.

Nurses came and went throughout the night, and each time they came into her room, Wade was on his feet, drilling them with questions. Once when Logan woke up enough to focus, she heard him talking. Knowing he was present to look out for her when she was so vulnerable gave her a whole new perspective on how much he meant to her, only she didn't know how to categorize it. She wanted to tell him, but she was too out of it to stay awake.

---

WITH DAYLIGHT CAME THE BEGINNING of a new agenda for Josh. He was getting ready to start what could prove to be an interesting day. He kissed Reenie goodbye and drove straight to the office. When he walked in the back door, Paul Robicheau was up and pacing his cell.

"I better be getting my day in court today," he yelled.

"A court appointed lawyer has your info. He should be here some time before arraignment, so you need to be thinking about how you're going to plead," Evans said.

Robicheau slapped the flat of his hand against the bars.

"Well hell, I'll be pleading innocent."

Evans grinned.

"You do know there's at least fifteen people in Bluejacket can attest to the opposite, not to mention the woman who flat out caught you trying to break into her car."

"I heard she got shot," Robicheau said.

Evans frowned.

"That's true, but she's nowhere close to dead. You take this to court, her testimony will nail your ass to the wall."

"Just my luck," Robicheau muttered.

His shoulders slumped as he backed up and dropped onto the cot.

Josh frowned. "Do you just hear your damn self?" he snapped.

"What?" Robicheau said.

"The fact that you need someone to die just so you can get yourself out of the mess you caused is disgusting."

Then Josh strode past the cells and into the precinct, slamming the door between them good and hard to punctuate his point.

"Loser," he muttered, and went straight to the break room for a cup of coffee which he carried to his office.

He sat down behind his desk, took a quick sip, and then set the coffee aside as he checked the clock. By the time he got the phone numbers to go with the names, it would be eight a.m. Since these were not social calls, he felt confident that proper manners did not apply.

He made the first call, then kicked back in his chair, waiting for it to be answered. He didn't know how Camren Stephens was going to react, but he'd soon find out.

CAMREN HAD JUST FINISHED SHAVING and was still getting dressed when his wife, Ashley, came hurrying into the room and pointed at their phone.

"Is the ringer still turned off on that phone?" she asked.

"Yes, why?" he asked.

"Because the chief of police is on the phone and wants to talk to you."

Camren frowned.

"Really? Wonder what he wants?" he said, then sat down on the side of the bed and picked up the receiver.

"Hello? Chief Evans?"

"Hello, Camren. Sorry to call so early, but we've got ourselves a little situation here, and I need your help."

"Of course. Happy to help. What do you need?"

"I need you to come in to the office this morning and answer some questions for me. How soon can you get here?"

Camren frowned.

"Come to the office to answer questions? What kind of questions?" he asked.

"Unfortunately, they have to do with your first wife's death. It won't take long, and I'm sure you can clear up the inconsistencies in the report. We didn't have a proper police chief at that time, and some of the paperwork wasn't done."

"Oh. Well. My goodness, yes, I guess I can do that," he said. "I'll be there as soon as I finish getting dressed."

"Thank you," Josh said, and disconnected, wishing he could have seen Camren's reaction.

"What did he want?" Ashley asked.

"To talk to me about Julia's death."

Ashley gasped.

"What? Why?"

Camren shrugged.

"He said something about the man who was standing in as chief at the time didn't finish up some of the paperwork properly."

"Oh. Well, I guess that's okay," she said.

Camren frowned.

"What the hell do you mean, you guess it's okay? You don't pass judgment on me."

Ashley frowned.

"Well, what you do reflects on me, too, smart ass. So, if you're in trouble, I have a right to know." Then her eyes narrowed. "Is there something you need to tell me?"

"Yes! Get the hell out of the room!" he shouted, and started toward her.

She backed out and then slammed the door between them.

He glared, and not for the first time, wondered why he'd bothered to remarry.

———◆———

THE CHIEF DECIDED TO SKIP Roger Franklin. His wife had not died under suspicious circumstances. He'd had no life insurance policy on her, and he had never remarried. If necessary, he could always go back and do it later, but the police did not have a file on her death because it had happened in a hospital, so he couldn't use the interim police chief story as an excuse.

The next person he called was Peyton Adams, and Peyton was a loose cannon. There was no way to tell how he would receive this, but that was beside the point. There wasn't anyone madder sadder, or more indignant than Logan Talman, and she had the right to feel that way.

———◆———

PEYTON WAS AT THE BREAKFAST table having waffles with his wife, Candy. Sophie, their cook, had just brought a fresh plate of bacon strips to the table when the landline rang in the house.

"I'll get that for you, sir," Sophie said. She came back holding a cordless phone. "Chief Evans for you."

Peyton frowned as he put the phone to his ear.

"Hello, Josh."

Josh frowned. By using his first name, Peyton thought he'd taken the power out of his call.

"Hello, Peyton. I'm calling on business. I need you to come by the office this morning and answer some questions for me."

"Questions? What questions?"

"Regarding the death of your first wife. During the time of her accident, there was an interim police chief who did not properly close out some of his cases, so that duty now falls to me."

"Oh, are you serious?" Peyton drawled.

Josh frowned. Peyton's sarcasm was obvious.

"Actually, yes, very serious," Josh said.

That was not the response Peyton had expected, and he began shifting his attitude.

"Well, I suppose I can stop by—"

Josh interrupted.

"You do understand this isn't really your decision. I require you to do this, if that makes it easier for you."

Peyton heard a tone in the voice that made him nervous. It had taken forever to clear her death, and now this was popping up. God almighty, what was going on here?

"I can be there a little after nine."

"That's fine. You may have to wait. You're not the only one I'm calling."

"Okay," Peyton muttered, and blinked when the line suddenly disconnected in his ear.

"What's going on?" Candy asked.

Peyton handed the phone back to Sophie, who walked out of the room.

"The strangest thing. It has to do with Mona's drowning. There was a temporary police chief when it happened who didn't close the case properly, and Evans said he needs to ask me some questions."

"That's so strange," Candy said. "Are you okay? I mean, is this going to be upsetting for you?"

"You're so sweet," Peyton said. "No, it's not upsetting. Just strange."

He put a couple of slices of bacon onto his plate and poured more syrup on what was left of his waffles before finishing his breakfast. A short time later, he was out the door.

# CHAPTER TEN

CAMREN STEPHENS WAS STILL PISSED off at his wife when he left the house. This wasn't the first time they'd crossed purposes, and it likely wouldn't be the last. She was bossy and too worried about her social standing to suit him. They lived in Blue-fucking-jacket, Louisiana for God's sake. Not New York City. There was no society page in the *Bayou Weekly*, and no events to cover that would have put them there.

He drove with the windows down and the wind blowing in his hair because it made him feel young. That's what he'd done when he was in high school. It was a subconscious move, adding to his illusion that the last thirty years had not passed, and that he still had enough hair for the wind to blow.

He was coming upon the Adams' property when he saw Peyton getting into his car. He honked and waved, and Peyton turned and waved as Camren drove past.

He reached the police station a few minutes later, parked at the curb, and combed his hair before getting out. There was a sweat stain down the back of his short-sleeved shirt and stains under both arms. It was the mark of summer in this part of the country and nothing to fret about as he headed into the building.

Arnie, the clerk, was at the desk as Camren entered.

"Morning, Arnie. I'm here at the request of your chief."

"Yes, sir. He told me you were coming in. Just a second, and I'll let him know you're here."

Camren sat down and moments later, Josh Evans came up the hall.

"Camren, thank you for coming. My office is this way."

Camren followed, his nose wrinkling slightly at the faint odor of urine and cleaning solvents, then remembered the jail was at the back of the station. Likely that's what he smelled.

"Would you like some coffee?" Josh asked, as he motioned for Camren to sit down.

"No thanks, Chief. I'm already over my limit for the day."

Josh sat, then pointed to a video camera on a tripod behind his desk.

"I'm going to film this interview for the sake of expediency," he said. "Please state your name for the record."

"My name is Camren Allen Stephens.

Josh nodded then opened a file already on his desk.

"Again, I do apologize for having to do this. In fact, I was unaware this problem even existed until I was going through some old files for research on another issue. You do understand this was all before I came on board as chief, but it's still my duty to rectify mistakes."

"Certainly," Camren said, then shook his head. "I still miss her. Oh, don't get me wrong. Ashley and I are fine, but I did not give Julia up willingly. The whole thing about killed me."

Evans was listening, but he was also watching the expressions on Camren's face. If he was lying, he was good at it.

"I understand. So, let's get to this. The sooner we're through, the better. Let's see...the first omission was no paperwork done on the follow-up after the autopsy report."

Camren frowned.

"What do you mean? It was horribly cut and dried. She died from head injuries when she hit the tree."

Evans nodded.

"Yes, the head injuries are noted, and the autopsy report did state cause of death was severe trauma to the brain."

"So, what's the problem?" Camren asked.

"There's no explanation for the amount of Diphenhydramine and Doxylamine in her system."

Camren frowned.

"That has to be wrong. Julia didn't do drugs."

"Did she take sleeping pills?" Evans asked.

"Sometimes, why?"

"Those are drugs in antihistamines, but they are also drugs in sleeping pills. And she had a high content of both. The fact that this was never called into question before ruling her death as accidental, is where the error lies."

Camren's eyes were widening in both shock and growing horror.

"Are you telling me my wife fell asleep at the wheel because she had taken too many sleeping pills?"

"According to this report, it looks that way," Evans said.

His voice was shaking now.

"On purpose?"

"Well, that's what I'm asking you. If she didn't do it on purpose, the only other explanation is that someone snuck them into the coffee she took to work, and we know she had coffee from home with her because the photos at the scene reflect that."

Camren jerked as if he'd been slapped.

"Are you accusing me of murdering my wife? You are, aren't you? Oh my God! No! I would never do that."

"Then let's work this out," Josh said. "I know it's been a long time, but can you remember anything about that morning?"

Camren started to answer, only nothing came out but a choked sob, so he took a deep breath and tried it again.

"I remember everything about that morning. I went over it for weeks, months...once in a while, I still dream about it, but in the dream, I always stop her from leaving home."

"Tell me," Josh said.

"I was sick. I'd been under the weather for a solid week and hadn't gone back to work. I still had the weigh station and sporting goods store back then."

"The weigh station, meaning the one where the gator hunters brought in their catch during hunting season?"

Camren nodded.

"Anyway, we had breakfast together as always." Camren closed his eyes as he spoke.

The chief knew Camren was watching it happen all over again by the movement of his eyes beneath closed lids.

"I ate cold cereal. Julia ate scrambled eggs. She was on a diet at the time, one with no carbs, no sugar. I had forgotten to take my medicine, so I went to get it. I came back to the table with it and—"

"What medicine were you taking?" Josh asked.

"Some over the counter stuff for sinus infection," Camren said, and kept talking. "I have this thing about pills. I can't swallow them properly. So, I dropped them in my hot coffee and let the gel capsules dissolve while I was still eating."

"You always put pills in something to dissolve them?" Josh asked.

"Yes. They won't go down any other way. So, Julia finished her eggs, carried her plate and cup to load in the dishwasher. I finished my cereal and took the dirty bowl to the counter so she could load it, too."

"Where's your coffee cup?" Josh asked.

Camren paused, again closing his eyes, trying to remember.

"I guess I carried it to the counter, too, but I still hadn't finished. I needed to drink it all to get the full dose of medicine."

"So, then what happened?" Josh asked.

Tears started rolling down Camren's cheeks.

"Someone rang the doorbell. I went to answer. It was the UPS man with the present I'd ordered for her birthday. I had to sign for it, and then I took it to the library and hid it behind the wet bar." He glanced up. "It's still there. I know it's stupid, but I can't bring myself to throw it away, and I can't bear to look at it. It's caused more than one argument between me and Ashley, too. Anyway, by the time I got back, Julia was on her way out the door. She had her coffee in one hand and her briefcase in the other. She said she thought she was coming down with what I had, said she took something for it, and that she loved me and would see me after school." He wiped a hand across his face and looked up. "You know the rest."

This had been an eye-opening interview, and Josh didn't think Camren grasped the meaning of what he'd said.

"So, did you finish off your coffee?" he asked.

Camren frowned.

"Did I what? Finish my coffee? Uh...I guess. I know I emptied the pot. I always do. I drink too much coffee," he said, and shrugged.

Josh pulled out the case file for the wreck, removed the two photos of the interior of the car, and laid them in front of Camren.

"Do you see anything specific in these photos that shouldn't be there?"

Camren gasped.

"Are these from the wreck?"

"Yes, the interior view of the front seat."

Camren's hands were shaking as he pulled them closer.

"There's her briefcase...and a shoe. Oh my God, one of her shoes. My baby...my sweet Julia. Why am I looking at these? Damn it, Chief! Why are you putting me through this?"

Josh tapped the photos.

"Just keep telling me everything you see, and if there's anything there that shouldn't be, tell me."

Camren shuddered, then looked down.

"I see a dark stain on the upholstery, probably from her coffee cup. Oh, and there's her cup in front of the—"

Camren let out a cry of such pain, Evans knew it was not faked.

"That's not her cup! That's my cup! It has a "C." Hers had a "J." She took my cup, with my medicine in it."

"You told me that she said she thought she was coming down with what you had and took something for it."

Camren gasped.

"Oh my God. She took my coffee cup and took pills with it, then took it with her, didn't she? That's what really caused the wreck, isn't it? She took double the antihistamines. Why is this happening?" He started to sob. "This is like losing her all over again."

Josh felt bad for Camren Stephens, but he was satisfied for now with the answers he'd gotten about the file.

"I'm so sorry. I can't imagine how painful this has to be for you, Camren, but I'm grateful for your help. Will you be okay to drive home? I can have an officer drop you off if you want?"

Camren shook his head and wiped his face with his handkerchief.

"No, I'm okay. More than anything, it was a shock."

"Oh...one more thing. Which one of you drove the Silverado you owned at the time?" Evans asked.

"I did, why?" Camren asked.

"No big reason. Just a footnote."

"Okay. Can I go now?"

Evans nodded.

"Yes, and thank you again for helping clear this up."

Camren got up, his head down and his steps slow as he walked back to the front lobby with the Chief beside him.

Camren left the building without acknowledging the clerk or the man sitting in the waiting area, but Peyton Adams saw him, and the emotional condition he was in, and frowned.

*What the hell is going on?*

Then Josh called for him.

"Peyton, thanks for waiting. Let's go to my office."

Peyton brought attitude with him and made certain the chief was aware of it as he took his seat on the other side of the desk. When he realized their conversation was going to be recorded, his heart skipped a beat.

"What's going on here?" he asked.

Josh wasn't surprised by Peyton's challenge. It was nothing more than he'd expected. As soon as he had the camera reset, he took a seat.

"Please state your name for the record," Josh said.

Peyton lifted his chin and stared straight into the camera.

"Peyton Carl Adams."

"Thank you. Now, what's going on is exactly what I told you over the phone, and because it's related to a previously closed case, I am videoing the interview so no one can claim misunderstanding later."

Peyton frowned.

"Is that what you and Camren were doing?"

"I'm not going to comment on that. Would you want me to talk about your business with other people?"

Peyton shrugged.

"Point taken, but it was a nightmare going through this the first time, so you should understand my reluctance to revisit it."

Josh tapped his pen against the desk in frustration.

"And I'm sure you can imagine my dismay finding out this case was never properly closed. I don't enjoy this. Quite the contrary. I am not heartless, and knowing I have to resurrect family tragedies does not make me happy, either."

Peyton sighed, then finally sat all the way back in his chair.

"Noted. So, ask away."

"Thank you," Josh said, and then opened the case file. "According to the autopsy, your wife, Ramona, died from drowning. Blood was found on the side of the pool and in the water at your home where it was supposed she slipped and fell, hitting her head before falling in and drowning. Is that correct?"

Peyton nodded.

"Please speak aloud for the camera," Evans asked.

Peyton's eyes narrowed, but he complied.

"Yes, that's correct."

"It also states that Ramona's seventeen-year-old daughter, Caitlin Justice, found her after coming home from a football game."

Peyton grimaced.

"Yes, bless her heart. It was horrible for her."

Josh tapped the open file before him.

"It just states you were out of town. There is no mention of where you were, or follow-up notes to verify your whereabouts. Where were you when it happened?" Josh asked.

Peyton's face reddened in anger.

"I was in New Orleans on business."

"Where were you staying?"

"With friends. Their names were Sam and Alana Owens."

Josh looked up from the file. "Were?"

Peyton nodded. "They died in a plane crash two years ago."

Josh frowned. "Is there anyone living who could corroborate this?"

"Hell, I don't know...Oh, wait. Yes. Maybe. Their son, Larry, was in and out that night, but we did speak. However, I have no idea if he'd remember a house guest their parents had ten years ago."

"I'll worry about that. Do you have contact info for him?"

"No. I barely knew him. I have no idea where he lives now," Peyton said.

"So, his name was Larry Owens?" Josh asked.

"Yes," Peyton said.

"How were you notified of the death?"

"Caitie called me in hysterics. At first, I couldn't understand what she was saying because she was crying, but when it sank in, I couldn't believe it had happened. Mona was a strong swimmer.

It would be later before I learned she had hit her head and fallen in. This did explain my disbelief as to how she'd died."

Josh watched the anger on Peyton's face shifting to sadness as he continued. "There is a mention of a very high blood alcohol level at the time of her death."

Peyton shrugged. "It started from an accident she had about six months prior. There should be a record of it at the high school, and at the hospital. She slipped down the front steps at school when it was raining and landed on her back. They took her to the ER by ambulance."

"I'll check," Josh said. "So, she started drinking after that because...?"

"Because the pain pills didn't kill the pain, so she added alcohol. Then the doctor quit giving her pain meds because he could not find the source of pain, and thought she'd just gotten addicted. When that happened, she chose liquor as the means to numbing her misery. It became a problem, but we were working on it. She had agreed to rehab, and we were getting ready to admit her when she died."

"I see," Josh said, and made a note to set up a time to speak to Caitlin. "By any chance do you have a phone number for Caitlin. I'll need to talk to her, too, since she was the one who found her mother."

"I think I do," Peyton said, and scanned the contact list in his phone. "Yes, here it is," he said, and read the number out to Josh, watching as he made a note of it.

"Thank you," Josh said, and then glanced up. He was taking a chance asking this question, but he wanted to see if it made Peyton nervous.

"So, which one of you was driving the Silverado at the time?"

"We all used it, but I guess I drove it more, why?" Josh shrugged.

"Just a footnote to the case file. I guess we're done here. As soon as I can verify your whereabouts the night of the incident, I can close this down properly. I really appreciate you coming in."

Peyton relaxed.

"Sure. Glad I could help," he said. "Are we through?"

"Yes, I'll walk you out," Josh said, and opened the door for him.

They walked to the front without talking, but Peyton did stop and shake his hand before he left. Josh gave him points after the fact and went back to the office to call Caitlin Baptiste.

Caitlin had just dropped her boys off at her mother-in-law's house for the day. One of their Baptiste cousins was having a birthday party and their grandmother was taking them to the party later, and then they were going to spend the night. They loved spending time with Johnny's parents, and Caitlin and Johnny loved a night to themselves.

She was getting ready to stop by Friendly's Grocery to get some flowers for Logan before she went to the hospital when her cell phone rang. She glanced at Caller ID and frowned. Why would someone from the police department be calling her? She pulled over to the curb in front of the Catholic Church and parked so she could answer.

"Hello," she said.

"Caitlin?"

"Yes."

"This is Chief Evans. I need to talk to you a bit about something. Could you come to the office?"

"Yes, I guess, but what's it about? Am I in trouble?"

He chuckled. "No. I'll explain it after you get here."

"Okay. I'll be there in a few. I'm already in the car heading downtown. Won't take me long to get there."

"Great. I'll wait for you in the lobby of the station."

"Okay," she said, and disconnected, then worried all the way to the station anyway.

But as promised, the chief was waiting for her when she walked in.

"Morning, Caitlin. How are the boys?"

"They're great...at their Grandma's today to go to a family birthday party, and then spending the night with them later."

Josh grinned. "Ah...you and Johnny have a night to yourselves. Going out to eat?"

She grinned. "Yes, if I can talk him into it."

"Well then, let's go back to my office and get this over with so you can be on your way, and I can get my paperwork cleared up."

"What          paperwork?"          Caitlin          asked.
"I'll explain it all," he said, and led the way down the hall, then

seated her in the same chair the others had been in.

When he turned the video camera back on, she frowned. "You're filming me?"

He sat. "It's the easiest way to record your comments."

Caitlin didn't understand, but waited.

Josh leaned across the table, hating to begin this because he guessed this was likely to be emotional for her, but considering what was at stake, he couldn't avoid it.

"Please state your name for the record."

Caitlin blinked. This sounded so court-like, as if she was on trial for something. It made her nervous, and she was already beginning to pick a hangnail as she answered.

"Caitlin Elizabeth Baptiste."

Josh nodded.

"Thank you. Now...here's what's going on. A couple of days ago, I came across some old case files that had not been properly closed. It's all before I took office, and one of them has to do with your mother's death."

Caitlin's eyes immediately welled.

"Oh no. What's wrong?"

"I know you found her, but I have to verify where Peyton was when her accident occurred. The records state he was out of town, but do you know where?"

She took a tissue from her purse, dabbed at her eyes, and then scrunched it between her hands, her voice already beginning to shake.

"He was in New Orleans on business. He goes now and then because that's where his stockbroker is located. Sometimes the stockbroker comes here, but most times he goes there. Mother always teased him saying he could have done everything over the phone, and that he went for the food and Beale Street."

"What do you mean?"

"Oh, Peyton is a huge jazz fan. He has this really big collection of classic albums and a turntable to go with them."

"I see. So, did you know where he was staying? Which hotel?" Evans asked.

"Not a hotel. He never stayed at the hotel. There were two or three couples who were friends with Mother and Peyton. He would stay over with one of them. I think that trip he was staying with the Owens, but I'm not positive. It's been a long time."

"I understand," Evans said. "I have to ask you some personal things about your mother. The autopsy stated cause of death was drowning, and that she had hit her head on the side of the pool. But her blood alcohol level was three times the legal limit, and there was no follow up on that. What can you tell me?"

"She was drinking a lot the last few months of her life, which really changed her personality. It was hard."

"So, was it something she'd hidden, or something new?"

"It was new. She had an accident at school that hurt her back. The doctor gave her pain pills at first, but physical therapy didn't help, and so she chose to add liquor to pills. Her doctor quit renewing the prescription when he found out she was drinking. He couldn't find a reason for her supposed pain and thought she'd just become addicted. When he did that, she turned totally to liquor to dull it."

"Did that adversely affect her marriage in any way?"

Caitlin shrugged. "Nothing I saw. Peyton sympathized. We both saw the pain on her face. It wasn't faked."

"It says it took a long time for the life insurance company to pay on her policy."

Caitlin nodded. "They didn't want to pay, tried to say it was suicide, but there was that head wound and the blood on the side of the pool and in the water. They finally had to pay up."

"It was a big payoff," Josh said.

"Half went to me, and half to Peyton."

This was news that wasn't on Logan Talman's list.

"The information I had just listed Peyton."

"Well, that's because he was the recipient, but he gave half of it to me anyway."

"Oh...okay. That was really nice of him."

She shrugged.

"Peyton is a good man, but he never wanted to be a father. By the time the insurance company finally paid off, I was already living with Johnny. After we married, we bought the little house where we're living with part of the insurance money and put the rest in savings for the boys' college."

Josh hid his surprise. Both of the men who'd received big insurance payouts were looking better than he'd first imagined.

So, what was he missing?

"Who was driving the Silverado owned at the time?"

"All of us did at one time or another. I drove it to school some, but I guess Peyton drove it the most."

"Okay then," Josh said, made the last few notes he was taking, and then closed the file. "That's all I needed to ask you, and thank you."

"You're welcome. Can I ask you a question?"

"Sure," Josh said.

"Who shot Logan?"

"I don't know, but I'm working on it," he said.

"Are all of these questions related to her?"

"I can't comment on an ongoing case," he said.

"Do you still need me to ask her about her brother?" Caitlin asked.

The Chief took a deep breath. Damn. "Not at this time, but I'll let you know if I do."

Caitlin leaned back in the chair and glared. "Fine. You know why she's here, don't you? It has to do with Damon. She did tell me one thing early on, and that was why they left town so fast."

"What did she say?" Evans asked.

"You already know the answer to that, don't you? Are we through here?" Caitlin snapped.

"Yes, ma'am."

"Then I'll be going. I was on my way to visit her when you called."

Josh sighed. "Don't drill her on anything. The less you know, the safer you'll be."

Caitlin blinked as she absorbed the horror of what he'd said, and then clutched her purse up against her breasts and walked out.

He got up and turned off the camera for the last time, then went to refill his coffee. He had a knot in his belly and the beginnings of a headache, but then he thought of Logan. She had a whole lot more to deal with than a headache, which shifted his focus from his aches and pains to the business at hand.

He took a quick sip of the coffee and frowned. Arnie was a damn good clerk, but his coffee sucked. He stirred in a little sugar hoping to mask the burned taste, then went back to his office and began running down leads on Larry Owens' location. He still had to verify where Peyton had been the night Mona died.

# CHAPTER ELEVEN

———◆———

L OGAN ATE BREAKFAST BETTER THAN she'd eaten supper the night before, but she still had no appetite, which was
beginning to bother Wade. He used his fork to point at her plate.

"You need to eat some more of your eggs," he said.

"They have no taste. They're overcooked."

"Besides that?" he asked.

She poked the eggs with the tip of her finger then watched
them spring back up – like rubber. "Isn't that enough?"

"I'm sorry, Logan. Is there a café in town that delivers?" he
asked.

"There's Barney's, but I don't know if they deliver," she said.
"It doesn't matter. I'm not going to be in here long enough to
worry."

He frowned. "Who said?"

"Me," she said.

"You will leave here when the doctor dismisses you and not an
hour sooner," he said.

She shrugged, shoved the tray table to the side, and closed her
eyes.

He knew that move and grinned. When she didn't like something, she ignored it. There was a knock at the door and then it
opened enough that Wade saw Caitlin's face.

"Come in. She's not asleep. She's just sulking."

Logan glared at him, then saw her friend and grinned. "Yay!
Someone who's going to be nice to me."

Caitlin smiled. "I'm so nice I brought you fresh doughnuts

from the deli at Friendly's. I was going to bring flowers and then saw these."

"Thank God," Wade drawled. "The sulk had to do with the poor quality of the eggs."

Caitlin giggled.

Logan managed to grin. "I'm awful, and I'm sorry Wade."

He winked and patted her arm. "I was just teasing you. I'm so happy you're alive that as far as I'm concerned, you can be a bitch for the rest of your life."

Caitlin handed Logan the sack of fresh glazed doughnuts.

"Oh my gosh! They look and smell heavenly," Logan said. She pulled one out of the sack and took a big bite, then rolled her eyes. "This is so good. Thank you for thinking of me, Caitie. Want one, Wade?"

"Do bears—"

"Never mind. Of course you do," she said, and handed him the bag. "Caitie, how about you?"

"I had two on the way over here, so I'll pass."

"Wow, these are amazing," Wade said, and finished one off before Logan had taken her second bite. He took one more and then handed the treats back to her. "Keep these away from me."

"You look so much better, but how are you feeling?" Caitlin asked.

"Good, considering," Logan said.

"Do you know when they'll let you leave?"

"Not yet, but I'm asking the doctor when he makes rounds. I haven't even been up to walk yet."

Caitlin nodded. "That's because you nearly bled to death," Caitlin said. "But, when you're released, will you be going back to Dallas then?"

The smile slid off Logan's face. "Not yet."

"Still chasing ghosts?" Caitlin asked, unaware of how close her offhand remark was to the truth.

Logan couldn't look at Wade for fear she'd cry. "In a manner of speaking. Where are your boys?"

The question shifted Caitlin's focus as she began explaining what was going on, and how happy she was to spend some alone time with Johnny tonight.

About fifteen minutes later, a nurse came in to help Logan

bathe, and sent Wade and Caitlin out of the room.

Caitlin kissed Logan goodbye as she left, and Wade wanted to kiss Logan goodbye, too. Instead, he just pointed toward the hall.

"I will be right outside the door."

"Would you bring me a Pepsi from the vending machine when you come back?" she asked.

"Absolutely," Wade said, happy to give her something she wanted.

As soon as they were gone, the nurse untied Logan's hospital gown and let it fall down around her waist.

"I can't get in the shower?" Logan asked.

"No, honey. Not today. I'll wash what you can't reach, and then we'll change your dressing when we're through."

"Can you wash the blood out of my hair?"

"Oh my. I didn't notice...your hair's so dark. Of course I can."

Logan knew she'd obviously been bathed by someone else when she was little, but this was the first time, and hopefully the last time, someone bathed her as an adult. And when the bath was finished, the nurse left to get a basin and came back with help. Between the two nurses, Logan's hair was finally clean.

———◆———

AFTER THE MORNING INTERVIEWS, EVANS changed his mind and called Roger Franklin, only to find he was at home with a broken foot. So, the chief went to him instead. The excuse he used was really close to the truth. He told him he was investigating an old, unsolved crime, and that one of the few clues that he had was that it had happened in 2008 and the perpetrator had driven a late model Chevrolet Silverado.

Roger was a kind man. One could say he was also quieter than most, but he was forthcoming without reservation, which left the chief with no new information.

Only the two divorced men remained.

He knew Tony Warren worked at the *Bayou Weekly*, so he just dropped by the newspaper office for an impromptu visit.

Tony wasn't any happier to see the chief than Peyton Adams had been when he got the call, but he willingly went outside and got in the police cruiser with the chief.

"Okay, I'm here, so what's going on?" Tony asked, and then caught a glimpse of his reflection in the window of his door and frowned. There were smudges from newsprint on one side of his face and near the widow's peak in his hair, which was as white as driven snow. The premature loss of hair color, coupled with his black, bushy eyebrows, was somewhat startling. "God, I look a mess. Sorry about that."

The Chief waved off the comment.

"Don't worry about it. Just let me ask the questions and I'll be out of your way."

"I'm listening," Tony said.

"A couple of things I need to know. Do you still own the Silverado you once drove?"

"No. My wife—my ex, she wanted it in the divorce because she was all about not only getting away from me, but living off the grid in Alaska. She thought the pickup would be more useful for what she'd need to haul, like the amount of things she'd have to stockpile."

Josh nodded.

"So, do you ever hear from her?"

Tony shrugged.

"Once a year, I get a card on my birthday. There's a Saskatchewan postmark, and that's all I know."

"Really?" Josh asked. "Do you keep them?"

"Yes. Call me a sap, but I didn't want the divorce, she did. I'm not pining, understand, but I guess I'm happy she communicates. At least I know she's still alive, you know?"

"I would like to see those postcards for myself."

"Yeah, sure...whatever. I may have a few in my desk here. I don't clean it out any better than I clean my house. Give me a second to go look."

He got out and hurried into the building, and a couple of minutes later, came back. He got back in the car and handed them to the chief.

"I had three. There are more at home, but they all have the same postmark. Other than that, I have no idea where she is."

Josh turned them over, read the brief messages that went with the Happy Birthday greeting. Same handwriting. Same postmarks. Different dates. He handed them back.

"Thank you. That's basically all I needed to know."

Tony started to get out of the car and then stopped.

"What's this all about, chief? Am I in trouble for something I don't know about?"

"No. I know this all seems strange, but it has to do with a case. I'm looking for a pickup like the one you used to own, and the guy who owned it. Just running down the list of names I was given."

"Oh. Okay then."

"Thanks for your help," Josh said.

"No problem," Josh said, and went back to work.

"That went nowhere," Josh muttered. "One more left. Maybe something will click there."

———◆———

DANNY BALES WAS, AS HE liked to say it, between jobs. His wife was the fry cook at the Shrimp Shack, and she'd given him fair warning before she left for work to mow their yard. So he was willingly complying.

He'd already finished mowing in the back and was halfway through with the front when the police chief pulled up in his driveway and got out. At that point, Danny guessed his day was about to get interesting. He cut the engine to the lawnmower, then pulled a rag from his hip pocket and wiped the sweat off his face.

"Morning, Chief," Danny said.

"Good morning, Danny. Glad I caught you at home. I need to talk to you."

"Sure thing," Danny said, and motioned to the empty lawn chairs beneath the shade tree near the porch. "Have a seat here in the shade. Can I get you a cold drink?"

"No, I'm good, but you look pretty hot. Get one for yourself if you want," Josh said.

"I'm okay for a bit," Danny said. He sat down, then slapped his knees and grinned. "Can't imagine what I know that you don't, but ask away."

"This all relates to an open case I'm working on, and I'm going down a list, eliminating names as I go."

Danny frowned.

"Well then let's get busy and eliminate mine. I don't want to be on no police list."

Josh began to explain.

"This relates to the summer of 2008. At that time, you owned a late model white Chevrolet Silverado, right?"

"Yep, I did," Danny said.

"And that was before you and your first wife divorced?"

"Yes. We were still together that summer. It was later in the year before me and Connie finally called it quits. She took our girl and moved to California. I stayed here."

"I assume you stay in contact with her some since your girl is with her."

"Yep, I do. We always liked each other. We just couldn't live together. Angela is sixteen now and comes here every Christmas and Easter."

Josh nodded.

"Did your wife take the truck in the divorce?"

"No, I kept it. I rented it out to people who needed to haul something. Made extra money every month. I got a twenty-dollar bill and a full tank of gas every time someone used it. But someone wrecked it in 2013."

"Who was that?"

"My ex-brother-in-law...our illustrious mayor, Barton DeChante."

Josh's heart sank. The list just exploded exponentially. If it was Danny's truck that Logan Talman had seen back in 2008, it could have been anyone driving it.

"Do you remember any of the people who rented it back in the summer of 2008?"

Danny shook his head. "Lord no. That's too long ago."

"Well then, thanks for the info. I'll let you get back to work."

Danny frowned.

"That's it? That's all you needed to know?"

Josh nodded.

"What's going on?" Danny asked.

"I can't comment on anything at this time. Have a nice day,"

Josh said, and left.

Danny wasn't happy. He thought if the chief wanted information from him, the least he could do was tell him why.

Josh was disappointed and dreaded telling Logan the latest twist. Instead of going back to the office, he decided to go check on her. If she was doing okay, he'd tell her what he'd learned.

———————◆———————

L OGAN HAD JUST FINISHED HER first walk and was glad to get back in bed.

"You okay?" Wade asked, as he helped straighten her covers.

"Yes, just tired."

"I'm going to change clothes in your bathroom. The guard knows not to let anyone in the room, but if you need me, just call out. I'll hear you."

"Okay," Logan said, and watched him take his bag into the bathroom to change, admiring his long legs and tight butt. As tall as she was, she usually made men uncomfortable being taller than them. Not only was Wade inches taller than her, but he had no problem with his self-confidence. She appreciated that.

It took her a couple of minutes to readjust the sling on her arm, and after she got comfortable, she settled down to rest. She was drifting off to sleep when she heard a knock at her door.

Before she could focus, Wade came out of the bathroom clean shaven and barefoot, wearing a different pair of jeans and carrying a shirt.

"I've got this," he said, and slipped on the shirt.

In all the years Logan had known Wade Garrett, she'd never seen him with his shirt off. Once seen, there was no way to forget the fine-tuned body and rock-hard abs.

She could hear him talking to someone, and then moments later, Wade came back with Chief Evans behind him.

"Good morning, Mrs. Talman," Josh said.

"Please...just Logan, okay?"

"Logan it is. I came by to see how you're doing," Josh said.

"Actually doing pretty good. Pain is manageable, and I just had my first walk. The food sucks, but don't tell anyone I said so," she said.

He grinned, then glanced at Wade, who was now wearing a shirt and putting on his boots.

"Uh, I have an update about the men on your list."

"Tell me," Logan said, and raised the head of her bed to a sitting position.

"I have pretty much cleared the three men with deceased wives and had moved on to the two men whose wives had divorced them. Tony Warren's missing wife, who went off the grid, sends him a birthday card every year. He has a whole handful with Saskatchewan postmarks.

"But the hitch in depending on the list to find your killer happened when I interviewed Danny Bales. He readily admitted to owning a pickup like the one you saw, and then unknowingly cleared himself. First off, he and his ex-wife have a good relationship and share a child. But this is what threw me. He said he rented out that truck all the time to anyone who needed to haul something. Said he got twenty dollars and a full tank of gas, and they brought it back when they were through. He doesn't remember who rented it during the summer of 2008, but that practice went on until 2013 when it was wrecked. This opens up the possibilities to nearly anyone in Bluejacket, including the mayor, who happens to be his ex-brother-in-law, and the one who wrecked it."

Logan's expression was one of pure dismay.

"Oh no. I was so sure that would be the link I needed."

"I'm sorry, but don't think I'm quitting on this. It's just a rough patch," Josh said.

Logan swallowed past the lump in her throat. All this meant was that she needed to up the ante.

"I think it's time to publicly announce why I'm here," Logan said.

"No!" Wade said.

Logan frowned. "You don't make my decisions."

Wade turned away, and walked to the window, leaving her and the chief to finish the conversation.

Logan knew he was mad, but he may as well get over it.

Josh shook his head. "I don't know if—"

"Hear me out," Logan said.

Josh moved to the foot of her bed. "I'm listening."

"Why would I need to keep it secret anymore? It's obvious the killer knows I am a threat to him because he already made a move. But what if there are other people in town who could provide new information? It can't make anything worse and it might help."

"Exactly what would you want to say?" Evans asked.

"Just let it be known that my brother was murdered in the summer of 2008, and that I was there and overheard it all go down, but never saw the killer's face—just heard his voice. Say that all I saw was someone driving away in a white, late-model Chevrolet Silverado, and I came back to find out who did it. Just saying that lets the killer know I can't identify him, so it might get him off my back."

Wade turned around. "That isn't a half-bad idea. I'm all for anything that would take the pressure off of her."

"We could divulge that information and see what happens," Logan suggested.

"You do know that the next question will be what happened to your brother's body?" Josh said.

Again, Logan had a ready answer. "When it comes to that, then I will make sure gossip gets around that I buried him that night where it happened, but I'm not sure of the location. Then let it be known that we're going to begin looking for the location as soon as I'm better, because I think there's evidence buried with him that might lead to the killer's identity."

"Is there?" Wade asked.

"There were bullet casings within the tarp in which I wrapped him. Maybe they'll match the casings you found where I was shot," Logan said. "And in the meantime, the chief can put up trail cameras on the crime scene. I'll show you where it is the minute they let me out of here. Then whoever shows up and starts poking around will add to the evidence proving who killed him, because the killer and I are the only ones who know where he was murdered. You can arrest him, and Wade and I can go home to Dallas."

Josh couldn't believe he was actually considering this.

"This will involve the Parish Sheriff, since anything outside of Bluejacket City Limits is out of my jurisdiction, and maybe the Louisiana State Bureau of Investigation, as well. Exhuming human remains takes a certain kind of skill to keep from damaging evidence."

"Fine. I don't care who's there. I just want to make sure there are people who can make the arrest. Then we can recover the body," Logan said.

"If there's anything to recover," Josh reminded. "He's in the swamp. Nothing stays below ground for long."

"I've already been back to the location. He's still there because I told him I'd be back," Logan said. "Just let me do this."

The chief glanced at Wade, then back at the woman in the hospital bed.

"You're one tough lady," he said.

"Not by choice," Logan said.

"Then I say yes," Josh said.

"Let me start the revelation," Logan said. "My friend, Caitlin, wants to know what the big mystery is about my return. Let me tell her. She'll spread the news naturally, rather than us making some big announcement that might spook the man we're after."

Josh nodded. "I like that."

"Oh, and while I'm thinking about it, what happened to my purse and car keys? My Colt was in that purse along with all my identification."

"It's in the evidence locker."

"Thank goodness," Logan said. "I would appreciate it if you could get it to me. I need Caitlin's number."

"I have her number," Josh said, and pulled it up on his phone and wrote it down for her on a pad of paper. "I'll get your things to you today. As soon as you're able, we'll set up trail cameras." Then he glanced at his watch. "I'd better get back to work, and you need to rest."

Wade saw him to the door, then came back to the bed and took her by the hand.

"I'm sorry I butted in."

She leaned back against her pillow and closed her eyes, but it didn't stop the tears rolling down her face.

"Oh hell, Logan. Don't cry," Wade said.

She clutched his hand tighter and shook her head.

Wade couldn't stand it. He dropped the bed rail and scooted

onto the bed beside her. When he did, she surprised him by leaning forward against this shoulder. He didn't have to think about
it as he wrapped his arms around her, cradling her head beneath
his chin. He felt her exhale softly, and then the tension in her
muscles began to ease.

"If you weren't here, I couldn't be this strong," she said.

He leaned back enough so he could see her face. Her dark eyes
were glittering with tears, and her chin was trembling.

"Ah honey, I've always been here. You just didn't look," he
said, then brushed his lips across her forehead and eased her back
down onto the pillow.

She said nothing as he lowered the head of her bed and straightened her covers, but her gaze never left his face.

"Sleep," he said.

She closed her eyes because she had to. It was too scary to look
at him as just a man and not a friend.

---

WHILE SHE WAS SLEEPING, AN officer came by with her
belongings, pointing out an added charger cord from the
chief so she could charge her phone. Wade thanked him, took the
phone and plugged it in to start charging, then put the rest of her
things in his bag.

A nurse came in just before noon with meds, then helped her
wash up before the lunch trays arrived. Wade made himself scarce
while the nurse was there, but Logan knew he was outside and
no farther away than the sound of her voice.

Not once in the years she'd known him, not even after Andrew's
death, had he ever crossed a line beyond friendship. And yet from
what he'd alluded to, he'd loved her all along.

Part of it made her sad, and part of it was almost exciting. She'd
never thought of anyone mattering to her as much as Andrew,
but she was coming to realize there were many levels of love.

Andrew had been the bigger-than-life, love of her life, but his
life had burned out too soon.

Wade was the enduring kind. And after spending the last two
years widowed and alone, there was something to be said for love

that lasts.

The nurse paused by her bed. "Logan, is there anything you need?"

"When is the doctor coming by?" she asked.

"It will probably be evening. There was some kind of emergency surgery this morning, which changed his normal routine."

"Okay, thanks," Logan said.

"Certainly. Food should be here soon. Chicken and dumplings today, and I have to admit, they are actually quite good. Maybe you'll be able to eat a little more this time."

"I'll try," Logan said, then saw her phone was charging on the table beside her bed. Chief Evans had made good on his promise.

Wade came in carrying two cold cans of Pepsi and two Snickers candy bars.

"Oh my gosh! Real food," Logan said.

Wade laughed. "No. Real junk food, which is what we eat on the job, right? You can have the cold Pepsi now, but save the candy for after you eat. They're already handing out food trays on this floor."

"Deal, and thank you," she said, and took a drink of the cold pop. "Mmm, good and cold, and still has the fizz."

He was watching the way her nose wrinkled from the spritz of carbonation in the drink and thought she was beautiful, then purposefully made himself change the subject.

"Your stuff came while you were asleep. The chief also sent you one of his charging cords so you could recharge your phone. I plugged it in while you were sleeping. Your other things are in my bag."

"I saw that. Much appreciated. Oh, I need to call Caitlin and ask if she can come back," Logan said.

Wade retrieved the pad with the number and then moved the hospital phone to where she could reach it.

She quickly put in a call to Caitlin's number.

Caitlin answered on the second ring. "Hello? Logan? Are you okay?"

Logan grinned. "Hello to you, too, and yes, I'm good. If you can, I'd like for you to come back to the hospital after you eat lunch. There's something I need to tell you."

"Is it about all this?"

"Yes."

"Johnny just came home for lunch. I'll be there as soon as we've eaten."

"Okay. See you then," Logan said, and disconnected.

"Feeling better?" Wade asked.

She allowed herself the freedom to look—really look at his face before she answered, and even then, it was just a nod.

Wade's heart skipped. Something was different. An awareness that hadn't been there before. And then the door opened and a nurse came in with one tray, and the officer guarding the door carried in the other.

Logan eyed the officer.

"Do you have food to eat, too?"

He smiled.

"Yes, ma'am. I brought my lunch, but thank you for your consideration."

The door closed behind them, leaving Wade and Logan alone to eat.

"Nurse said it was chicken and dumplings," Logan said, as she lifted the cover from the food.

Wade was already eyeing his.

"If she says so," he muttered, but then took a bite and perked up. "Tastes way better than it looks."

Logan sighed. "I am not nearly as convinced as you are. Did you eat all the doughnuts Caitie brought?"

He grinned sheepishly.

"That's why I brought you the candy bar. Penance for poaching your treats."

She laughed.

Wade watched her settling into a comfortable spot to accommodate the sling before digging into her food.

"You're getting better with your left hand," he said.

She nodded, and forked up a bite of the dumplings.

"Needs salt," she said, took another bite, then made a face at Wade to let him know she knew he was staring.

He grinned, then settled in to eat.

She watched him when he wasn't looking, wondering why she'd never noticed how handsome he was. Maybe it was true what he'd said. Maybe she hadn't seen him before because she'd never looked.

She took a quick sip of sweet tea, thinking it was strange how much better the world seemed when she wasn't in it all alone.

# CHAPTER TWELVE

———◆———

CAITLIN WAS ON EDGE AS she hurried down the hall to Logan's room. She didn't know what prompted her sudden need to confess all, but was grateful Logan trusted her enough to share.

The current officer on duty looked up from the book he was reading and recognized her.

"Afternoon, ma'am."

"Hi, Stuart. What are you reading?"

"A book on family law. I'm taking online classes."

"Good for you," she said.

He smiled, then went back to reading as she knocked before entering.

The television was on. They were watching the game show Wheel of Fortune, where contestants spun a wheel for prizes while trying to guess a phrase slowly being revealed by how they answered. Wade quickly hit mute when Caitlin came in.

"Hi," Caitlin said, glanced at the screen, saw the blank spaces in the phrase being revealed and said, "Oh, Family Jewels. It's Family Jewels."

"Aagh, Caitie!" Logan said, and then laughed out loud at the look on Wade's face. "Wade, you should have gotten that," she said, which made Wade grin as he stood and stretched.

"Afternoon, Caitie. I'm gonna leave you two ladies alone to visit. I'll be outside if you need me."

Logan watched him leave, and then turned her focus to Caitlin.

"I saw that look," Caitlin said.

Logan shrugged.

"He's an old friend. Come sit with me like we always do," she said, and patted the side of the bed as she turned off the television.

Caitlin scooted onto the mattress to sit at Logan's feet, and Logan started talking, beginning with the phone call Damon got in the middle of the night to her driving out of Bluejacket the next morning.

By the time Logan's story ended, Caitlin was crying.

"It breaks my heart to think of you out in that swamp all alone. How sad and scared you must have been, and burying Damon all by yourself. Oh honey, I don't know what to say."

Logan shrugged. "I won't lie. It was a nightmare. Chief Evans is talking to everyone in the area who owned a late model Chevrolet Silverado in 2008. Since I can't identify the killer on sight, that's about all we have to go on at this time."

Caitlin wiped her eyes and then blew her nose. "Are there a lot of names on that list?"

"Not a lot," Logan said.

"Maybe something will pop up soon."

"I sure hope so," Logan said. "I want this over with."

"What about Damon's body?" Caitlin asked.

"I don't remember the location. We're going to search for it after I'm better. I want the killer caught, then I'll deal with recovering Damon's body."

Caitlin started crying all over again. "I'll say prayers," she said.

Logan nodded. "Good idea. If you have any friends on a prayer chain, let them know what's going on and ask them to pray, too."

Caitlin's eyes widened. "You don't care if other people know all this?"

"No," Logan said. "I should have been upfront from the start, but I wasn't sure who I could trust. I was afraid if I told the whole story outright that the killer would just disappear, and I'd never know who did it. Now this has happened, and I have to take the chance that someone else knows something that might help."

Caitlin got up and hugged her gingerly, careful not to hurt her. "I will get the word out. That much I can do."

Logan nodded. "Much appreciated. Just tell them to contact Chief Evans if they have information to share. And on another note...you and Johnny have fun tonight."

Caitlin arched an eyebrow. "I intend to make sure we do," she said, and left with purpose in every step.

Wade returned within a couple of minutes of Caitlin's exit. "Everything okay?"

Logan nodded. "It's as good as done. I have to admit I am so heart-weary I can't think. This is how I felt the first six months I was in Dallas. I knew what happened, but I had no way to fix it. What if I can't find his killer?"

"Then we'll recover your brother's remains and have them sent to Dallas. At least you can have a proper burial and let God take care of the killer."

Logan drew a deep, shaky breath and blinked away tears.

"Yes, I think I could live with that outcome," she said.

"Then let it be for today, and we'll see how this plays out. I'm not going anywhere until you do."

This time there was no blinking the tears away.

He sat down on the bed beside her again and opened his arms. She leaned in, rested her cheek against his shoulder, longing to feel the weight of his arms as he held her. She didn't have long to wait.

———◆———

CAITLIN CALLED THE WOMAN WHO was in charge of the prayer chain at their church, then called her three sisters-in-law and the friend who babysat her boys, then Johnny.

The woman with the prayer chain spread the news to the twenty-five women on it, who told their husbands, who told their friends.

Her sisters-in-law told their neighbors, who told their neighbors.

T-Boy heard it at the gas station while he was filling up and was shocked by the story, unable to imagine the strength and fear that Logan had endured that night. He was the first to spread the news on the southside, and it finally became apparent to the residents in their old neighborhood why Logan and Damon had disappeared. They were indignant on Logan's behalf, and a little ashamed that she hadn't felt safe enough with any of them to ask for help and had been so scared she'd run away to save herself.

Everyone who heard the story told it to someone else, and by nightfall, it was the news on everyone's lips. They were talking about it over dinner at Barney's, talking about it at every business, and talking about it on the streets.

Big Boy was putting gas in his car when he heard two men on the other side of the pumps talking about it. It made his gut knot to the point of nausea. His hands were shaking as he finished fueling up. When he pulled away from the pumps, instead of going straight home, he drove out to the bar at the edge of town.

The lot was filling up fast as he parked and went inside. A few customers looked up. A couple of them said hello, a few more waved and offered him a seat at their table, but he wanted to be alone and took a seat at the bar.

"Whiskey...neat," he said.

The bartender poured the shot and pushed it toward him.

Big Boy downed it like medicine and tapped the empty shot glass on the bar. The bartender gave him a refill and a bowl of pretzels, the only hint to take it slow he was going to get.

He took the suggestion and popped a pretzel in his mouth, trying to decide what his next move had to be. If he hadn't missed his shot at the motel, none of this would be happening.

The only good news he'd gotten from what he'd learned was that while Damon's sister overheard the whole meeting, she hadn't seen his face. Since she couldn't identify him, he should be safe.

He reached for another pretzel and was slowing down on the drink when he overheard a conversation at the table behind him, and learned there was one more facet to the story that made his blood run cold. She'd seen what he was driving.

Then his phone signaled a text.

*Where are you? We're going to be late for dinner. And don't tell me you forgot.*

Big Boy groaned. Oh shit! The Lowry's shrimp boil! He sent her a text right back.

*I'm on the way home right now. Be there in ten minutes.*

She sent back a heart emoji.

He slapped a twenty-dollar bill onto the bar and walked out, unaware that the entire evening would be more conversation about what he was trying to forget.

———◆———

LOGAN'S SURGEON, DR. SILAS, FINALLY got around to making rounds as they were serving the evening meals. His nurse was beside him as they moved from room to room, and when they arrived at the room Logan Talman was in, he noted the guard on her door, which made what he'd heard today a little clearer. They nodded at each other as he and his nurse walked into the room.

Dr. Silas noted Wade's presence as he reached his patient's bed. "Good evening, Logan. You are looking much better today. How do you feel?"

"I feel pretty good. When will I be able to leave?"

Dr. Silas smiled. "What? You aren't happy with the accommodations?"

She said nothing as he began using his stethoscope to check her heart. He eyed her latest blood pressure reading, checked her heart rate, then turned to the nurse.

"Carol, I'd like to check the wounds."

Carol untied the hospital gown at the neck, revealing both the front and back dressings at her shoulder.

"No fever to speak of," he said, as he pulled the dressings down both front and back to check the wounds, then left it to the nurse to replace the dressings.

"Both wounds are looking good. No appearance of infections. The stitches will dissolve. If you are still doing this well tomorrow, I'd consider letting you go home if you won't be alone."

"Home is Dallas, Texas," Logan said. "I'm at the Bayou Motel."

"But she won't be alone," Wade said.

Dr. Silas glanced at the man across the room. "I don't know that a motel will be the best place to recover."

"It's all I have access to here. It will be fine," Logan said, and then looked at Wade. "And as he said, I won't be alone."

Finally, Dr. Silas nodded. "Yes, well, if you haven't developed any more issues, I'll sign your release papers this time tomorrow."

"Thank you," Logan said.

He nodded, and then he paused, eyeing her carefully. "I heard quite a story about you today. Is it true?"

Logan was glad to know it was already spreading. *Good job, Caitie.* "Not sure what you heard, but I am here to find my brother's killer."

"So, you did witness it?" Dr. Silas asked. "I overheard it," Logan corrected. "I never did see his face."

"Amazing," Dr. Silas said. "I wish you success and no more injuries."

"I wish that, too," Logan said.

And then they were gone.

She looked at Wade. The intent expression on his face was telling. "What?" she asked.

He heard the anger in her voice. He'd heard it countless times before, but it had usually been directed at someone on a job site who'd just challenged her authority.

"There is no 'what'," he said.

She sighed. "Then *why* are you looking at me like that?"

He folded his arms across his chest.

"Because if I looked at you in the same way as I think of you, you might have me arrested."

Shock rolled through her in waves—turning her whole body hot, then cold, then scared.

"See," Wade said. "Scared you senseless." The door opened and a nurse came in carrying a tray of food. "Ah...and supper is served."

He pushed the tray table across Logan's bed to accommodate her food tray, then went out with the nurse to carry his own tray into the room.

"Need anything? Help opening something? Something cut up?" he asked.

She took the lid off her food, saw baked fish, macaroni and cheese, and green beans cooked to a mush with a small bowl of red Jello.

"My compliments to the chef," she muttered.

Wade chuckled.

She looked up, arched an eyebrow, and then smiled. "You disagree?"

"I'll let you know later," he said, eyeing his yellow Jello. "I'll trade you yellow for red," he said.

She nodded.

He made the trade, then used up the one packet of salt on the fish and the pepper on the macaroni and cheese.

"Want my salt for the green beans?" she asked.

"There's no amount of salt, or anything else for that matter, that will help them one bit."

"I hear that," she muttered.

He grinned.

And the uneasy moment between them was gone.

———◆———

B IG BOY COULDN'T DECIDE WHETHER he was suffering indigestion or having a heart attack. The evening at the Lowry's shrimp boil had turned into a nightmare. Listening to people he'd known most his life talking about the poor kid who'd witnessed her brother's murder. One man made big claims about what he would have done - how he would not have hidden when he realized someone he loved was about to be killed. Then others laughed and jeered at the man for making such a claim.

Big Boy felt obliged to comment, if for no other reason than to not call attention to his silence.

"How would you have defended yourself?" Big Boy sneered. "Jumped out from beneath that tarp and yelled 'Boo'? You're a dumb ass, Frank. She didn't have a weapon. And she was just a girl."

Big Boy's wife dug a piece of crushed ice from her glass and threw it at him.

"Just a girl? On behalf of women everywhere, I resent that," she said. "She was a warrior. Buried her brother's body, then drove herself back home and had the strength of will to get herself out of Bluejacket before the killer came looking for her."

They all laughed, and Big Boy laughed with them, then leaned over and kissed his wife's cheek.

"I'm sorry, sweetheart. I didn't mean that like it came out."

She giggled, and kissed him back, and the moment passed.

One of the other men added some information that Big Boy

hadn't heard.

The chief had a list of names of people in the area who'd owned late model Silverado pickups back in 2008, and he was interviewing all of them. The hair crawled on the back of Big Boy's neck. That could be bad—really bad for him.

Later, as they were on their way home, his wife gave him a curious look.

"Hey honey?"

"Yeah?"

"You said that girl 'jumped out from beneath a tarp'."

"Yeah,　　　　　　　so　　　　　　　what?"

"I never heard that part about a tarp," she said.

The heartburn hit boil as he managed to shrug off her comment.

"So? The version I heard did. Gossip is alive and well in Blue-jacket, I guess."

She laughed.

"I didn't think of that. No telling how many versions of the truth are happening tonight."

"That's for sure," he mumbled, and then pointed. "We're home sweet home. I had a good time, but I need something for heartburn. It's been killing me all night."

"Probably that cayenne I saw Jeannie Lowry put in the water before she dumped in the corn and potatoes. I thought they were a bit spicy myself, but I like things hotter than you do."

"Lord," he said, rubbing the front of his chest as he pulled up beneath the portico and parked.

He unlocked the door and then helped her up the steps and into the house, still rubbing his chest.

"Poor baby. I'll go make you something for it right now."

"Thank you, Sugar. You are the best."

———◆———

LOGAN WAS ASLEEP, DREAMING OF the ride out to the bayou.

She heard the night sounds, felt the heat, and lived the fear of what was happening all over again.

She could hear the man telling Damon to kill his wife and how much money he would earn. She had to stay still. Stay quiet. It was dark beneath the tarp, and she felt spiders running up her arms, then realized it was just sweat running down them. Then in the dream, Damon was refusing the money and the job, and she was thinking, now we can go.

Because logic has no place in dreams, she never expected what came next. She heard the man telling Damon that he couldn't let him go now. That's when she realized what was about to happen. She had to save her brother.

In dreams, events can often fix what life could not. She could hear some small animal in the throes of a death squeal as she rose from the back of the pickup like an avenging angel—a double-barreled shotgun aimed at the man with a gun.

Enraged by her abrupt appearance, the killer swung his gun toward her just as she pulled both triggers. The blast of the barrels threw him backward, obliterating his face.

She was climbing out of the truck bed, and Damon was running toward her when the man with no face rose up and shot her brother in the back. Damon died with his arm outstretched toward her. She was trying to reload her shotgun when she heard someone calling her name. She opened her eyes to see Wade standing over her bed, shaking her awake.

"Oh my God," she whispered.

"You were crying out," Wade said.

"It was a dream, just a dream," Logan said. "Please, turn on the lights!"

He reached above her bed and pulled the chain, instantly sending a bright circle of light into the middle of the room. Then he poured cold water into a cup and lifted her head so she could drink.

She took one sip, then another, and then the third before the dream began to fade.

"Thank you."

He eased her head back onto the pillow and then went to the sink, got a wet washcloth and came back to the bed and began washing her face, as if she was a baby.

Logan saw everything in his eyes a woman would ever want to see in the man she loved. She took the washcloth from his hand, dropped it on the table, then pulled his hand to her face.

"You scare me, Wade Garret. You make me feel again. I thought I'd buried my heart, but it's still there."

Wade cupped her face, then leaned over and kissed her. Before she could catalog the feeling, he stepped back.

"Never fear the heart that loves you," he said, then rubbed his thumb across her lower lip. "Do you think you can go back to sleep?"

Mesmerized by his gaze, she shook her head.

"Want to split a candy bar?" he asked.

"What? Did you just say candy bar?"

"We have to do something. I suggested the candy because I really want to crawl in bed with you, and you're not ready for that."

"Then raise me up, you crazy man. I'll eat candy with you and save that thought for another day."

Wade opened the top drawer of the little bedside table, pulled out the Snickers candy bar, and tore off the paper. He broke it in two pieces and handed one to her.

They took a bite at the same time, then ate in silence, watching the changing expressions on each other's faces.

---

IT WAS JUST AFTER MIDNIGHT when a new shift of nurses came on duty.

Logan had fallen back to sleep, and Wade was standing at the window.

"Everything okay?" the nurse asked as she came into the room.

Wade glanced at Logan and then back at the nurse.

"Yes, ma'am. Everything is good."

# CHAPTER THIRTEEN

———◆———

DAYLIGHT BROUGHT ANOTHER ROUND OF thunderstorms.

Josh Evans was still at home when his cell phone rang.

He looked at Caller ID and frowned. They were already calling him from the police station with something that couldn't wait until his arrival, which did not bode well for his day.

"Hello, Arnie. What's up?"

"There are people here at the station," Arnie said.

Josh frowned. "Okay...so how many people and what do they want?"

"There are about thirty in here with me, but there's a line out the door."

"What the hell?"

Arnie winced at the tone in his boss's voice.

"They all claim to have tips about Conway's murder. Some have tips about who shot Logan Talman, or they saw something that might be of interest. We've already had to break up one fight between two guys who decided to blame each other for the murder, while neither one is ready to blame the other for shooting Mrs. Talman."

"I did not see this coming, but I should have," Josh said. "I'll be right there."

Josh's wife, Lorene, walked up behind him and wrapped her arms around his waist. "Trouble already?" she asked.

He turned around. "More like chaos," he said, rolled his eyes, and gave her a quick kiss.

"Don't forget your poncho. It's pouring," she said.

He grinned. They didn't have any kids, but there were days when she treated him like one.

"Yes, ma'am," he said, winked and left on the run.

---

BIG BOY WOKE UP IN the middle of the night, bathed in a cold sweat. There were so many loose ends to the mess he'd made of his life, he didn't know what to do first, cut all ties and run, or start tying knots and see how many held.

One big problem he had to fix now had to do with that damn pickup. And that's all because of the woman. Why couldn't she have just stayed in Dallas? Why did she have to come back and stir up the past?

And, if all of this mess hanging over his head wasn't enough, last night he couldn't get it up. Sugar claimed she didn't mind and went for one of her sex toys, but he minded. Hell. What kind of a man was he if he couldn't perform? Stress. It was all this fucking stress.

He spent the rest of the night downstairs in the den, watching TV and dozing in the recliner. By the time the sun was up, Big Boy had figured out how to take himself out of the picture. All he needed to do was remove one more player from the chain of events that had led him to the bayou that night.

---

WHEN THE CHIEF GOT TO the station, he saw a line of people out the door and halfway down the block, all willing to stand in the rain to say their piece, and it was his job to hear them out and take their statements.

"God give me patience," he muttered, and drove around to the back to park.

His poncho was dripping rain as he came in the back door. He saw the empty jail cell, which told him Paul Robicheau was no longer their guest. Likely bonded out and already back on the streets of Bluejacket. That was encouraging.

He got to his office, hung up the dripping poncho, and poured himself a cup of coffee, then called Arnie.

"I'm here. Send the first one back."

"Yes, sir," Arnie said.

Moments later, Josh heard footsteps coming down the hallway. He got up and opened the door.

"Good morning," he said. "Have a seat."

And so it began.

———————◆———————

WADE HAD ALREADY SHAVED AND downed one cup of coffee by the time Logan woke.

"Good morning," Wade said, and patted her arm.

Logan smiled sleepily as she raised the bed to sit up.

"Morning. Have you heard from McGuire this morning? Is everything going okay on the job sites?" she asked.

"It seems to be. He said the guys all send their best wishes and to hurry home. They miss your steely gaze."

Logan laughed. "I do not have a steely gaze."

Wade grinned.

She              frowned.              "Do              I?"

"Sometimes," he said. "It scares the hell out of all of us when we see it."

"Then good," she said. "I need some kind of edge to keep fifty men on five job sites in line. Oh, who am I kidding? You're my edge, and I know it. If it wasn't for you standing between me and them, half of them would have already quit. They don't like having a woman for a boss."

"I like it," Wade said.

"Thank you. I like having you around, too."

The door opened and a nurse came in with a handful of clean towels and washcloths and laid them aside.

"Good morning, Logan. These are for later. I need to check your stats and breakfast is on the way."

"I'm going to step out and leave you two on your own for a bit. You know the drill, Boss Lady. Within the sound of your voice,"

Wade said, and left the room.

Watching him leave, Logan wished she had the freedom to walk out with him. She was sick of this inactivity and even more tired of being disabled, even if it was a temporary thing.

"Why does he call you 'Boss Lady'?" the nurse asked.

"Because I am his boss. I'm a contractor. I build housing additions, and he's my general manager."

"Wow. That is awesome. You have a big footprint in a man's world and have men working for you. Way to go, lady! Now, let's get you up and get this show on the road."

———◆———

BIG BOY HAD HIS GUN and the silencer beneath the seat, and he had lifted Sugar's little spray can of mace to bring, too. He didn't know exactly how this was going to happen, but he intended to have as many options with him as possible.

By the time he arrived at Barney's for breakfast, the rain had passed. He saw a couple of friends from the Lowrys' shrimp boil last night as he walked in, and at their invitation, pulled out a chair at their table and sat down.

Junie came sailing by with a coffee pot and filled his cup.

"Know what you want to eat?" she asked.

"Yes, ma'am. Eggs over easy, bacon, and biscuits with a side of white gravy."

Junie nodded and went to turn in his order as Danny Bales walked into the cafe. He saw Big Boy and the other men at the table, nodded and smiled.

"Want to join us?" Big Boy asked.

"I appreciate the offer, but I'm pickin' up an order to go. I'm on my way to Buford Point to do a little fishing before the day gets too hot."

"Hell, Danny, this is summer in Louisiana. Is it ever any other way?" Big Boy asked.

Danny laughed.

"You'd be right about that, but unless one of you is willing to give me a job, I'm going fishing." Then he saw one of the waitresses coming out of the kitchen with a sack. "That looks like my breakfast. Y'all have a good day."

Their food came to the table as Danny left, and Big Boy spent a solid hour eating and talking. By the time he was ready to leave, his mood was positive. He got in his car, checked the fuel, then headed out of town toward Buford Point.

———◆———

EVEN THOUGH IT WAS BARELY past ten a.m., Danny was already one beer into a six-pack, with one fish on the stringer. He heard a car coming through the trees and frowned. Damn it. Someone was going to set up in here and ruin his spot.

Then he recognized the vehicle and relaxed. Whatever he wanted, he wouldn't be here long. That man did not like to sweat.

"What the hell are you doing here?" Danny yelled, and waved him over.

Big Boy felt of the pistol wedged into the back of his pants and kept walking. The thought of doing this up close and in broad daylight made him nervous. He had to get it done and be gone before someone else got the same idea Danny had.

"Catch any yet?" he asked.

"Got one," Danny said. "Want a beer?"

Big Boy pulled the gun and aimed.

Danny's eyes widened in disbelief.

"What the hell, Dude?"

"Sorry," Big Boy said, and pulled the trigger, putting a neat round hole in Danny's forehead.

Blood splatter dotted the trees and the bushes behind where Danny had been sitting, while the force of the impact put Danny on his back, still in the folding chair with the fishing rod on the ground beside it.

Big Boy turned to leave, and as he did, saw the float bobbing on Danny's rod, and then watched it disappear beneath the water, taking line with it.

"You got one," Big Boy said, and then ran back to his car and drove away.

———◆———

IT WAS A QUARTER TO twelve, and Josh had just finished taking the last statement regarding Damon Conway's death and sent the man on his way, when Arnie buzzed him on the intercom.

"Chief. Call for you from the Parish Sheriff's office on line three."

"Thank you, Arnie," Josh said, and took the call.

"This is Chief Evans."

"Josh, this is Sheriff Elway."

"Hey, Carl. How's it going?"

"Not too good right now," Elway said. "Some kids down at Buford Point went fishing this morning and found the body of one of your citizens."

"Oh, no. Who was it?"

"Danny Bales."

Josh immediately flashed on the interview he'd just had with him.

"What happened? Did he drown?"

"No, but there's a bullet hole in his forehead. Danny knew his killer. Looks like the shot just laid him backwards, still sitting in the chair. I need you to notify his next of kin. Will you do that for me?"

Josh sighed. This was the part of the job he hated most.

"Of course."

"There's not a shred of evidence here and no witnesses. Was anything going on there in Bluejacket that would lead me to a suspect?"

Josh thought about the Conway case, and the fact that Danny had rented out the Silverado he owned on a regular basis.

"Maybe," Josh said. "We have a big thing going on now that just came to light. A ten-year-old murder we just found out about, and the relative who brought this to light is in the hospital after being shot, too."

"Damn. Sounds like someone is trying to get rid of witnesses," the sheriff said. "Well, we're about to transport the body to the Coroner's Office. Tell his widow we'll be in touch when the body is ready to be released."

"Yes, sir. I sure will. Good luck."

"Same to you. Keep me in the loop. Sounds like our cases might be connected," and then he hung up.

Josh replaced the receiver, then buzzed Arnie.

"Yes, Chief?" Arnie said as he answered.

"I'm going to have to make a death notification, so I'll be out until after lunch. When you get a chance, mop up the puddles down the hall and in my office."

"Yes, sir," Arnie said.

Josh got up and then reached for his hat. Damn it to hell, he did not want to do this.

---

THE RAIN HAD MOVED ON, and the landscape was already steaming. The vapor was visibly rising as Josh drove down Main, then parked at the Shrimp Shack. He'd been through the drive-thru here so many times over the past few years without thinking about the woman cooking the food that he bought, and now he was going to have to break her heart. It wasn't good police procedure to let personal feelings spill over into ongoing cases, but right now he was enraged.

Bluejacket was home to a whole lot of people, and none of them should have to live in fear. He needed to find this bastard and find him quick. He radioed his location in to dispatch, and then grabbed his hat and got out.

The scent of hot grease and fried shrimp met him at the door. The six tables inside the shack were full, and there was a line at the register waiting for take-out orders, as well as the line of cars going through the drive-thru. He glanced past the owner manning the register to the kitchen behind him.

Stella was in high gear, putting potatoes into one deep fryer and breaded pieces of shrimp into another. There were two others making shrimp Po-Boys as fast as the shrimp came out of the fryer. And he was about to bring everything to a screeching halt. He took a deep breath and then moved through the diners, past the line waiting for pickups, to the owner.

---

R ORY MARTIN WAS A FIFTY-SOMETHING Cajun who'd been running the Shrimp Shack most of his adult life. He'd seen the chief come through his drive-thru many times, but he couldn't remember one time when he'd come inside to eat. He knew from the moment he walked in that he was here on business. Rory was scared, afraid the bad news Chief Evans carried on his heart was going to be for him, and he started praying when the chief came toward him.

"Hey, Chief," Rory said.

Josh nodded, then lowered his voice. "I need to talk to Stella right now, and she will have to leave, so if there's anyone you can call to take over for her, do it now."

Rory's eyes widened. "Oh Jesus, Chief. Yes, okay. One of the guys can take over for her until my wife can get here. I'll call her now."

Rory picked up his phone and called home.

"Lara, it's me. I need you down at the Shack, ASAP. I'll explain when you get here."

Then he hung up the phone.

"I'll get Stella now."

"Yes, please, and someone get her things and bring them outside to my car."

Rory was pale and shaky as he went back to the kitchen.

Josh saw Stella look up, then Rory pointed to the register where Josh was standing. That's when the smile on Stella's face disappeared. Rory took off her apron, then held her hand all the way to the register.

Josh put a hand on Stella's shoulder.

"I need you to come outside with me for a bit."

Stella moaned and nearly went to her knees.

Josh took her by the arm and led her through the room, desperate to get her outside before she fell apart. He opened the front door of his cruiser to get her out of the heat, then got in with her, started the engine, and turned up the fan speed on the air conditioner.

"Stella, I am so sorry to have to tell you this, but I just got a call from Sheriff Elway. Some fishermen found Danny's body at Buford Point this morning."

Stella screamed, and then covered her face and started to sob.

"No, no, no! I don't understand. He was just fishing! What happened?"

"They don't yet know who did it, but it appears that Danny was murdered...one shot to the head."

Shock spread over Stella's face so fast that it stopped her tears.

"Murdered? What the hell?" she cried. Then she gasped. "Danny said you were questioning him about a case you were working on. Is that right?"

"Yes, ma'am. I did do that."

A dark flush spread up her neck to her cheeks.

"Is he dead because of that?"

"I don't know that, Stella, but it's a possibility."

"Oh my God!" Stella screamed. "What hell are you working on?"

"Murder, ma'am."

"Danny didn't kill anyone!"

"I know that."

"Then what!" she cried.

"We only know a little bit about the killer we're looking for. The murder happened in 2008 and the killer drove a late model Chevrolet Silverado to the crime scene. I spoke to Danny only because he was one of several people in the area who owned one. This is when he was still married to his first wife."

"Connie. Oh my God! I'm going to have to call Connie. She's going to have to tell Angela her daddy is dead. Oh my God, that damn truck. He loaned it out to everyone and their hound dog. One of them was the killer, right? That's why he's dead! The killer didn't want Danny to start naming names."

Josh was surprised that Stella made that connection, but couldn't confirm it until they proved it.

"Right now, everything is still supposition."

Stella's chin came up.

"That woman who was shot at the motel...it was her brother who was murdered, right?"

"Yes, ma'am. That's now public knowledge."

Stella nodded, then wiped her eyes.

"I need to go home now."

"I'll take you," Josh said.

"Thank you, but I'll drive myself. I need my own car at home." She shuddered, then choked on a sob. "Find the bastard."

"Yes, ma'am, we're trying."

Stella looked up as Rory came out of the Shack carrying her things. She moaned. "Oh my God, why am I not waking up?"

"Sheriff Elway said to tell you he would notify you when Danny's body is ready to be released."

She shuddered. "This is really happening, isn't it? I mean, I'm not dreaming...right?"

"Yes, it's really happening, and no ma'am, it is not a dream."

"God help me," she whispered, and got out of his cruiser.

She paused in front of Rory. Josh knew she was telling him what had happened. He saw the shock on Rory's face, and then he hugged her. He was still hugging her when his wife arrived.

Josh sat in his car, still watching as the tableau unfolded. The shock on Lara's face seeing Stella in her husband's embrace. Then hearing the news and taking Stella in her arms.

At that point, he'd seen enough. He backed up and drove away, but instead of going back to the station, he went straight to the hospital to update Logan Talman.

———◆———

LOGAN WAS WALKING BACK TO her room with Wade by her side when they saw Chief Evans get off the elevator.

He spotted them, waved, and started toward them, then stopped at her room to wait.

Logan eyed the look on his face and grabbed Wade's arm.

"Something has happened," she said.

Wade heard a hint of panic in her voice and put his arm around her waist to steady her.

"Then let's get back to the room, okay?"

She nodded, but the sick feeling in her stomach was there again. When they got to her room, the chief opened the door and then stepped aside to let her pass.

"Thank you," Logan said, and got back in her bed. After she'd taken a deep breath, she prepared herself for the worst.

"What happened?" she asked, and felt Wade's hand slide beneath the hair at the nape of her neck.

Josh leaned against the foot of the bed, his gaze fixed on her.

"Remember when I told you one of the men who owned a Silverado had rented it out multiple times?"

"Yes, Danny Bales," Logan said.

"Danny was murdered this morning."

Logan reeled as if he'd just punched her. Wade moved closer. This nightmare kept getting worse and there was something Logan had to know. "Is it my fault for telling the story?"

Josh frowned. "Hell no, it's not your fault. Do you think it's your fault your brother is dead?"

"No, but—"

"Well, it's also not your fault that a murderer decided to kill someone else. He tried to kill you to shut you up, but you survived. He's in a panic, trying to tie up loose ends. But that's just an opinion right now. We have no proof."

"What do I do?" Logan asked.

"When do you get to leave the hospital?" Evans asked.

"Dr. Silas said he'd release me this evening when he made rounds if I didn't have any problems."

Josh frowned. "And do you have any problems?"

"No."

"She's doing amazing," Wade added.

"I'm not sure if you'll be up to this, but the sooner I can get those trail cameras up, the better. The killer is going to realize you will be searching for your brother's body, and he's going to go back to the scene of the crime to make sure there's no way to link him to the site. Understand?"

She nodded.

"Only you and the killer know where the murder happened, right?" Josh asked.

"I told no one, but I told Wade *how* to find it if anything happened to me."

Josh shifted his focus to the man behind her, but all he did was move closer to her.

"Wade told me you had the directions tattooed on your belly,"

Josh said.

Logan nodded. "Yes. The date he was killed, and the miles from the city limits north to the location of the body."

Josh looked at her with renewed respect. "I have to say, I don't think I've ever met anyone as determined to bring someone to justice as you are. You would have made a good cop."

Logan didn't hesitate. "Is the Hummer still at the motel?"

Josh nodded. "Yes, and I sealed the door to your room so that no one could enter. If you'll call me to let me know when you're being released, I'll gladly come get you both and drop you off at the motel."

"Thanks, Chief," Wade said.

"My pleasure," Josh said, then glanced at Logan. "See you this evening?"

She nodded. "And I will take you there tomorrow," Logan said.

———◆———

STELLA DROVE HOME IN A daze until she turned onto her block and saw their house. Danny's pickup was gone, and for a second, the thought went through her head that she didn't know where he was and needed to text him. And then she remembered.

The loss washed through her in waves as she pulled into the drive and parked. She fumbled for her keys and then stumbled getting out.

Her next-door neighbor saw her and waved, but Stella was afraid to lift her arm for fear she'd break apart in a million pieces, so she just kept putting one foot in front of the other until she was inside.

The moment she walked in, she saw one of Danny's older tackle boxes that he'd decided to leave behind. The sudden pain in her chest was so sharp she thought she was having a heart attack, but then it passed. She went from the living room to the kitchen and saw his coffee cup from breakfast still sitting beside the coffee-maker. That brought on another heart pain to breathe through.

She started down the hall to the office to get Connie's phone number, only to come face to face with her sons' graduation pictures on the wall next to hers and Danny's wedding picture.

The boys had been teenagers when she and Danny married. She stopped, caught in the smile on his face.

"Oh Danny, how am I going to do life without you? How am I going to tell the boys that you're gone?"

But there was no answer to the question, and so she moved to do what had to come next. She made it to the office, collapsed into the chair behind the desk, then broke into tears again as she went through the address book for Connie's number.

It wasn't until she'd already started the call that she thought to check the time. It would be much earlier in California, but not too early. She sat listening to it ring and praying for grace to get through this without coming undone. Just when she was afraid it was going to go to voicemail, she heard a breathless hello.

"Hi, Connie. It's me, Stella."

"Well, hi girl. What's going on?"

Stella took a deep breath, and then the words were too ugly to be said. So, she started to cry.

Connie gasped. "Stella! Honey! What's wrong? Has something happened to Danny?"

"He's dead. He was at Buford Point fishing and someone shot him."

"No, no, oh my God! Was it a hunting accident?"

"No. It was outright murder," Stella said.

"Oh Lord," Connie moaned. "Why? What's happening there?"

Stella grabbed a handful of tissues, wiped her eyes, and blew her nose.

"It's tied up to something that happened the summer of 2008. Someone was murdered then, and no one but a sixteen-year-old girl knew it. She didn't know who it was, but she knew what he drove."

Connie gasped. "Oh hell, no! Tell me it wasn't that damn Silverado he farmed out on a regular basis."

"It was, and the police chief thinks the killer is trying to get rid of any loose ends that might tie him to the old crime. So that sixteen-year-old girl grew up and recently came back here to find the man who murdered her brother. He ambushed her at the motel here in town."

"Oh my God!" Connie cried. "He killed her, too?"

"He tried. Shot her in the back, but she survived."

"I'm coming, Stella. I may not have a right, but I'll stand with you until this is over if you'll have me."

"I wouldn't have it any other way," Stella said.

"I'm sorry. I'm so sorry," Connie said. "Now I have to find a way to tell Angela. Blessings to you and the boys," Connie said. "I'll try to get there sometime tomorrow."

"Okay," Stella said. "See you soon." Then she hung up the phone and burst into tears, sobbing until her head was throbbing and her eyes were nearly swollen shut. She wanted to die, too, but she still had to call their boys.

# CHAPTER FOURTEEN

———◆———

FROM THE MOMENT THAT BULLET went through Danny Bales' head, Big Boy felt a relief that carried him all the way back to Bluejacket on an emotional high. As he was passing the Bayou Motel, he saw that big black Hummer still parked in front of room 4A and grinned. There was nothing left for her to do but go home. Gossip said she'd buried the body, but had been so scared and in shock that she couldn't remember where. Even if she did find it, there was nothing on a stack of bones with Big Boy's name written on it. It was all good now.

He parked, got out, and strode into the house with his head up and a defiant jut to his jaw.

Sugar was in the kitchen with Ruthie, their cook, and when she saw Big Boy, she frowned.

"Where have you been? Our lunch is all cold and—"

"Hush it, woman. I was out on business all morning. I'm tired and hungry, and I don't want to hear any of your sass."

Sugar blinked. "I'm sorry, honey. I was just worried, that's all," she said, and threw her arms around his neck.

He gave her a kiss and a smack on the butt, then set her aside.

"Ruthie, heat up my food. Whatever it is, it'll be fine. I'm going to wash up."

"Yes, sir," Ruthie said.

Big Boy went to their bedroom, took off everything he'd been wearing, tossed it all into the laundry, and washed up before he put on fresh clothes to go downstairs.

Sugar was waiting for him at the foot of the stairs. She slipped her hand in the crook of his arm and began chattering about the morning she'd had and the sale coming up at her favorite boutique in New Orleans.

———◆———

LOGAN WORE HER BLOOD-STAINED BOOTS, a pair of Wade's jeans, and one of his shirts back to the motel. She sat in the back seat, listening to Wade and Chief Evans making plans for tomorrow. All she could think about was that there would be no police on her door tonight, and that the killer was still out there, leaving bodies in his wake.

The Chief unsealed the door to her room then went inside to make sure nothing had been disturbed. From what he could tell, it looked the same as the day he'd locked it.

He came back and handed the room key to Logan. "There will be an officer patrolling this parking lot off and on all night, and every night until you two go home. Call me any time if something comes up. I'll bring coffee and doughnuts in the morning. Try to get some sleep."

"Thanks, Chief. See you in the morning," Wade said, then helped Logan into the room and locked the door behind them.

Logan went straight to the little closet and got a pair of shorts and a shirt, then underwear from the dresser and disappeared into the bathroom to change.

Wade didn't know what to make of her being so quiet, but he'd seen her this way before, so he guessed if she wanted him to know something, she'd tell him.

She came out a short while later carrying his clothes and handed them to him.

"I didn't get anything on them, and thank you for letting me wear them out of the hospital."

"You're probably the only woman I know who could have pulled that off. My inseam is 38. You have long legs, my friend."

He laid the clothes on the back of a chair and then couldn't think of anything else to say that wouldn't get him in trouble.

There was a tense moment of silence as they stared at each other, and then Logan handed him her sling.

"Would you help me get back into this?"

He took it, slipped her arm into the pocket, then moved behind her to make sure it wasn't going to rub on her neck as he separated the Velcro strips.

"Can you hold your hair back for a minute while I fasten this?"

She grabbed the length and pulled it over her shoulder as he fastened the strap on the sling.

"You're good to go," he said, and brushed a kiss on the side of her neck, right below her ear. "Remember, Dr. Silas sent some pain pills, plus a prescription, which we can get filled tomorrow. Do you need one?"

She was still struggling with the kiss when she realized he'd just asked a question that required an answer.

"Need what?"

"A pain pill," he repeated.

"Not right now," she said.

"Then why don't you rest a while?"

"What about you?" she said. "There's no comfy recliner in this room. Just two straight-back chairs and a bed."

"There are two sides to a bed, and I will honor my side."

She turned around. There was no guile in his voice or expression. Just Wade being Wade. She finally relaxed.

"Okay, but there are only two temperatures in here. It's either hot or cold, and I opted for cold when I got here."

He pointed to the bed. "There are covers."

He pulled the blankets back and waited.

She moved past him to the bed, then eased down and stretched out.

"I'm tired," she said. "I think I'll rest for a little while. Turn on the TV if you want. I sleep with it on at home all the time."

Wade tucked her in, and then turned on the television and sat down on the other side of the bed, leaned against the headboard, and turned down the volume. He didn't care what was on. He just wanted to watch her sleep.

CONNIE BALES HAD HELD HER sixteen-year-old daughter until she cried herself to sleep, and then got down to business.

She called a friend who worked for American Airlines and explained why they needed to get to New Orleans tomorrow. Within the hour, she had two tickets to their destination, and a rental car waiting for them upon arrival. Because these were hardship tickets, the airlines waived the higher cost and also put them first class. The drawback was catching a flight at six a.m., but she was grateful they had one at all.

She and Angela spent the rest of the day tying up loose ends here, and then packing for the trip tomorrow. By the time she finally got to bed, she was exhausted and sad—so sad.

She set the alarm and then fell asleep, only to wake up hours later in a panic, remembering the fight she and Danny had had about that Silverado that wound up being the last straw in what was left of their marriage.

She was too wired now to go back to sleep, and it was only a couple of hours before her alarm would go off, so she made some coffee and cried while she waited, knowing they were going back to chaos.

———◆———

JOSH EVANS GOT A TEXT from Wade Garrett. They were at the motel, dressed and ready to go.

The chief responded to the text with a thumbs up emoji, and left his house pulling a small flat-bed trailer with two four-wheelers on it. He drove straight to Friendly's Grocery for the fresh doughnuts and coffees. Next stop, the Bayou Motel.

There were a half-dozen trail cameras in the trunk of his car, along with an axe and his hand-held radios. He didn't know what all they might need, but he didn't want to be there without it. He hadn't slept worth a damn last night. The murder of Danny Bales had hit him hard. He would never get used to giving people bad news.

When he got to the motel, because of the trailer, he parked at the office and walked down to their room.

———◆———

IT HAD BEEN A LONG time since Logan had slept with a man, however innocently. She was far too aware of the body heat, the soft sound of his breath, and the covers stretched over two people instead of one, to get much sleep.

She got up once to go to the bathroom, and when she came out, he was waiting to help her back in.

"You okay, honey? Do you need something for pain?"

"I'm okay, but yes, where are the pain pills?"

"On the table. Get in bed. I'll get them and some water."

She sank down onto the side of the bed, then waited.

He came back, dropped two pills into the palm of her hand, and handed her a cold bottle of water from the mini-fridge.

"Thank you," Logan said, and downed them, then took another long drink of the cold water before handing it back.

He set the bottle on the nightstand, then eased her down onto the bed.

She patted his hand as he was pulling up the covers and closed her eyes.

Wade paused and smiled.

"Thank you, too," he whispered, then turned out the lights and got back in bed.

It took a couple of minutes for him to settle, and then when he did, he fell back into a deep, dreamless sleep.

The next time he woke, it was just after seven a.m. He rolled over to wake Logan, and she was already awake looking up at the ceiling.

"Hey you."

She turned her head and smiled.

"Hey, yourself. I've already showered. Woke up before six."

"Were you in pain?" Wade asked.

"It wasn't that. Just thinking about this morning."

Wade leaned over and kissed her, softly, slowly, and then stopped before it got intense.

"Think about that, instead," he said, then threw back the covers and got out of bed.

Logan's lips were still tingling when she heard the shower come on, then groaned and made herself get up and start dressing. Chief Evans would be here soon.

She was ready by the time Wade came out of the bathroom with nothing but a towel wrapped around his waist. She looked up and then groaned.

"You make being a man look damn interesting, Wade Garrett."

He grinned, grabbed some clean clothes, and then started to go back into the bathroom to change.

"Oh, you don't have to do that," Logan said. "I promise I won't look."

Then to prove her point, she got up, pulled up one of the straight back chairs, and sat down in it to watch TV, giving Wade the rest of the room to dress.

He shrugged, dropped the towel, and started putting on clothes, wishing he was taking hers off instead. When he was finished, he sent Chief Evans a text that they were ready, and got a thumbs up in return.

"Chief Evans will be here shortly," he said.

Logan nodded, but she had that faraway look again, and there was nothing he could do to make it better.

They were both staring blankly at the early morning news when there was a series of sharp raps on the door.

"That'll be the chief," Wade said.

Logan stood as Wade let him in.

"Ready?" Josh asked.

When she didn't answer, Wade looked over his shoulder. Logan had her arm out of the sling and was buckling on her holster. They watched her slide the Colt into place, and drop a box of ammo into a shoulder bag before replacing her sling.

"Do you have water, Chief?" she asked.

Josh nodded. "And transportation. Two four-wheelers. It may be a little rough riding out there, but at least you won't have to walk."

"Thanks," Wade said. "Got the room key?"

She pointed. "It's in the bag."

Wade picked it up.

"Then let's go," Josh said. "I want to get out of town before anyone notices we're all leaving together."

He led the way to the cruiser, seated Logan in the back beside the box of doughnuts, handed her a tall to-go cup of coffee and a roll of paper towels.

"Knock yourself out," he said, grinning.

"Save some for me," Wade said, and got into the passenger seat beside the chief.

Logan tore off a couple of paper towels, picked up two doughnuts with the towel, and handed them to Wade.

"How many do you want, Chief?"

"Just one for now. I had a bowl of cereal at home."

Josh took the doughnut and laid it on the dash, then started the cruiser and looked up at Logan in the rearview mirror.

"Which way?" he asked.

"You need to be on the northbound highway out of Bluejacket, and once you pass the city limit sign, drive nine miles north," Logan said.

He nodded, and off they went. As soon as they passed the city limit sign, he started watching the miles.

Logan ate two doughnuts and was still working on her cup of coffee when Josh spoke up.

"We just passed the eight-mile mark."

"There will be a blacktop road on your left at the nine mile. Turn left, which is west, and go two miles."

"Yes, ma'am," Josh said.

Wade kept looking over his shoulder, making sure they weren't being followed, and each time, he and Logan locked gazes. It was obvious to him that the closer they came, the more tense she became.

"Turn here," she said, and the chief signaled the turn, then eyed the speedometer again to mark off two miles.

Wade glanced back over his shoulder again and then caught a glimpse of Logan's face. She looked like someone was driving her to her death, and he didn't like that.

"Logan!"

She blinked, then focused. "What?"

"Wherever you are in your head, this time you're not alone, remember that."

Her eyes welled. She nodded.

"Coming up on two miles," Josh said.

"I'm watching," Logan said. "Slow down, look to your left... south...look south...STOP! We're there," she said.

The chief frowned. "I don't see a road."

"It's there. I've already walked in. These fences weren't here ten years ago. I don't know who owns this land now, but the fencing was put up after I left."

Evans marked the location on his GPS.

"Give me a few minutes, and I'll find out who owns this." He got out and walked away, punching in numbers as he went.

Logan and Wade sat without speaking, waiting for him to come back.

"Are you feeling okay? Is this going to be too much?" Wade asked.

Logan nodded. "I'm okay, just dreading the inevitable a little, you know?"

Josh came back, opening the door abruptly. "This land is owned by some holding company called Delta Ventures, Incorporated. I'll delve into it more after I get back into town. Right now, I need to figure out how to get four-wheelers in there."

"Cut the wires," Wade said. "I can make it look like someone ran off the road and hit a fence post."

Josh frowned. "I'm supposed to be upholding the law, not breaking it."

"I don't think cut fencing is comparable to murder," Logan said.

Josh couldn't argue with that. Instead, he opened the trunk of his car to grab bolt cutters, and then headed across the ditch to the fencing. He cut all four wires right up at the fence post, dragged them back into the weeds, then pushed the post over onto the ground.

Logan got as the men began unloading the ATVs.

Wade eyed the ditch and frowned. "That's too rough a ride for you. Wait here a minute," he said, and took one across the ditch and came back for her.

"Hang onto me as we cross the ditch. You don't want to slip and fall on your shoulder, okay?"

She grabbed him around his waist, and held on tight as he took her down the ditch and then past the fence line.

Josh locked his cruiser, and was tying the duffle bag full of trail cameras to the back of his ATV as Wade got in the driver's seat.

"Get on behind me," Wade said, as the chief crossed the ditch in his four-wheeler, and rode up beside them.

"You know where you're going. Lead us in," the chief said.

Logan threw one long leg over the seat and settled into the seat, wrapped her good arm around Wade's waist, and off they went.

It took far less time to make the trip in on the ATVs than it had the day Logan had walked it. The old road became visible when they finally got into the trees, and Wade followed it all the way to the water.

Logan tapped his shoulder.

"Stop here," she said, then dismounted and walked a few yards away.

The chief rolled up behind them and killed the engine.

The heat was palpable. Gnats and flies swarmed the new offering of bare flesh. Wade caught a glimpse of a big snapping turtle sliding off of the bank into the water, and a little farther down, Josh spied a gator barely visible in the water.

"Gator out there," he said, pointing.

"Jesus," Wade muttered. "I keep picturing her here, alone and in the dark, digging a grave."

"What's she doing?" Josh asked.

Wade looked back at her and shrugged.

Josh called out. "Logan, is this the place?"

She nodded without turning around.

Wade didn't realize until he walked up behind her that she was crying, but when she turned to face him, there was defiance in her stature.

"He died here," she said, pointing down, then she walked over to the grove of cypress with the men following. "I dug the grave here by the light of a full moon. After I was through covering him up, I marked an X on the back of this tree with the shovel blade. It's there. This is the spot."

Wade looked back at the distance between where her brother had died and where she'd buried him and shook his head.

"How did you get him this far?"

Logan's eyes narrowed, as if she was reliving it. "There was a heavy tarp over his tools in the pickup bed. It's where I hid. I took it off, rolled him onto it, and then used it like a sled to drag his body to the grave." She shuddered. "The killer won't know this part. All he knows is where my brother died. You need to set up some of the cameras to catch that view. He'll assume I buried him where he dropped. And it's been ten years, so he won't be expecting to be able to see it."

Evans grabbed a couple of cameras and moved off into the woods, cursing swamp grass and snakes as he fastened them to trees where the killer wouldn't see them, then began working his way around the small clearing, putting up a trail camera every twenty or so yards while keeping an eye out for gators until the site was encircled with the cameras.

"We're done here," Josh said. "Let's get before someone sees us in here."

They loaded up on the ATVs, and this time Evans led the way out. He crossed the ditch and then drove the ATV back onto the trailer.

Logan rode the ATV up out of the ditch with her jaw set, ignoring the pain. But when she dismounted at the blacktop, she crawled back in the cruiser as Wade loaded the second ATV. She was hurting and she was weak, but it was done. She set what was left of the doughnuts into the floorboard and then curled up in the backseat and began taking slow, deep breaths, trying to ward off a growing ache in her shoulder.

Wade leaned over the seat after he got in. "I brought your pain pills."

"They'll make me sleepy," she said.

"So what," Wade said, and shook two out and handed them to her, watching until she popped them in her mouth and washed them down with water.

"Oh my God, my shoulder hurts like a bitch," she muttered, then eased back down against the seat.

Josh started the car, and then jacked up the air conditioner as high as it would go so Logan could cool off quicker.

"Are you okay, ma'am?" he asked.

"I'll be fine, just shaky. There's a place a little farther west where you'll be able to make a turn without backing up."

"Thanks," Josh said, and took her at her word.

Sure enough, the blacktop ended at a big, open space, free of fencing or roads. Evans took the turn wide, and the trailer made it with ease.

They passed the place where they'd ridden into the swamp on their way to the highway. The ATV tracks were visible, and, unless someone looked very close, it appeared as if a couple of reckless riders went off the road, knocking down the post and breaking the wire on impact.

Lulled by the pain pills and the hum of the wheels on pavement, Logan fell asleep, and woke up as Wade was about to carry her into the motel. She was too weak to argue.

He laid her down on the bed, took off the gun and holster, and then her boots, before pulling up a blanket.

"I'm okay," she mumbled, and felt his lips on her forehead as she drifted away.

# CHAPTER FIFTEEN

———◆———

D ANNY BALES EX-WIFE, CONNIE, AND his daughter, Angela, landed in New Orleans before noon, picked up their rental car, and drove into Bluejacket just before three p.m. Connie was still reeling from the shock, but she'd thought about this all through their flight, and there were things she needed to get off her chest. As soon as she hit Main Street, she drove straight to the police station and went inside.

The door banged shut behind them as she and her daughter walked up to the desk.

"I need to talk to the police chief."

Arnie eyed the sun-bleached blonde in a turquoise sun-dress and sunglasses pushed back on the top of her head, and then at the teenager with purple hair beside her before he realized who they were.

"Connie Bales, is that you?"

"Yes, Arnie, it's me and this is Angela, Danny's daughter."

"I'm very sorry for your loss," he said. "Just a minute and I'll ring the Chief."

He buzzed his office.

"What's up, Arnie?" Josh asked.

"Connie Bales is here. She wants to speak with you."

"I'll be right there."

Moments later, they could hear the long, steady stride of Josh Evan's footsteps coming up the hall before he appeared in the lobby.

"Ma'am, I'm Josh Evans, the police chief here in Bluejacket.

You needed to speak with me?"

"Yes. I'm Connie Bales, Danny's ex-wife, and this is our daughter, Angela."

"Good afternoon, Angela. I'm sorry about your father."

"Thank you," she said, and leaned closer to her mother.

"Chief, I need to talk to you," Connie said. "Angela, you stay here in the lobby, okay?"

She nodded, pulled out her phone, and sat down.

"Then follow me," Josh said, and led the way into his office.

The second they were both seated, Connie started talking.

"Stella told me what's been going on in town. She said you're working on a case involving a man who was murdered back in 2008."

"Yes, ma'am."

"What was the date of the murder?" she asked.

"July 29, 2008."

"Oh God, I was right," Connie said, then put her hands over her face and dropped her head.

"What's going on?" Josh asked.

"That's the same night Danny's nephew, Jody Bales, was killed over on the southside."

"Are you saying there's a connection?"

"No, not in the way you mean. But that night, our whole family was in an uproar. The police were all over town trying to find who'd shot him. A couple of teenagers witnessed it and ran, not wanting to be involved, then one came forward later and named the shooter who was subsequently arrested and went to trial and then later, to jail. But by the trial occurred, I was already gone from Bluejacket. The connection is the damn pickup that Danny persisted in renting out earlier that same night, and the fight we had over it the next morning."

"But what does that have to—"

Connie held up a hand.

"I know I talk around a story before I can get it told, but it's how I am. Bear with me."

"I'm listening," Josh said.

"The guy who rented it the night before, brought the pickup back the next morning, and it was a mess. Mud and swamp grass packed up beneath the undercarriage, and a hole in the oil pan.

He just parked it at the house and left without talking to either one of us, and Danny blamed me."

"Why?" Josh asked.

"Because it was my brother, Barton, who had rented it. Danny called him on it after jumping all over me, and Barton told him to take the truck to the car wash and stop bitching about it."

Josh was stunned, trying to take in everything she was saying.

"Barton DeChante, our mayor, had the pickup that night? You're sure?"

Connie's fingers curled into fists.

"Yes, I'm sure. Danny's nephew murdered on the same night Barton pulled that stunt and left me to deal with it. I was so mad at both of them I didn't speak to Danny for a week, and I've never spoken to Barton since."

Josh was trying not to get too excited, but this was the best lead they'd been given.

"I didn't move to Bluejacket until about eight months later, so I don't know the back history of a lot of the residents, but Barton is married, and our killer was looking for someone to kill his wife," Josh said.

"Oh...Stella told me some years back that Barton's wife left him and he remarried. I haven't met wife number two."

"When did he lose his first wife?" Josh asked.

"I'm not sure. Danny and I were going back and forth to court trying to iron out all the stuff regarding Angela, but I remember something about her leaving him for another man. Stella said Barton caught her with the guy, and then they were both gone."

"Do you remember the man's name?"

"No. You'd have to ask around. He was kin to some family here. That's all I remember."

"I'm going to ask you not to repeat this," Josh said.

Connie nodded.

"I understand. And I am sorry to God if my suspicions are all wrong, but Barton has a mean streak. He was mean when we were kids, and he only got worse as we got older. You know that old saying, you can choose your friends but not your family? Well, that was us. We didn't like each other and made no bones about it, and we still don't. Now, I've said what I came to say. We'll be at Stella's if you have any other questions."

He saw her to the front lobby, and then watched them driving away before he went back to work, but he couldn't stop thinking about the ramifications. Barton DeChante? Lord, what a scandal this was going to be if there was any truth to it. He wondered if Arnie remembered anything about Dechante's wife skipping out with another man. He'd lived here all his life.

He started up the hall and found Arnie in the break room getting a cold Mountain Dew.

"Hey Arnie, I need to ask you something."

"Yes, sir?" Arnie asked.

"Do you remember anything about Barton DeChante's first wife? Was there a story about her running off with some man?"

"Oh yeah...that was a while back, maybe 2008."

"Tell me what you know. Like who was the man? Someone said he was related to a family in Bluejacket."

"Yes, the Baptiste family. It was quite a scandal because Justin Baptiste was married, too. When they ran away together, it not only broke up Barton's marriage, but Justin's as well."

Josh resisted the urge to grin. He knew where he was going next.

"I'll be out for a while. Radio if you need me."

"Will do," Arnie said, and carried his Mountain Dew back to his desk while Josh went out the back door.

He glanced at the time as he got into the car. It was a little early, but Johnny Baptiste might already be home. He'd swing by the house first before checking his job site.

The adrenaline rush of being on a killer's tail was a high that never got old. Just like he'd been when he was a little boy, Josh had always wanted to be the cop who caught the bad guy.

He upped the fan on the air conditioner and accelerated, then braked almost immediately to miss a mangy cat that ran out into the street. The cat appeared to have missed a few meals and was obviously a stray. He could almost count the ribs as he drove past.

He took a right turn at the next block, and saw Johnny pulling into his drive from the other direction. Josh pulled up right behind him and got out.

"Hey, Chief," Johnny said.

"Johnny, do you have a minute? I need to ask you a couple of questions about your cousin, Justin."

Johnny frowned.

"The family doesn't talk about him anymore."

"Has anyone heard from him since he left?"

"Not that I know of. We all thought he would surely stay in touch with his Mama. He was her only son."

"Was he really having an affair with Mrs. DeChante?"

"I didn't know about it beforehand. I never saw any sign, but Barton said he saw them together and then his wife up and disappeared the same night that Justin disappeared, and well...one plus one makes two, you know?"

"You mean it was all just on Barton DeChante's say-so? No one else ever saw them together?"

Johnny's eyes widened as he realized where the Chief was going with his questioning.

"Are you saying it wasn't true?"

"I'm not saying anything," Josh said. "I'm just asking. Do you know if Justin packed a bag when he left?"

All the color faded from Johnny Baptiste's face.

"Lila didn't believe it for the longest time."

"Who's Lila?" Josh asked.

"Justin's wife. She didn't believe he was cheating on her. She kept telling the family he didn't even pack a bag, but Granddaddy was still alive then, and he was a strict-by-the-bible, church-going man. He kept saying, 'Thou shall not covet thy neighbor's wife', over and over, mad at anyone who disputed his beliefs. It was easier to let it be than argue."

"Okay then," Josh said. "Thank you, Johnny. Thank you very much, and I'd appreciate it if you wouldn't say anything about this just yet."

Johnny glanced back at his house to make sure the kids were still inside.

"Uh, Chief...if Justin didn't go with Faith, then what happened to him?"

"How do you know Faith went anywhere?" Josh asked, and then got back in his cruiser and drove away.

LOGAN ROLLED OVER ONTO HER bad shoulder and woke up with a gasp.

Wade was lying on top of the bedspread beside her, minus his shirt and boots, and sound asleep. She eased out of bed, careful not to wake him, and went to the bathroom, then stopped and made a face at herself. Her hair was a mess.

She dug her hairbrush out of her toiletry bag and began trying to brush out the tangles, but doing it with one hand wasn't happening. She was muttering to herself about shaving it all off when Wade appeared in the doorway. He took the hairbrush out of her hand, closed the lid on the toilet and pointed.

"Have a seat and turn around."

She sat facing the wall with her back to the door, and when he made the first brush stroke through her hair, she winced.

"There are tangles," she said.

"Yes, baby, I see them. I am trying not to pull."

"Okay. Sorry."

He laid his hand on the crown of her hair. "No apology necessary. Let's talk, maybe that will take your mind off of what I'm doing."

"Okay. About what?" she asked.

"What are you missing most about Dallas?" he asked.

"My pool."

He chuckled. "Agreed."

"What are we going to do about supper?" she asked, as he kept brushing.

"I haven't the faintest idea what choices I have here. I came straight out of a chopper and into the hospital. I'd seen nothing but hospital food until the day Caitie brought doughnuts. Then we ate the chief's doughnuts. Is there anything else good to eat in Bluejacket besides doughnuts?"

Logan laughed. "Barney's. Best gumbo in Louisiana. Good food all the way around. If you can make me presentable, we could go there to eat."

"Sure, why not?" Wade said. "I think since it's now a known fact that you did not see your brother's killer, you are safe enough."

"Good. I've eaten every meal there since I got here, except once when I got a shrimp Po-Boy at the Shrimp Shack drive-thru."

"How's your shoulder feeling?" Wade asked.

"It hurts. I need to take some pain pills before we leave."

Wade laid down the brush and then ran his fingers through the long dark lengths, feeling for tangles.

"I think you're good to go," he said.

She got up then paused, looking at him without saying a word.

"What?" he asked.

Finally, she shook her head. "Nothing...just admiring the view."

She saw his eyes flash, then his hands were on her face and his mouth was on her lips, and she was lost.

Wade was the one who finally stopped because they'd gone as far as she could go.

"When you're well," he promised, and rubbed his thumb across her lower lip.

Logan shivered. A promise of things to come.

"Pain pills," she mumbled. "And shoes. I need shoes."

He'd never seen her quite like this. A little rattled with a well-loved look on her face. And it was only a kiss.

———— ◆ ————

BEING BACK IN THE HUMMER, and doing something as ordinary as going out to eat made Logan feel bare to the world, like she'd come out of hiding without any clothes. Before coming back to Bluejacket, safety had meant wearing a hard hat on the job, or wearing eye protective gear when grinding down metal. Here, it had a whole other meaning. She'd known coming back would have a measure of risk, but she'd underestimated the danger. At least she had backup now that Wade was here.

"Are you okay?" he asked.

"Yes. It feels good to be out of the hospital."

"It's even better to know you're alive. The chopper flight to Bluejacket was the worst ride of my life."

"I never thought of your side," Logan said. "I just remember waking up and hearing your voice, then seeing your face and knowing I was no longer alone."

"You don't have to be alone, Logan...ever again. But it's your choice."

Her heart skipped as she met his gaze. "I hear you," she said.

He glanced at the worried look on her face and then winked, which made her smile. After that, she was fine.

As they passed the bank, someone she didn't know waved. She waved back, even though they couldn't see her through the tinted glass.

"Barney's is in the next block," Logan said. "See that building with the yellow sign on top? It used to have the word Barney's Café on it, but the café part weathered off years before I left."

"I see it," Wade said, and turned in to the parking lot with ease.

He got out first, then came around to help her.

"You ready to face an audience?" he asked.

"I've had one ever since I got here. Now at least they'll know why I came."

They entered Barney's to the sound of laughter, dishes clinking, and someone yelling, "Hey Junie, bring me some tea."

Wade grinned. "I like it already."

But as they paused to look for a place to sit, the laughter faded, the room grew quiet.

"There's always a table in the back of the room. For some reason, no one sits there but me," she said.

Wade put a hand in the middle of her back as they began winding their way through the diners to reach it.

Someone touched her arm in passing.

Then a woman whispered, "God bless you."

Another called out, "Welcome home," which brought tears to her eyes as they kept moving.

Someone started clapping, and then the whole room broke out in resounding applause.

Logan turned to face them, trying desperately not to cry.

"Thank you," she said. "This is my friend, Wade Garrett. Wade, these are my friends from home."

He smiled and took off his hat.

Then someone one yelled out. "Bring me their ticket. I'm buying their meal."

It was George Wakely, the plumber Damon used to work for.

"Thank you, Mr. Wakely, but I'll warn you ahead of time. This cowboy is hard to fill up."

Wade grinned, as he hung his Stetson on the corner of the

extra chair at their table, and helped her get seated. After that, the room returned to normal chaos, and Charlotte came with menus and two glasses of sweet tea, dripping with condensation.

Charlotte set the glasses in the general vicinity of where Emily Post long ago decreed drinking glasses should be, and then handed each a menu.

"We all said a bunch of prayers for you, girl. It is good to see you up and about."

"It's good to be up and about," Logan said, and then introduced Wade. "Wade, this is Charlotte. Damon and I used to live just up the street from her and her family."

"Nice to meet you, ma'am," Wade said. "What do you recommend?"

Charlotte smiled. "If you're a meat eater, which I suspect you are, Barney's makes one fine chicken-fried steak. And as always, the fish on the menu is fried."

"Got it," he said.

"Take your time. I'll be back to get your order in a few," she said, and hurried off to deliver some orders to a nearby table.

"This is a great place," Wade said.

Logan looked up, trying to see it from his viewpoint, and saw ordinary people doing ordinary things. Safety. Maybe it was still here after all.

"Yes, it is a great place, but I had to lose it to appreciate it."

When he reached for her hand, there was no mistaking the look on his face, which ended a few dreams some of the male diners had been having.

They ordered, and when their food came, they hungrily dug in. But there was no privacy to the meal. Someone who was leaving would stop at their table to tell Logan they were praying for her, while others just arriving quietly apologized for what had happened to her here, and all of them left their sympathies for the loss of her brother.

The news of Danny Bales' murder, coupled with what had happened to her and the reason why she'd come back, had everyone jumpy. Facing the fact that there was a killer in their midst was both shocking and shameful. They'd thought themselves above big city woes, but they'd been wrong.

———————

L ONG AFTER LOGAN AND WADE had returned to the motel, and long after the chief had gone home to his wife, Big Boy was celebrating.

Sugar was giving him a blow job, and in return, he was buying her a diamond ring.

Tit for tat, and all that.

It's how Big Boy rolled.

But if he'd known he was already in the police chief's sights, his sleep might not have been as dreamless.

———————

T HE MOOD AT THE BALES' house wasn't jovial. Stella and Connie, two women who had loved the same man, had been drawn together in a common rage. Grief had taken a back seat to the anger. Stella wanted to know who, and Connie feared she already did.

Stella's sons were due in tomorrow from New Orleans. Danny had been a good stand-in for their absentee father, and they were grieving his loss.

Angela was quiet and weepy. This house and the little town had been the source of much happiness on her visits back every year, and now she didn't know how to feel.

That night after everyone had gone to sleep, she crawled in bed with her Mama. "I can't sleep," she whispered.

Connie opened her arms. "Neither can I, baby," she said, and pulled her close.

"What's going to happen now?" Angela asked.

"What do you mean?" Connie said.

"Well, I always come here for Easter and Christmas, and that won't happen again, will it?" Angela asked.

"No, baby, it won't."

So, Angela cried, and her Mama cried with her.

THE NEXT MORNING WAS ANOTHER day of the same thing – heat and flies, and people moving about at a slow, lazy pace — except for the chief.

Josh left for the office right after seven a.m. and started running a search on Justin Baptiste. If he had truly run away with Faith DeChante, then there would be job history connected to their social security numbers on at least one of them, or both. While he was waiting, he left to stake out Barton DeChante's house just to see where he was going. It wasn't long before he saw DeChante come out of the house and head downtown. The chief followed from a distance, watching as he went through the ATM at the bank, then followed him straight to Barney's.

He waited until Barton was inside, then parked, went in and placed an order to go. He chose a seat close to where Barton was sitting with friends, taking his cup of coffee with him.

Both Roger Franklin and Tony Warren were sitting at the table with DeChante. Josh thought it somewhat ironic that he had suspected both of those men first, while Barton had never been on his radar.

"Morning, Chief. We heard about that Bales fellow who lived on the southside. Really a bad thing. Does Sheriff Elway have any suspects?" Roger asked.

"It was tragic for his family," Josh said. "However, that's not in my jurisdiction, so I couldn't say what's going on with that case."

"One thing's for sure, this woman who drove in from Dallas has sure stirred up the ghosts in this town," Tony said.

"She didn't stir up anything that wasn't already here. Besides, she's one of ours, remember? She grew up here until life threw her a big ugly curve."

Tony cleared his throat and nodded, but it was plain to see that none of the three men at the table had the least bit of compassion for southside rabble. Josh should have been shocked, even disappointed in their rhetoric, but he'd heard it too many times before.

"So, when is she leaving?" Barton asked.

Josh had cast the lure by sitting down here, and now he was

about to reel him in.

"As soon as she can locate her brother's body. She said she buried him where he fell, but it was dark and she was scared. It's been ten years, and she's not a hundred percent certain where it is anymore, but we're going to try to help her find him. It's the least that we can do," he said, and watched the pupils dilate in Barton's eyes.

Barton lowered his voice a bit.

"This is a delicate subject, Chief, but did you explain to her how fast stuff deteriorates in this climate? Hell, we can't keep a body buried in a coffin around here, let alone a body just tossed in a hole. She has to know there might not be anything there anymore. I mean...he could have floated up, and critters would've dragged him off piece at a time."

Both of the other men nodded in agreement, which prompted one man with a story to relate about a great-uncle whose coffin floated out of a mausoleum after Hurricane Katrina, and never was found.

Josh let them talk, and then threw out his last cast.

"I don't know exactly why she's so sure he'll still be there, but she also seems to think the killer left evidence."

The chief watched the shock come and go on Barton's face.

"What kind of evidence?" Roger asked.

"She said he was shot twice, so she's hoping to find the bullets with the body or within the tarp in which she wrapped him. Lead and shell casings don't rot, you know."

Tony frowned.

"I don't get it. Even if you find bullets, you don't have anything to compare them to."

"Maybe we do and maybe we don't," Josh said, and then Junie came to the table with his breakfast order. "Ah...breakfast awaits. Gotta go men. Y'all have a good day."

"You, too, Chief. You, too," they said.

Josh got in his car and then backed out of the parking space and drove down the block, then parked again so he could watch where Barton DeChante went next.

Less than fifteen minutes later, DeChante came wheeling out of the parking lot and headed up the street.

Josh sat, watching as his car kept going north, past the Bayou

Motel and out of town.

He grinned, put his car in gear, and headed back to the station.

"Brought you some breakfast," Josh said, and dropped the sack at Arnie's desk.

Arnie beamed.

"Thanks, Chief! Seconds at breakfast are always welcome."

"You're welcome," Josh said, and went into his office.

The report he'd run on Larry Owens to verify Peyton Adams' whereabouts in New Orleans came back with an address and phone number, but he had a feeling he wouldn't need this anymore, so he filed it for future reference.

Then he checked the report he got back on Justin Baptiste's work history. It was just like the one he'd gotten back on Damon Conway. It all ended in Bluejacket. A chill ran up the back of his neck as he thought about what this meant. Then a few minutes later, he got the same report back on Faith DeChante.

"Godalmighty! Where did he bury all the bodies?"

————◆————

BARTON DROVE LIKE A BAT out of hell, flying past houses and billboards, and weaving in and out of traffic until he came to the blacktop leading out to his land.

He took the turn too fast and almost ran himself into the ditch, which scared him enough to slow down. But when he reached the two-mile mark and saw his fence broken and the four-wire fencing in a tangle, he jumped out on the run, cursing as he went. Then when he saw the ATV tracks in the tall grass, he got pissed all over again.

"Damn teenagers on those ATVs. I hope whoever hit my fence broke his damn neck," he muttered, and then realized since the fence was down, he could at least drive to the water, rather than walk.

It was a bit tricky getting a car across the ditch, but he made it, and then was so busy making sure he wasn't followed, that he never saw the ATV tracks going all the way to the inlet.

He hadn't been back here since the night it had happened, but he had a good idea of where they'd been standing. He walked the whole area with his head down, looking for signs, but all he saw was swamp grass and deadfall.

Convinced there was nothing here to see, he got back in his car and left, following his tracks back out, then got on the blacktop and headed home. He'd have to call someone to go out and fix that fence. If she did happen to make it out this way, there was no need making her search convenient.

He drove back to Bluejacket at a more sedate speed, and then went by the house, picked up his wife, and headed for New Orleans. It was an hour plus drive, but he'd been promising her a shopping trip for weeks, and today felt like a day to celebrate.

# CHAPTER SIXTEEN

JOSH GAVE THE PARISH SHERIFF a call, filling him in on what was happening with his case, and that he was almost certain the killers they were searching for were one and the same. After watching DeChante make a run north, he wanted to see what, if anything, they might have captured on camera. So, he took Kenny McKay back with him. When they got to the broken fence, he eased his car across the ditch. Then he saw car tracks going in and coming out over the tracks of the ATVs and grinned.

But Kenny was at a momentary loss.

"What are we looking for, Chief?"

"Kenny, we are looking to catch ourselves a rat," Josh said, and drove all the way to the inlet and parked.

"Follow me," he said, as he got out and headed for the first camera he'd put up. He took it down and went back to the cruiser to see what, if anything, they had caught.

At first, it was a small assortment of animals barely visible within the grass, and then he moved past the night shots, to the latest views of the day.

"Hey, there's a car driving up," Kenny said, pointing to the left of the small screen.

Josh grinned. Not only did he recognize the car, but he knew the driver.

Kenny moved closer to the screen.

"Danged if that doesn't look like the mayor. What would he be doing all the way out here?"

Josh said nothing as he watched the small screen, showing Bar-

ton DeChante walking in a circle right where Logan told him
her brother's body had fallen.

He stopped the camera and handed it to Kenny.

"Put this in the back seat of the cruiser then follow me. I need
to pick up the rest of the trail cameras before we leave. And mind
where you're putting your feet. You're just as likely to walk up on
a gator as step on a snake."

"Oh shit," Kenny said, and shuddered as he did what he was
told.

Thirty minutes later, they were on their way back to town
with all of the trail cameras. He needed to view the rest of them,
too, and see if they had enough evidence to get a search warrant.
They had recovered the shell casing from Logan Talman's shooting. The Parish Sheriff had recovered a bullet from Danny Bales'
body, and he was running a trace to see if Barton DeChante
owned a registered weapon. The only thing missing were bodies.
Barton had left one lying where he fell, but Logan had buried it.
Josh was hoping Barton had buried the others, instead of leaving
them to the gators.

He was at his desk going through everything he had to take to
a judge to get a search warrant, when Arnie came in and laid a
piece of paper on his desk.

"This just came in, Chief. Info on who owned Delta Indus-
tries."

Josh began to read as Arnie left, and when he saw the name, he
grinned. One more piece to add to the puzzle. The owner was
Barton DeChante.

———◆———

WADE AND LOGAN HAD DRIVEN to Barney's for breakfast, but rather than go back and sit in the motel, Wade
wanted to see where Logan had grown up, so he drove and she
blazed the trail.

They went past the park, then the high school and football
field. She showed him where her brother once worked, and the
big fancy house where Caitlin grew up, then they headed to the
south side of town.

It was immediately evident to Wade that the lifestyles here were far different than what he'd been seeing. When she directed him down the street to the house where she and Damon had lived, she began leaning slightly forward, bracing herself against the dash as if it would take her just that little bit closer to finding her brother.

All of a sudden, Logan pointed to a few men standing beneath a shade tree a few houses down and yelled, "Stop."

Wade hit the brakes, and when he did, saw one of the men turn around and look. Then he separated himself from the others and began walking toward their car.

"That's the man who saved my life," she said, and got out.

Wade parked at the curb, then got out and followed her.

---

T-BOY HEARD THE RUMBLE OF the engine before he looked to see who it was. When he recognized the vehicle, the ache in his chest was a reminder of how much he'd wanted her to love him. Still drawn to her, he headed for the car, hoping she was in it. He saw her get out, still the same tall beauty, but with her arm in a sling, and she was walking toward him.

They met in the middle of the street, like they'd done so many times before when they were young, only this time she was smiling.

"I've been told you saved my life."

T-Boy shrugged.

"I saw a friend down. What else would I do?"

"I am forever grateful," Logan said, and put her arm around his neck and hugged him.

It was a moment in time that T-Boy would never get back, and because she'd made the first gesture, he wrapped his arms around her and ever so gently, returned the hug. Finally, after all these years, he had the satisfaction of knowing what life would have been like if she had loved him as much as he loved her.

Then he looked over her shoulder and saw the big cowboy get out and start toward them. He was a damn fine-looking man, older than them, but with a look on his face that told T-Boy she was already taken.

He patted her on the back and stepped away.

"Reinforcements are coming to rescue you from the street thug," he quipped.

Logan knew it was Wade.

"He works for me," she said, and then Wade walked up beside her. "Wade. This is T-Boy. We grew up together, which is one thing, but he's also the man who kept me from bleeding out before the ambulance came. T-Boy, this is Wade Garrett."

Wade grabbed T-Boy's hand and shook it gladly.

"It is an honor and a pleasure to meet you, sir. I don't know what we'd do without this lady back home."

"Good to meet you, too," T-Boy said, and in that moment, wished with everything in him that he had made better choices.

T-Boy turned around and shouted at his friends.

"Hey, y'all. It's Conway, and she's here without that damn bat. Come say hi."

Logan looked up at Wade and grinned.

He shoved his Stetson to the back of his head, watching as people began coming out on their porches to see what was happening, then they saw who it was. They had all known she was here, now they knew why, and she was one of theirs.

People were crowding around her, everyone talking and laughing, but so careful not to bump her. It wasn't until Logan spilled the beans about T-Boy, that anyone knew the part he'd played in saving her life.

It was a moment T-Boy would never forget, being praised instead of cursed.

As for Wade, he had never seen Logan so at ease. This was who she was meant to be. A woman without secrets.

———◆———

JOSH EVANS HAD HIS SEARCH warrant, but he did not have his man. Barton DeChante and his wife, Sugar, were not at home.

Ruthie, their cook and housekeeper, was informing the chief that they'd gone to New Orleans to shop. He didn't need them to be present when he searched the house. Ruthie could receive the warrant, but he'd counted on rattling DeChante enough to hope he said something incriminating.

"When do you expect them home?" Josh asked.

"I got a call from Mrs. DeChante asking me to make something special for dinner tonight, so probably around five or six o'clock. I always serve dinner at seven."

"That's okay," Josh said, then he had a thought. "Say Ruthie, maybe you can help me with something. Did you work for the family when the first Mrs. DeChante was still here?"

"Miss Faith? Yes, I did. She was such a lovely lady. So sweet and soft-spoken."

"Were you here when she went missing?"

"No. Mr. DeChante had sent me and my husband on a seven-day river cruise on one of those paddle-wheelers. We had the time of our lives."

"Wow, that's great. Was it for something special? Your birthday...or your anniversary?"

"No. He just up and surprised me with it."

Josh nodded. Yet another clue to the man's plan to do what he wanted without witnesses.

"I see...so I guess you were shocked when you came back and heard the news about his wife."

Ruthie shrugged.

"I heard it, but I still don't know that I believe. Miss Faith wasn't like that."

"Then what do you think happened to her?" Josh asked.

Ruthie frowned.

"I don't rightly know. It still puzzles me some. I came back to her gone, and the Mister out rearranging his rose garden. He's in that garden all the time, and he's real fond of his roses. Why, some of them roots are nearly a hundred years old, he says."

Josh felt like sweeping Miss Ruthie up in his arms and dancing her about the foyer, but withheld the urge. Now he knew where the bodies were buried.

"Yes, ma'am. I've taken up enough of your time. Thank you again."

"You're most welcome," Ruthie said, and went back to the kitchen.

Josh left, making a call to the judge's office for a request to amend the search warrant he already had to include the exterior of the property and then told the secretary why, along with a message that he'd be by to pick it up shortly. After that, he made a call to Parish Sheriff Elway, as well.

———————◆———————

LOGAN WAS BACK IN THE motel and stretched out on the bed, exhausted but at peace. Wade was pacing the floor, talking in undertones so she couldn't hear exactly what was being said, but she knew he was pissed. She was thinking to herself that she would never want to see him this angry at her, and then she heard him say the name "McGuire" and knew it had something to do with her business.

She sat up in bed.

"Wade!"

He glanced at her and then he said, "Wait a second," and covered the phone. "What, honey?"

"What's wrong on the job site?"

He hesitated.

She stood up, and sling notwithstanding, held out her hand for the phone.

Wade walked straight to her.

"McGuire came to work drunk and was trying to load up one of our table saws in the back of his work truck when some of the men stopped him."

Her eyes narrowed.

"Who are you talking to now?"

"Enzo Behenja."

She took the phone.

"Enzo, this is Logan."

"Boss Lady. It is good to hear your voice. You are doing well?"

"I'm fine," she said."Is this true what Wade is telling me? That McGuire came to work drunk?"

"*Si, Señora*, and he wants to take a saw."

"What was he going to do with it?" she asked.

"Sell it. He told one of the bricklayers that you didn't pay him, and so he's going to take that in pay."

"Well, that's a lie," Logan snapped. "Call the police. Have him arrested for attempted robbery. And tell them he came to work drunk, and I'll be pressing charges."

"*Si, Señora*, I will do that."

"Thank you, Enzo. We'll be in touch. Here's Wade."

She handed the phone back to Wade and went to find her purse.

Wade told Enzo to call as soon as McGuire was arrested and removed from the property and ended the call.

Logan was already on the phone talking to her accountant to verify that paychecks had gone out on time, and that no one's pay has been withheld. When the call ended, she was madder than ever as she told Wade what she'd learned.

"McGuire tried to get her to cut him a check for expenses he claimed he incurred while standing in for you. She said he sounded drunk when he called, and when she refused, he started cursing her and disconnected."

Wade was still shaking his head. "I have never seen this kind of behavior from McGuire, have you?"

"No, and he stepped in for you a couple of times after Andrew was gone. With you gone, too, and me somewhere between here and dead, I think he thought it would be an easy snatch," she said.

"I'm sorry," Wade said. "I put him in charge."

"And I put him in charge once before that. Neither one of us saw this in him. It is what it is," she said. "But now who can we trust to keep things moving until we get home? Maybe you should just catch a flight home and—"

"Oh, hell no," Wade said. "I'm not leaving you own your own down here again. When I leave, you're coming with me."

Logan was secretly relieved.

"Hey, what about Sarge? I know he's retired, but Andrew used to say he was the best at running a crew he'd ever seen."

Wade nodded.

"Yes, good call. I have his number. I'll see if he's free and able."

"He doesn't have to be too able. Make sure he knows it's nothing but directing traffic, so to speak."

"I'll give him a call," Wade said.

Logan was hurting. She glanced at the time. The last pain pills she'd taken were before breakfast, so she took a couple more and lay back down, waiting for them to take effect and wondering if those trail cameras would work. She wanted justice for her brother, but now it was obvious she also needed to go home.

———•———

SUGAR BUBBLED WITH ELATION, TALKING about her new clothes, her new shoes, even giggling about the psychic they'd seen while they were there.

"Can you imagine? She said something momentous was waiting for us. I wonder what it might be," she said.

"I don't believe in that stuff," Big Boy said.

Sugar pouted.

"I don't care. I do, and you'll see."

He chuckled.

"Don't get yourself all in a snit. You have new stuff to wear to your next girls' night out. You'll be the prettiest one there. You always are."

Sugar giggled.

"Ooh honey, sweet talk like that will get you everywhere with me."

"Yeah...I know," he said, and then they both laughed out loud.

He was still in good spirits and wondering what Ruthie was making for dinner when he pulled into their drive.

"Oh my. It's good to be home," Sugar said, and unlatched her seat belt.

Big Boy's hand was on the door handle when he looked up in his rearview mirror and frowned.

"What the fuck?" he muttered, and got out.

———•———

CHIEF EVANS ROLLED UP INTO DeChante's driveway with lights flashing and his siren screaming, as did four of his officers in their patrol cars.

The chief got out with his warrants, saw the look on DeChante's face, and grabbed him before he could run.

"Barton DeChante, I have a search warrant to search your house and one to search the exterior of your property as well." He stuffed the warrants into DeChante's pocket.

"No!" Barton screamed. "Why? What are you doing? You're crazy. Let me go you fuckers! I didn't do anything wrong."

Josh calmly handed him over to one of his deputies.

"Please see that he doesn't run off. I'll have questions for him after the search."

Sugar was in shock up to the point they handcuffed her husband, and then she came to and ran forward, screaming as she went.

"What are you doing? Stop! Let him go, let him go!" she cried, and rushed up to the chief. "Whatever you're doing, this is all a horrible mistake."

"Move aside, ma'am. We have search warrants for your house and the outside of the property, as well."

"This can't be happening!" Sugar cried, as Officer Kenny McKay pulled her out of the way, while two others came up to assist the chief.

DeChante looked over the backend of the cruiser as a yellow backhoe appeared at the end of the block. When he realized it was coming toward his property, for the first time in his life, he was afraid.

"What are you going to do with that backhoe?" he cried.

Josh was in his face. "We're searching the premises, both inside and out, and have reason to believe you buried the bodies of your wife, Faith, and Justin Baptiste here."

Barton gasped, then began to shout.

"No. You can't dig in my garden. The roses alone are priceless. Some of the roots are a hundred years old. You can't destroy history!"

And just like that, without realizing he'd said it, Barton DeChante had just verified his guilt by admitting where the bodies were buried.

The backhoe came closer, and so did Sugar, still pleading for mercy.

"Please, please, Chief!" Sugar begged. "What can I do to make you see what a mistake you are making?"

"Tell me where your husband keeps his gun."

"In the library," Sugar said. "I'll even show you. It will prove you're wrong."

Big Boy was in shock. How did the bitch even know he had a gun, let alone where he kept it? Then he threw back his head and let out a scream of pure rage. The woman he'd killed for had just turned into his betrayer.

"You bitch, you bitch! What have you done? If you hadn't been so good at fucking, I would have already buried you, too."

Sugar gasped, staring at her husband as if she was seeing him for the first time, and at the same moment, Big Boy realized what he'd said. He dropped his head and closed his eyes as Josh read him his rights, while the backhoe came closer and closer.

Josh had the back door open, ready to load him up into his cruiser, when the backhoe reached the house. The driver bypassed the cop-filled driveway, and started up through the perfectly manicured lawn, leaving a ragged set of tracks.

Barton stopped just shy of stepping inside the car, watching in horror at the backhoe bouncing past the magnolia tree. Then it rounded the corner and was heading into the back gardens as it went out of sight.

Big Boy wailed, and then lowered his head and shook it like a dog shedding water.

"Stop him," he said.

Josh leaned down.

"I'm sorry, I didn't hear you. What did you say?"

"I said, stop him! Don't let him tear up the roses."

"Sorry, but we have bodies that are missing and families in grief. It is my job to find them and their killer."

"I did it," he said.

"Did what?" Josh asked.

"I killed them."

"I didn't hear you," Josh said.

Big Boy turned on him, screaming.

"I killed them. I killed Faith because I wanted Sugar, and I killed Justin because I needed a reason for Faith to disappear. Please, tell him to stop now. Don't let him dig up the roses."

Josh pressed him for more answers. "I suppose you killed Damon Conway because he turned you down when you asked him to kill your wife, and you killed Danny Bales because he would remember loaning you his truck the night of Damon Conway's murder."

Barton was in a panic. He could hear the backhoe's gears grinding and pictured his beautiful rose bushes being ripped to shreds. He groaned. There was no way out of this now. "Yes, yes, I did it...I killed both of them. Now please stop them from digging up my roses."

Josh nodded at one of his deputies.

"Go tell Henry to take the backhoe back to the City Utility Barn. We'll use it again when we exhume the bodies.

"Yes, sir," he said, and took off running.

"Just for the record, where did you bury the bodies?" Josh asked.

Barton's head dropped.

"Under the bench at the end of the brick path through the garden."

Josh grabbed him by the arm.

"Know that if you're lying, I will make it my personal business to not only dig up everything in that garden, but I will also set it on fire." Then he pushed Barton into the backseat. "Watch your head," he said, then slammed the door in his face.

---

A N HOUR LATER, THEY WERE back at the station, logging DeChante's gun and silencer into evidence, and booking him into jail. Later, locking him into a cell was the culmination of a week of hell, and he had the monster who'd caused it off the streets.

Wearing jailhouse orange, and still smarting from the humiliation of mug shots and fingerprinting, DeChante dropped onto the cot, shuddering to think of the vast number of degenerates who'd been here before him.

Josh walked out, locking the cell door behind him, then he went to his office and called Johnny Baptiste.

"Hello," Johnny said.

"Johnny, this is Chief Evans. How long will it take you to gather your family at your house?"

"I don't know for sure, Chief. At least an hour, maybe more."

"Then please start notifying them. I have something to tell the family, and I need to say it to all of you at the same time."

Johnny was nervous, but didn't hesitate.

"Yes, sir. They'll be here."

"See you later," Josh said, and next called Wade Garrett.

"This is Wade."

"This is Chief Evans. Are you both at the motel?"

"Yes, sir."

"I'll be there shortly. I have information," Josh said.

He disconnected, then made one more call to Stella Bales.

Unlike Wade Garrett, Stella was slow to answer, and when she did, he could hear a lot of noise in the background and guessed more family had arrived.

"Hello. Stella speaking."

"Stella, this is Chief Evans. Sounds like you have a lot of company."

"Yes, sir. We do."

"I am going to add myself to the mix, if you don't mind. I have some new information to give you."

"Yes, okay. We'll be here," she said.

Josh disconnected, then called home, listening to it ring and waiting for the sound of his Reenie's voice. And then she picked up.

"Hello."

"Reenie, it's me."

"Hi, sweetheart! Are you on your way home?"

"Not quite yet. I have to talk to a few families first, and then I'll be there."

"I heard all the sirens," she said. "Y'all did good, didn't you?"

He heard a smile in her voice.

"Yes, baby. We did good."

———— ✦ ————

WADE AND LOGAN WERE SITTING on the bed, talked out and anxious, while waiting for that knock on the door. "What do you think he's going to tell us?" Logan asked.

"You heard the same sirens I heard. I think it's going to be good news."

Logan leaned her head against his shoulder.

"I hope so. I just want to find Damon and go home."

"I know, and I want that for you... for both of us."

They were so intent on listening, that when the knock finally came, it made both of them jump.

But it was Logan who went to the door.

"Come in," she said, and then sat back down on the bed, leaving the chairs for the men to choose from, but Wade stayed beside her. When the chief began talking, Wade slipped his arm around her waist.

Josh had come here first out of respect for the fact that her brother was Barton's first victim. He pulled a chair up to the bed where they were sitting, and went straight to the reason he was here.

"Barton DeChante has been arrested for the murder of your brother, Damon, of his wife, Faith, of Justin Baptiste, and of Danny Bales."

"Oh my God, how did you know who it was?" Logan asked.

"Danny Bales' first wife arrived from California with a story about a man renting Danny's pickup the same night that Jody Bales was murdered on the south side"

Logan shuddered, and then looked at Wade.

"I never did know who that was, but I saw the body in the street. That all happened before Damon came home."

Josh heard her and nodded. "That same night, it was Connie's brother who had rented Danny's truck. He turned out to be the one wanting his wife killed so he could marry another woman, and we do have the right man. He confessed."

"Barton DeChante lived in that big house with the rose gardens, didn't he?" Logan asked.

The                 chief                 nodded. "Yes, which happens to be where he buried his wife and Johnny Baptiste's cousin, Justin. He spread a lie that they were having an affair and told everyone they ran away together. Then he killed Danny so he wouldn't put two and two together and remember he was the one who'd had the truck the night your brother was killed."

"You couldn't make this stuff up," Wade said.

"Truth. And Logan, just so you know, the Parish sheriff is notifying all the proper agencies, and if you're up to it, with your assistance, they will begin the recovery of your brother's body tomorrow."

"Yes, oh yes," she whispered. "Finally ... Yes, I'm up to it and yes, we'll be there. Just tell us what time."

"You two can follow me out in the morning. It'll probably be close to nine before all the agencies can gather in the same place. This is unusual to get this much cooperation from different agencies so quickly, but they're all sympathetic to your situation. I'll call you in the morning when I leave," he said, and then stood.

Logan stood up and shook his hand.

"I will never be able to thank you enough."

"I'm sorry we got off on the wrong foot, or this might have ended sooner," Josh said.

"It's over, and that's the main thing," she said.

Josh nodded, then shifted his gaze to Wade. "See you both in the morning," he said, and left.

Wade locked the door after the chief left and then turned and took Logan into his arms.

"You did it, Boss Lady. You found your brother's killer."

Logan laid her head on his shoulder as she settled into his embrace.

"Yes, and now all I need is to find my brother."

———◆———

JOSH DROVE TO THE BALES home next and had to park in the street because of the number of vehicles in their yard. He was walking toward the house when Stella and Connie came out to meet him.

"Whatever it is you have to say, would you come inside and tell all of us at once," Stella asked.

"Yes, ma'am," he said, and followed them inside.

Stella introduced him and offered him a seat, which he declined.

"I won't stay. I just need to give all of you an update. You'll get details later, but thanks to Logan Talman and Connie Bales, we found the killer."

Everyone in the room looked at Connie, who was in tears.

"Oh my God, was I right?" she asked.

He nodded.

She collapsed into a chair and started sobbing.

"What's going on? What are you saying?" Stella cried.

Josh couldn't imagine how this was going to play out, since the killer was related to Connie.

"We just arrested Barton DeChante on four counts of murder."

Stella gasped. "Barton? Four? He murdered four?"

"Yes, ma'am. Damon Conway, Faith DeChante, Justin Baptiste, and your husband, Danny."

Stella shook her head, unable to follow what he was saying.

"But Faith and that Baptiste man ran away together."

"No, ma'am. That's the story he put out to cover what he'd done. Unfortunately, Justin Baptiste's only crime was being in the wrong place at the wrong time. DeChante just used him as the excuse to explain away his wife's sudden absence. He buried them both in the rose garden. We'll be recovering their remains within a few days."

When the people in the room erupted in questions and tears, and all talking at once, he knew it was time to leave.

"My condolences to all of you. I have one more family to talk to before I can close my eyes tonight."

Stella grabbed his hand.

"Thank you. Thank you for giving our Danny justice."

"Yes, ma'am. Just sorry it happened at all," and then he was out the door.

Josh got in the car and then sat for a few moments, gathering his emotions. This was a hard way to end a day, but it was the best outcome any of them could have hoped for.

Two down and one to go.

He next drove to Caitlin and Johnny's house. There, the family cars were all parked along curbs up and down the streets. There were so many people in the house that some of them had spilled over onto the front porch, and others were in lawn chairs out in the yard.

Johnny came out of the house before Josh was up the steps and welcomed him inside.

"Here we are, Chief, at your request."

Josh stood at the door so that everyone could see and hear him. As soon as they quieted, he began.

"We just arrested Barton DeChante for the murder of Damon Conway and for the murder of Danny Bales."

There were gasps of shock and disbelief.

"The reason I'm telling all of you this is because the entire tragedy began because DeChante wanted his first wife killed so he could marry another woman. When Damon Conway refused, Barton killed him, which then meant he had to kill his wife on his own."

He heard gasps and whispers beginning and knew they were starting to understand why he was there.

"What you need to know is that Justin Baptiste was an innocent. He just happened to be in the wrong place when DeChante needed a reason to support his wife's absence. He killed and buried them both in his rose garden. Your Justin did not cheat on his wife. He was a victim, like the others. Details will be forthcoming, and we will be recovering all of the bodies in the coming days. Is Justin's wife here?"

A small brown-haired woman stood.

"I'm Lila Baptiste. I'm Justin's wife."

"Ma'am, my sympathies for your loss. The authorities will be notifying you when your husband's remains are recovered so you can properly lay him to rest."

"I thank you," she said. "I knew he had to be dead. I just didn't know what happened. I told them all he wouldn't leave me. I told them, and they still chose to believe the worst."

The family was gathering around the grieving widow as he walked out. He headed for home, needing the time he would spend with his sweet woman before the recoveries began.

He would be glad when this summer was over.

---

IT WAS A SOMBER NIGHT in Bluejacket.

Logan was in bed, trying to relax enough to sleep, and Wade was lying behind her, aware of her discontent.

Logan was mentally psyching herself up to face what ten years in the swamp would have done to Damon.

Wade knew she was bothered, and didn't know what to say to make it better.

"Boss Lady, I would do anything to take this burden from your shoulders, but I can't, and I accept that. This is your grief. I just want you to know that I'm here. Lean on me tomorrow. Don't hurt your recovery by overdoing it, okay?"

Logan heard the promise and felt the love.

"Yes, I hear you. And while tomorrow will be a sad and trying day, it's nothing compared to the night I rolled him in that grave. Okay?"

"Definitely okay."

Then she closed her eyes and finally slept, safely cradled in Wade Garrett's arms.

———◆———

MORNING ARRIVED WITH A CLEAR, cloudless sky, and air so thick and heavy from the humidity that you could almost taste the salt from the Gulf.

Wade and Logan followed Chief Adams out to the dig site without talking. Logan was mentally bracing herself for the day and grateful for Wade's presence.

The crime scene team from the Louisiana State Bureau of Investigation was already there and waiting. They would be heading up the recovery.

Officers from the Parish Sheriff's Department were there to provide protection for the recovery team and were standing guard with weapons drawn, ready to dispatch any gators or snakes if the need arose.

Chief Evans from the Township of Bluejacket was on scene, partly on Logan's behalf, and partly because he was the one who'd solved the cases.

As soon as Logan arrived, she was asked to spray-paint an X on the ground where Damon had died, and then spray-paint the area where she'd dug the grave. She handed a crime scene investigator a paper on which she'd drawn a diagram of the levels of layers within the grave, and what they would find before they reached the depth where the body would be, and she had been specific enough that she'd impressed the entire team by what she'd done.

She had written that they would first find the two small boulders she'd rolled onto the deadfall.

Then the layers of decayed deadfall, and then below all that, the tarp-wrapped body of her brother.

Once they settled her into a folding chair within some shade, had stomped down all the swamp grass to make sure the area was clear of snakes, they began to dig, going one slow shovelful of dirt at a time.

The day was like all others, already hotter than hell and turning blood to a languid liquid, making hearts compensate by beating faster just to finish a task.

And all the while that the sun moved higher toward its daily zenith, the temperature rose. Not even shade could provide any kind of relief from the thick, airless swamp.

Initially, Logan sat motionless and as the first layer was removed, she glanced up to see where Wade had gone, and instead caught a glimpse of movement in the trees beyond the clearing. Goosebumps rose on the backs of her arms as she stood up to look closer, but it was gone. She sat back down.

While the dig site was surrounded with the turmoil of too many people and ongoing racket, the swamp had become silent. The air grew heavier. Sweat rolled in rivulets.

When they found the boulders, the men who were digging were shocked at their size, and once again, she was eyed with new respect.

Logan didn't notice. She was on her feet again, staring into the trees beyond them. Something—no, someone was there. A glimpse of shoulder, a brief flash of long legs. The quickening of her heart took her aback.

Recognition!

Wade walked up behind her and handed her a cold bottle of water. She drank thirstily and gave it back without speaking.

Another hour passed, and then another, and they were down through two more feet of dirt and hitting rotted wood when Logan's gut began to knot.

She stood up again, watching him weaving his way toward her

through the trees. She knew him now. She felt the love. He was here to witness and to thank.

Suddenly one of the men down in the pit stood up.

"We've got him," he said.

Logan pushed out of Wade's arms and moved forward until she was standing at the edge of the pit.

"Ma'am, you need to get back," an officer said.

"I put him there. I told him I'd be back, now I need to watch you bringing him out."

Wade wrapped his arms around her waist, then whispered against her ear and pulled her back to a safer location.

"Lean on me."

So she did.

The digging crew abandoned their small shovels for even smaller trowels and brushes, until finally, the rotting tarp was clear of debris.

Four men slipped down into the pit and carefully lifted the tarp and its contents to the surface, while another group carried it away from the grave and gently lowered it to the ground.

When Logan finally saw the tarp come up from the hole, if it hadn't been for Wade, she would have collapsed. She was shaking now, and suddenly so cold.

Someone went to get a body bag, and while everyone else was focused on the tarp and its contents, Logan was looking into the trees.

She could see him clearly now, standing in a patch of shadow. He hadn't moved, but she heard the words.

*Thank you. Love you. Look forward, not back.*

Tears blurred her vision, and as they did, he faded away.

She felt the loss again, just as she had the night he took his last breath. She lifted her arm to wave, but he was gone.

"I love you. I miss you. Rest in peace."

# EPILOGUE

---

*Dallas, Texas—One year later.*

Sunlight reflected on the surface of the pool and into Logan's eyes. She shifted her stance and looked away, and when she looked again, Wade was climbing out of the water and walking toward her.

He was tall enough she had to reach to put her arms around his neck, but just right for making love. He loved her without caution, and she felt it all the way to her bones.

And then he held out his hand.

"Come into the water, darlin'."

When she took a step forward, sunlight caught on the diamond on her finger, and then all of a sudden, he'd swung her off her feet and into his arms.

She laughed, so full of joy she could not contain it.

"Crazy man. What are you doing?"

"You took too long making up your mind," he said, and still holding her in his arms, jumped into the deep end of the pool.

She shrieked, and then the water was over their heads as they sank down, down, until he touched bottom. Then he shoved off, and they were going up, up, up, shooting out of the water and into the sunlight, laughing.

*The End*

# ABOUT THE AUTHOR

Sharon Sala is a long-time member of RWA, as well as a member of OKRWA. She has 113 books and novellas in print, published in five different genres—Romance, Young Adult, Western, Fiction, and Women's Fiction. First published in 1991, she's an eight-time RITA® finalist, winner of the Janet Dailey Award, five-time Career Achievement winner from *RT Magazine*, five time winner of the National Reader's Choice Award, and five time winner of the Colorado Romance Writer's Award of Excellence, winner of the Heart of Excellence Award, as well as winner of the Booksellers Best Award. In 2011 she was named RWA's recipient of the Nora Roberts Lifetime Achievement Award. In 2017 Romance Writers of America presented her with the Centennial Award for recognition of her 100th published novel.

Her books are *New York Times, USA Today, Publishers Weekly* best-sellers. Writing changed her life, her world, and her fate.

For book list go to her website www.SharonSala.net

CPSIA information can be obtained
at www.ICGtesting.com
Printed in the USA
LVHW04s1343240818
587633LV00003B/236/P

9 781976 386671